YULE LOG BLAZING . . .

Pink tendrils of dawn peeped through the snow clouds as Eli Holten, Chief Scout for the 12th U.S. Cavalry, enjoyed his Christmas present. The warm, passionate body of Prudence Alden writhed against him.

They'd been in her small house in Eagle Pass since before sunset the previous day. *Seven times*, the scout dizzily enumerated. It gave him strong doubts how much more he could endure. There were limits beyond which no man could perform.

For a prim and proper school teacher, Prudence Alden certainly had some wild ideas about gift giving.

Sometimes, Eli thought giddily, it was indeed more blessed to give than to receive!

SIOUX SWORDSMAN

BY BUCK GENTRY

#24

ZEBRA BOOKS
KENSINGTON PUBLISHING CORP.

Special acknowledgment to Mark K. Roberts.

ZEBRA BOOKS

are published by

Kensington Publishing Corp.
475 Park Avenue South
New York, NY 10016

First printing: June 1987

Printed in the United States of America

This volume of the Scout's adventures is dedicated with deep gratitude to Jim and Barb Wilkerson, good friends and good neighbors.

BG

"Scouting for the Army was not an easy task. Most of your equipment was paid for from your own pocket. The work was hard, dusty, and dangerous. The rewards few and far between."

—Noah Jessup,
Frontier Scout

Chapter One

Bright moonlight shone down on a fantasy world of white. Stars twinkled frostily and the persistent wind even died, as though for a magical moment. Christmas had come to Dakota Territory, and along with it came six feet of snow on the level, with drifts from eleven to fifteen feet. On this most special of nights a hush gathered over the prairie. Thick ice covered the greasy grass on Montana's high plain and the sparse trees groaned and creaked under a burden of ice and snow. A short distance away, a dark lump, made of sod blocks and logs, rose above the uniform flatness. Smoke came from a stone chimney and thin voices could be heard, raised in song.

"*Stelle nacht, heilige nacht, alles schläff . . .*"

Hermann Richter and his family celebrated their second Christmas in America. While they did, a silent group of riders sat their mounts, clouds of vapor surrounding their faces, and watched the scene. A silhouette appeared for a moment in the bright yellow square of an oiled parchment window, then moved out of sight. The men's leader, *Pisko*, a noted warrior among the Miniconjou Sioux, grunted in satisfaction.

A heavily muscled arm came from under his thick buffalo robe and he waved his followers forward.

"*Fröliche Weinachten, liebchen*," Hermann said warmly as he handed his wife a carefully wrapped package.

"*Ach!* Hermann, you should not have done this," Frieda Richter exclaimed unconvincingly.

"What is it, Poppa?" ten year old Martin Richter demanded.

"Let her open it, *junge*," his father chided gently.

"Oh, Poppa, is it the pretty robe Momma saw in the catalogue?" Hilde inquired, wise beyond her thirteen years.

Hermann made a show of surprise, his mouth drawn into an "O", eyes wide. "That's for you to find out, *meine kleine Maus*."

Hilde produced a pout. "Poppa, I'm too old to be called 'little mouse.' "

His big arms enfolding his daughter, Hermann chuckled. "Not to me you aren't. And now, just for tonight, a little bit of *schnapps* for both of you."

With a suddenness that took the family's breath away, the front door slammed open. *Pisko, Tasa* and three Sioux braves entered the room, weapons ready. Their appearance created pandemonium within the small farmhouse.

"*Macht schnell*, Martin!" Hermann shouted. "*Nach unser Bersteet!* Take your sister with you. Momma, too."

Too late. In all the confusion the Richter family stumbled into each other while the Sioux warriors moved cat-quick to cut off any avenue of escape. A knife flashed in *Tasa*'s hand and Martin Richter fell to the floor, his shirt laid open and his pale white chest streaming blood from a long, diagonal slash. Hermann

Richter bellowed in rage and hurled a chair into the face of the nearest brave. He followed up by grabbing his rifle from over the fireplace.

In such close quarters, Hermann had little need to aim. His first shot crashed loudly in the low-ceilinged room. The slug chiseled out bone from the outer corner of one warrior's left eye-socket back past his ear. The Miniconjou spun away from impact and slammed against the wall. He slid to a sitting position while blood bubbled from the wound. Hermann chambered another round and leveled the muzzle at *Pisko's* belly.

The keen edge of a tomahawk bit into Hermann's right collarbone and he jerked in agony as he discharged the heavy Spencer. Its big slug cracked past *Pisko's* head and went harmlessly out into the night. Frieda and Hilde shrieked in terror. The dripping 'hawk raised again and Hermann feebly warded it off with the barrel of his rifle.

Pisko and *Tasa* shot Hermann at the same time. The bullets ripped into his body and sent the burly German farmer staggering toward the fireplace. Flames licked wildly upward, nourished by the increased draught from the open door. Hermann rebounded from the sandstone mantel he had so proudly carved and installed. His knees sagged. His vision began to swim, yet he managed to chamber another cartridge and raise his weapon lefthanded.

"*Schweinhunden!*" he bellowed.

Three shots sounded as one, the lesser two overridden by the roar of the Spencer. *Pisko* saw his bullet rip through the side of the big German's throat, to send a spray of crimson across the room. Gray Otter missed, for which error he paid with his life when the Spencer's heavy slug smashed into his chest and exploded a chunk of his spine out his back. A hollow, sickening sound followed when Runs Backward sank his tomahawk to the haft in the back of Hermann's head.

Tasa leaped over the quivering body of their enemy and ran to the doorway. There he beckoned to the remaining warriors to enter. All resistance had ended as he shut the door behind them. Fourteen leering Sioux gathered in a circle around the frightened, trembling females. Runs Backward reached out and plucked at a frill on Frieda's dress.

She instinctively struck at him and recoiled from his profane touch. That brought throaty chuckles from several warriors. Runs Backward took solid hold this time and yanked downward. Frieda shrieked and tried to cover herself as large, pale, moon-like breasts spilled out of the ruin of her bodice.

"Momma?" a terrified Hilde squeaked.

"Aaah!" a youthful brave named Snake Chaser sighed out. He reached forward and ran the backs of his fingers down Hilde's cheek.

"Oh, Momma!" Hilde wailed.

Snake Chaser ripped Hilde's dress open to the waist, followed by her chemise. Her tiny, pubescent breasts poked out impudently. Despite her fear, Hilde flushed red with shame. Snake Chaser jerked aside his loincloth.

"You lak?" he asked in his limited, broken english.

"*Nein, nein*," Frieda pleaded.

"Momma, *hilfst du mir*!"

Frieda could only utter a thin, high wail, totally unable to aid her daughter as three warriors began to tear away the remainder of her clothing. If only she

introduction had been so gentle, for the next three braves who had their way with her lacked the sensitivity of Snake Chaser. The pain returned and with it the sickness and terror. Before the ordeal ended, Hilde prayed for death. It came at last, as it did for her mother, with a hatchet buried deep in each of their skulls. Unnoticed where he lay in a heap by the hearth, Martin Richter remained utterly motionless until the Sioux departed.

Then he vomited wretchedly and sobbed uncontrollably at the horror he had witnessed. His father butchered, his mother and sister violated over and over before his eyes, specters of those unspeakable scenes repeated in his brain. Shaken to his depths, Martin found himself unable to stand. He even lacked the energy to cover the bodies as decency demanded. Outside delicate snowflakes began to sift lazily out of the thick, gray clouds.

Pink tendrils of dawn peeped through the snow clouds as Eli Holten, Chief Scout for the 12th U. S. Cavalry, enjoyed his Christmas present. The warm, passionate body of Prudence Alden writhed against him as she rode his massive shaft like a bucking bronc. She crouched over him, hard brown nipples of her swaying breasts brushing his chest as she surged back and forth.

"Aaaah! Eeeeei! Oooooh-aaaaah, oooh-aaah, eeeeeeeei!" she wailed.

Holten matched her thrust for thrust, driving his mighty pillar ever deeper within her fevered passage. They'd been making love in her small house in Eagle

Pass since before sunset the previous day. Seven times the scout dizzily enumerated. At least seven. It gave him strong doubts as to how much longer he could endure. There were limits, beyond which no man could perform. For a prim and proper school teacher, Prudence Alden certainly had some wild and erotic ideas about gift giving. Sometimes, Eli thought giddily, it was indeed more blessed to give than to receive.

"Now . . . ah! Now . . . deep . . . deeper . . . make-it . . . hurt!" Prudence panted out as yet another of her seemingly endless climaxes built to a crescendo.

"Hell, sweetheart, it hurts already," Eli grunted as he attempted to meet her demand.

Unaccountably, Prudence began to giggle. Holten joined her. The mood faltered, weakened, threatened to slip joyously away. Until . . .

"Ayyyyyyyiiiiiiiii!" Prudence shrieked as she exploded into belly-cramping completion. "Harder . . . harder . . . oh, Eli, make it NOW!"

What had begun as bursts of cannon fire had declined to fretful spurts of damp fuse. Despite this, Eli hurtled into his own oblivion, mustering sufficient force to prove himself a good soldier.

"Oh, Pru, Pru, you're going to be the death of me," Eli mourned in gratitude when his senses returned to near-normal. "But what a way to go."

"You don't think this has taken a lot out of me?" Prudence came back. "Lord, Eli, mine, I've never been so thoroughly, completely and satisfactorily loved in my life. And believe me that covers a lot of years of loving."

Eli wrinkled his brow. "How can that be? You can't be more than, ah, twenty-two."

"You hit it right on the button, Eli. This is my third year of teaching and my first independent assignment. But neither age nor occupation have anything to do with, shall we say, twelve wonderful years of love?"

"Twel—I don't believe it. Granted you have a skill I find remarkable in any woman. A certain ability to give and take in equal portion. But twelve years certainly belies your given name."

"Prudence? No, it doesn't. I've been quite prudent in the *who* I've loved with. It's the *how many* that sort of gets into a fuzzy area."

Holten patted her sleek, firm rump. "That must have been a great deal of fun."

"Oh, it was. Some day I'll tell you all about it."

"In the meantime, I think we ought to get a little rest, have some breakfast. Before we wear ourselves out."

"You needn't worry about that. This time let me do all the work."

"This . . . time?"

"Oh, yes," Prudence murmured as she slid free of him and knelt between his upraised knees. Her warm, moist hand wrapped around his member and squeezed it to new life. Then long swaying wings of her rich blond hair slithered tantalizingly over his bare abdomen as she lowered her head and flicked her tongue over the tip of his throbbing shaft.

"You like? Yes, you like indeed," Prudence teased as she went to her work with a will.

"Pru . . . ah, people have been known to die of overexertion," the scout cautioned.

"Not from this means. At least I've never seen it written up that way."

"We, ah, ought to, er-ah, that is, we've not had anything to eat since early yesterday. I'm getting weak in the knees."

"The weakness hasn't spread up this far, I'm happy to report," Prudence responded.

"Pru! I . . . ah, that is . . . oooooooh," Eli groaned. "That's it. Good, oh, so good. Yesssss, aah, yessssss."

Unnoticed, an hour fled by in such pleasurable pursuits. Slowly, achingly, the scout began to sense the rising of his response. His heart pounded and wild images flitted through his mind. Like Eros reviewing a parade on Olympus, he saw the image of every woman he had ever made love with. They slid slowly through his mind as Prudence's lips slid slowly up and down his fiery lance. He would never have believed any man could have enjoyed so many conquests. Then the pounding insistence of his rapidly approaching climax shattered Eli's reverie.

"Aaaaah! S-so good, Pru. Now, now, *now*!"

Eventually, Prudence arose from the crumpled, damp sheets and made them breakfast. Despite the chill in the room, with snow piled half-way up the windows, they ate in the nude, enjoying the healthy glow of their bodies. Prudence spread marmalade on a biscuit half and pursed her lips.

"It looks like a long, hard winter," she observed.

"That it does. Won't be much doing for the troops at Fort Rawlins."

"Or for their chief scout," Prudence added. "In light of which, I want you to make me a promise."

"Anything," Eli answered unthinkingly.

"Now that you've opened your present and have sampled what's in store for the months to come, I want you to promise me you'll stay here with me until winter breaks."

Eli blinked, jerked out of his lethargy. "But that'll be nearly Easter time."

Prudence brightened. "Won't it be wonderful? Easter sounds like a quite reasonable time. Then, after that, we can . . . whenever we can."

Recalling nearly eighteen hours of non-stop love, Eli suppressed a groan. "Until Easter . . . if I can live through it."

Chapter Two

Watery sunshine sparkled off the Montana snowfields. A steady *drip-plop* sounded from the eaves of the headquarters building and barracks of Fort Keogh. Although hardly felt by the soldiers of the Ninth Infantry Regiment, the warm rays melted the long icicles that hung from each rafter end. The wide, iron wheel-and hoof-pounded trail that led past the fort had been turned into a black quagmire. The viscous gumbo mud splashed high on soldiers' boots and horses' hoofs as the wood detail returned shortly before noon.

"Ain't a hell of a lot out there that's not covered by snow," Sergeant Bascomb of K Company confided to the regimental sergeant major. "We got enough for headquarters and officers' row."

"An' do ye think we'll be for gladly freezin' our arses off in the sergeants' billets tonight, Bascomb?" Sergeant Major Quinlan sneered. "Ye'll be dividin' that sorrowful lookin' load up between headquarters, the senior sergeants' quarters an' yer own barracks. Then, if there's a wee bit left over, ye might see it gets to the carp'rills."

"What about our officers, Sergeant Major?"

"Devil take 'em. There's ice in their blood, so they'll not know the difference, I declare. But, if yer conscience is botherin' ye, or ye want to make sure ye get papers for yer next furlough, then ye might squeeze out a little for them, as needs be."

"I've a feeling the corporals will be cold tonight."

Quinlan gave a heavy sigh and an expression of blank innocence. "That they may, lad. That they may. Now get along wit' ye."

"Corporal of the Guard, Post Number Two!" a young voice sang out from above the gate. "Horse and rider approaching slowly. Looks like a small boy, or a woman."

"Stand ready, sentry," came the reply. "Guard Mount, two men to the gate to make ready to open."

"Wonder what that'll be?" Quinlan asked the empty air.

Shivering and hollow-eyed, his coat and shirt soaked with blood, Martin Richter walked a shambling plow horse in through the gate at Fort Keogh. The thin, black-haired boy raised his face to gaze at the Stars and Stripes, then made a feeble gesture behind him, to indicate half the prairie.

"Indians. The Sioux. They—th-they attacked our place," he said in thickly accented English. "Hunnerds of 'em. *Meine Pappa, und Mutti, und schwester Hilde, sind alles gestarben.*" Silently, tearlessly, he began to sob.

Adroitly, the Officer of the Day, Lieutenant Hildebrand, recognized the situation and moved to rectify it. "Sergeant of the Guard, my compliments to Bandmaster Schweiger and I need him here at once."

"Yes, sir!" Sergeant Pallesier responded with a snappy salute.

Three minutes later a portly, white mustachioed man with huge European sidewhiskers, and the three downward-pointing light blue chevrons of a sergeant on his sleeve, waddled to where a number of troopers grouped around a small boy on a sway-backed horse. He snapped a Prussian-precise salute to Lieutenant Hildebrand. His multiple chins jiggled as he arrested his movement.

"Vass iss it, *Leutnant* Hildebrand?"

"We've a boy here who apparently doesn't speak much English." Quickly he outlined what was known.

"*Ach, zo . . .*" To the chest-heaving boy he snapped, "*Achtung! Was ist los, Jungen?*"

In broken words, painful with grief and personal agony, Martin Richter recounted the raid by Miniconjou warriors. While he related it, his tear ducts slowly recovered and scalding streams ran down his smooth, rounded cheeks. When he came to the tomahawk murders of his violated mother and sister, he seemed to collapse inwardly. Howling in sorrow, Martin Richter tilted forward and hugged the neck of his hungry, exhausted horse.

"*Sie sind verwundet,*" Schweiger exclaimed, feeling the pain vicariously.

Martin felt his chest. "*Das ist garnichts.*" His voice raised to the edge of hysteria, as Martin screamed in anguish, "*Miner Stamm ist Todt! Ich bin ganz allein!*"

"Sergeant Major," Lieutenant Hildebrand spoke commandingly. "Get this boy inside. Strip him of these clothes, and have that wound treated. Then warm him with a hot bath and get some soup down him. See if you can find him something to wear from the women along Soapsuds Row. Then he'd better tell his story to Colonel Miles."

"Me auldest lad's his exact size, sir," Sergeant Major Quinlan responded. "I'll send to me wife for some britches, a shirt an' coat."

"See that you do it all quickly. We don't want to lose the little tyke, now he's made it this far."

"It's all but accomplished now, sir," Quinlan answered with a brisk salute.

Half an hour later, Colonel Nelson A. Miles listened with growing concern to the child's testimony, as translated by Bandmaster Schweiger. When the narrative had concluded, the stocky, granite-faced Miles inquired further.

"What about his background? Where's his family come from? What about his religion?"

"He speaks high Cherman mit a touch of Bavarian aczent," Schweiger offered. "Let me try . . . *Bist du auf Byrn?*"

"*Jawohl, Herr Capitän.*"

"Humph," Schweiger snorted at his unofficial promotion. "Bavarian chure enough. *Aber,* he's so tired *und* frightened he can hardly talk clearly."

"It happens, I believe, Sergeant Schweiger," Nelson Miles put in, suppressing a grin.

"As to his religion, sir," Sergeant Major Quinlan put in, "he's a Cat'olic sure enough. After I got him undressed an' the doc was treatin' him, he was recitin' the *Ave Maria.* An' he had a felt phylactic o' the Blessed Virgin around his neck on a grubby string. I took the liberty o' replacin' that wit' a cheap silver chain me Patrick had to spare."

"That's, ah, all quite well and good, then. Thank you, Sergeant Major. In your, ah, obvious concern for the boy, would you have room in your home, as well as your heart, for him?"

"Wit' five lambs o' me own to feed, sir, another one would hardly make a dent. Me wife an' I would be happy to take him in, if that's the Colonel's desire, sir."

"Then see to it, Sergeant Major. With the matter of the boy disposed of, there'll be a lot doing around here from now on. Department headquarters sent me out here to effect a removal of the remaining wild Sioux to the reservations. Then they sat on orders putting the regiment in the field. It's about time we got on with the job I was sent here to do. I want you to draft a letter to department headquarters for me, Sergeant Major. Outline the events of the attack and give the family's name. Perhaps there are relatives who can take care of the boy. Also request that we be put immediately into the field to staunch this before a regular blood bath develops."

"Yes, sir. I'll do 'em one that'll rattle their false teeth, sir."

"I'll settle for getting them off their dead asses, Sergeant Major. But one way or the other, I mean to go after these renegade Sioux."

Harley Winslow bolted from the telegraph office and clumped noisily across Main Street at an angle. The early morning commerce in Valentine, Nebraska had barely begun and Harley wanted to get his news to Everett Lockwood at the mercantile before someone else had the opportunity. Suddenly Harley, whom everyone considered a couple of scoops shy of a full bowl, began to giggle. How could it be? he wondered. Ol' Everett Lockwood would be glad to get the news he carried, but it would sure make him mad.

Everett Lockwood owned and operated a large dry goods store in Valentine. His sons clerked for him and rumor had it they were paid lower wages than an outsider would demand. He also ran a group, or so it was said, which monitored the moral climate of Valentine. Men who met in secret and went abroad at night with hoods over their heads. Three families of colored folk had once lived in the north-central Nebraska community. They all departed after one of them had his home burned down. Credit for the deed went to the nightriders, who called themselves the "Nebraska Rangers."

Since then, ugly signs had been posted at each end of the three-track railroad yard in Valentine. Crudely lettered in bold, black paint, they read:

NIGGER!
DON'T LET THE SUN SET
ON YOUR BLACK ASS
IN THIS TOWN!

Somehow, though he knew himself to be of Scotch-

Irish and English descent, the signs made Harley Winslow nervous. If they didn't want darkies in the place, who might they turn on next? A loud, wet *plop*! close by gave Harley a scary turn. He looked jerkily to the right to see the cause.

The thick snow coverings on the roofs of the town's buildings had begun to melt, revealing black splotches of wet shingles below. Some of the load on Jensen's barber shop had let go and fallen to the ground. Harley gave an edgy snort and hurried on.

"Mister Everett, Mister Everett!" Harley yelled as he entered the mercantile and set the bell above the door jangling wildly.

"What is it, Harley?"

"Mister Everett, I was over at the telegraph office when this message came on the wire. It's the Sioux, Mister Everett. They done gone an' kilt a family on Christmas Eve. Folks named Richter, up in the Territory."

Everett Lockwood's eyes glowed. A soft smile played over his lips and he seemed to be seeing something in the far, far distance. Richter was a German name, he knew, and he didn't much care what happened to a family of sauerkraut slurpers. *How* it happened, though, was of considerable importance. He reached into the coin till and flipped a piece of silver to Harley.

"Thank you, Harley."

"Gosh! A whole quarter. Thank *you*, Mister Everett."

"Where, exactly, was this, Harley? Do you know?"

"Oh, yes, Mister Everett. Out Montana way, around Fort Keogh."

"You're a good man, Harley, no matter what the

others might say. I appreciate you bringing this to me. Now, I want you to go find Paul May, Ephram Sprague, Clem Wells and Jim Bench. Tell them to come here right away. There's another twenty-five cents in it for you if you hurry."

"Oh, yes, sir, Mister Everett."

After the store had emptied of two woman customers and Harley Winslow, Everett Lockwood turned to his eldest son. "Ralph, we've got a marvelous opportunity here. The boys have been getting a little stale of late. With the Sioux acting up out west, we have an ideal situation to show everyone the importance and the power of the 'Rangers.' "

"I thought the army was supposed to handle the Sioux," Ralph responded in a pouty tone.

Everett Lockwood looked at his angular, bony son. Even though Ralph had passed twenty-five by two years, he somehow missed the look of adulthood. A lank lock of dirty-blond hair hung over his high forehead and his small, pursed lips gave him a little boy image. The senior Lockwood read weakness in the lines of his son's face. Although Ralph had laid on with a will when the Rangers had horsewhipped that darkie, Everett suspected that his son was a bit of a coward. Ha! Being a *bit* of a coward was like being a bit pregnant. A man was either yellow or he wasn't. It all seemed, somehow, to revolve around Ralph's vaguely effeminate features. Everett curbed his ruminations and made a bitter answer.

"Colonel Nelson Miles was *supposed* to handle the Sioux. Only the big brass back at the Department of Dakota Headquarters and in the east in Washington have been dragging their heels. Now that someone has been killed, even they can't delay any longer."

"How many of the Rangers do you think would ride with you for something like this?"

"All of them. You included, Ralph."

"Who'll run the store?"

"Harold and Tommy, naturally."

Paul May and Jim Bench entered the mercantile. Both had anticipatory smirks on their faces. Bench, the more talkative, broached the subject in a rush.

"You got work for the Rangers, Ev?"

"Crudely put, but accurate, Jim," Everett responded coolly.

"More niggers tryin' to move into town?" Paul May inquired, his broad, jowly face reflecting a certain native cunning and cruelty.

"Nothing like that, Paul. It's the Sioux. Some renegades off the reservations massacred a white family out near Fort Keogh. It appears, as usual," the senior Lockwood invented, "that the army isn't going to do anything about it. So, I propose that the Rangers take a hand and show what real Americans can do about this outrage."

"What outrage?" Clem Wells asked as he entered.

Jim Bench quickly told him. Clem produced a broad grin. "When do we ride?"

"Soon as possible. Tomorrow morning as I see it," Everett Lockwood responded. "With twenty-five men we ought to be able to round up all the hostile Sioux and chase them clear t'hell and gone back to the reservation."

"What's left of 'em, you mean," Paul May said

through a snicker.

"The Sioux are tough," Ralph Lockwood inserted quietly.

"Yes, but we're tougher, son. Don't ever forget that," Everett countered with ringing confidence.

Chapter Three

Every blade of the tough gamma grass, each thistle stalk and sage bush bowed to the weight of the white blanket that gently muted the harsh prairie into a uniform plain across the Montana landscape. Ice crystals and snowflakes glittered in the air, whirled by the brisk wind into individual points of brightness. From across the drifts and mounds a thick black column of smoke rose straight into the sky. Puffs of steam accompanied it. A smile lifted *Pisko's* thin lips. Before long the white men would know of his anger again.

"They do not move," *Tasa* remarked unnecessarily.

"Much snow on the iron road," Night Hawk answered his friend.

"They'll be easy to kill, *Pisko*?"

"Oh, yes. Entirely too easy."

"I'll shoot the iron horse," Elk Tail enthused.

"We'll all shoot it," *Pisko* agreed.

Chuffing as though with impatience over the enforced delay, the Baldwin No. 6 locomotive sat on the track. A high, curved wooden plow, metal tipped, extended in front of the cowcatcher. Dougal MacDougal, the engineer, sat on his padded seat in the cab of the 4-6-0 heavy duty loco. He swore softly to himself while men labored with shovels to clear the drifted snow from the deep cut through which the railroad ran. It would be a good half an hour before the *General Halleck* could continue the job it was supposed to do. The Union Pacific had a schedule to maintain and there would be a train along behind them before long. Come snow or high water, the track across Montana to the next division point had to be kept open.

"At least we're warm," his fireman observed. "Those poor devils'll be froze stiff before we get that drift cleared."

"Rocks. That's the trouble," Dougal declared with finality. "Somehow a whole lot of rocks got mixed into that snow. Slamming a shovel into a big one in this kind of weather could near to break a finger."

"All we've got to do is stay warm and dry up here and keep the boiler under quarter pressure," the soot-smeared fireman answered.

Bored with watching the laborious progress, Dougal MacDougal raised his eyes to scan the rim of the cutbank and the sky beyond. In an instant he tensed, eyes opened wide, mouth formed into an astonished "Oh."

"Benny, my good lad," Dougal said softly. "I think we're in for some terrible trouble."

"How's that?"

"It's the Sioux. About thirty of them, spread out along the ridge yonder."

"Jesus, Mary, and Joseph!" Benny blurted out.

"You might be adding all of the saints to your petition, Benny. It looks like we'll need every bit of help we can get."

At the center of the file of Indians, one man raised a feather-decorated rifle over his head and uttered a high, wild yip, like that of an amorous coyote. Dougal's hand closed on the wooden handle of the steam whistle control and he released five fast blasts, four shorts and a long, the danger signal. In the same instant, the Sioux started down the steep incline. Gandy dancers and their foremen looked around in doubt at the shrill warning of the whistle. Whoops and hollers sounded louder and they located the Sioux.

To a man they began to run toward the train, shovels abandoned. Several arrows made a morbid hum through the air and a couple of rifles cracked. Unbidden, Benny began to heave hunks of wood into the firebox to build up enough pressure for the locomotive to move. An arrow clanged off the metal side and caused Benny to wince. From the crew box, Dougal produced a rust-sprinkled sixgun.

"We'll give 'em what for, Benny. They'll not be likin' to attack the Union Pacific again."

Lead slugs spanged and yowled off the curved sides of the huge Baldwin boiler. Benny ducked low and continued to throw chunks of oak into the blaze. Dougal took refuge behind the thick iron plates of the cab's sidewall and fired at a bronze figure he saw sweeping by.

With a final yip, the Miniconjou brave fell from his pony's back. One less of the heathen devils, Dougal thought. The return fire increased in volume as workmen located their weapons and exchanged shots with the Sioux. Spread out in two directions, the warriors raced toward the ends of the work train. Needles flickered on gauges and the pressure indicator stopped short of the halfway mark. Dougal eased open the reverse valve.

Steel wheels spun on the rails, while steam hissed out through a dozen escape ports. The engineer added a trickle of sand and opened the valve a bit more. Another squeal of metal on metal, louder because of the friction of the quartz grains. The locomotive strained backward. Couplers clattered and the four-wheeled trucks began to squeak in protest as the train got under way. It looked good to Dougal, very good. Then painted warriors appeared in the entrances at both sides of the cab.

One drove a stone war club down on the exposed head of the fireman. Benny didn't make a sound as he crashed to the floor, blood welling in the deep pocket in the back of his skull. Over his dead form, another brave fired a tack-studded Sharps.

The heavy .56 caliber ball slammed into Dougal MacDougal's stomach a moment after he'd triggered a round from his Remington. The .44 bullet blasted through his killer's right eyesocket and turned the brain behind it into pudding. He fell heavily against the warrior behind him.

With hoots of victory, the Miniconjou fighting men began to hurl more wood into the fire. Outside, their companions blazed away at the metal monster. Several, including Red Buffalo and Elk Tail, boarded one of the cars. Hideous screams began a moment later. Still more billets of oak went into the maw of the roaring furnace. Lost His Name bumped unknowingly into the dump valve and water poured from the dome-topped reservoir. Steam pressure continued to build. With it, the speed of the work train increased.

Frightened by this phenomenon, the Sioux warriors made hasty retreat by jumping clear of the swaying cab. Already the needle on the steam gauge had reached the red line. It quivered there a moment, then ticked over to + 20. Back in the cars, the last of the workmen died. Red Buffalo hastily scalped him and made ready to abandon the accelerating coach.

The steam gauge read +80.

Four Miniconjou flung themselves into the snow from the rocking train. They rolled in white clouds of disturbed flakes, and came to rest, laughing at the exhilarating sensation.

The steam gauge took a final, fateful leap to +100.

Elk Tail hesitated. He was moving faster than ever in his life and the blur of motion disoriented him. Trembling slightly, he flexed his knees and leaned out from the vestibule.

"Jump!" several of his friends called out.

"Hurry!" a wiser head cautioned.

With a howl and a deafening roar, the over-heated boiler exploded.

A white ball of death-giving vapor expanded outward with a rush, scalding the flesh on two warriors close by the track. Concussion shook the ground and knocked Elk Tail free from his perch. He went sprawling into the snow, astonished as his brothers over this unexpected event.

The medicine of the iron horse white men was indeed powerful.

Eli Holten ran a fingertip around the dark brown, perfect circle of the aureola of Prudence Alden's right breast. "You were going to tell me about that twelve years of love you've enjoyed."

"Was I?"

"That's what you said the other day."

Prudence and the scout lay partway under the big goose-down comforter on her sumptuous bed. They had made long, slow love for an hour and nestled close now to enjoy the gradual descent from the delirious heights.

"If I tell you, you'll have to reveal all your dark secrets, too," Prudence teased.

"Pru, that's not fair. I haven't any dark secrets to tell."

"Oh, I bet you do."

"You got my curiosity going the other day. The least you can do is satisfy it a bit."

"Just a bit?" Prudence wrinkled her pretty little nose. Her breasts jiggled in suppressed merriment.

"Well, in the beginning, there was this older boy. He was twelve, I think, and I was ten. We were in my Uncle Dan's tool shed. We got to playing 'Show Me Yours and I'll Show you Mine,' and daring each other. I took to feeling tingly all over, so I hopped up on this bench, about waist high to him, and pulled off my bloomers. I spread my legs and gave him a little peek and I thought his eyes would pop.

"Right away he jerked open the buttons on his pants and took out this long, pink, ah, *thing*. It stood right up on its own and poked out toward me." Memory faded Prudence's voice as she returned to that summer afternoon, reliving the event as she told the scout about it . . .

. . . "D-do you like it?" Jimmy asked breathlessly.

"It's so *cute*," young Prudence squealed in delight.

She reached out and, instinctively, curled her fingers around the hard, hot shaft. Slowly she stroked downward, and the shock of her delightful contact caused the red-headed lad to drop his trousers around his knees.

"Y-you touched me, ah, Pru. You still are, for all that. C-can I, er-ah, touch you?"

Pru shrugged in coy indifference. "Sure. Go ahead. Use your middle finger. Rub it along the crack and it'll open up."

Shaking slightly, Jimmy followed her instructions. Prudence giggled and scooted closer.

"Move your hand a little faster, Pru," Jimmy directed. "Up and down. That's it. Oooooh."

"Does it tickle and make you feel good all over, Jimmy?"

"Yeaaaah."

"That's how it feels to me. See, I told you it would open up. And I'm gettin' all wet."

"Yeah, I can feel it," Jimmy replied dreamily. His heart pounded so hard he thought it was in his throat.

"Come a little closer," Prudence urged, directing the

boy by his rigid phallus.

They both shivered when his rock-stiff flesh met her yielding cleft . . .

. . . "After that it didn't take long," Prudence summarized as she returned to the present. "At first all he'd put in was the tip. Then I grabbed him by his behind and pulled him hard against me. There was just the tiniest bit of pain when Jimmy pushed all the way in. He waited a little while, shivering and shaking, then took hold of my bottom with both hands and began to pump his hips back and forth and I thought I'd died and gone to heaven. He kept saying over and over, 'Our folks will kill us, our folks will kill us.' But neither one of us could stop, even if we'd wanted to."

"Something like this?" Eli Holten asked as he rolled onto her supine form and pierced the leafy portals of her moist passage.

"Oh, yes, exactly like that. It's sooooo gooood, Eli!"

Teasingly, he denied her his fullness for an excruciating fifteen minutes, driving only a bit more at a time into her quivering center. Her legs twined around him and shook with delirious passion, while she raked her nails along his back.

Unknown to Eli and Prudence, their joyfully uninhibited bedroom gymnastics had an audience. The breath caught sharply in young Lonny Cramer's throat as he lay on the snowdrift and peered through the window into his teacher's bedroom. He'd never seen so big a pecker as the one on the man folks called Eli Holten. In all of Eagle Pass, Lonny bet himself, there wasn't another one so big around and long. Lonny gagged and thought his heart would burst through his chest when Eli slid that big thing between Miss Alden's legs. As it buried itself in her soft flesh, a biting cramp developed in Lonny's lower belly and pain radiated from the rigid shaft that bulged his trousers.

Oh, and oh, now! Eli began to glide in swaying strokes and Lonnie heard Miss Alden squeal, in delight or pain he did not know, and saw her begin to hump her hips in time with the man atop her. Revulsion swept over Lonny and he wanted to squeeze his eyes tight shut. But he couldn't! For some mysterious reason he could not take his eyes from the grotesque sight before him. So nasty and dirty! Lonny tasted bile at the back of his throat. It had to be the Deathly Sin that Preacher Williams always hinted about to the boys at Sunday school.

Even worse, what eleven-year-old, Sunday school class president, Lonnie Cramer couldn't understand, was why, when watching something so repulsive and sinful, his little pecker was stiff as an iron rod. Stiffer than it had ever been. While he gazed in rapt concentration upon the loving couple, his hand strayed absently to the source of discomfort.

He began energetically rubbing on it through his whipcord trousers and longjohns. That set off a rippling cascade of the most delightful sensations! Which told him that this, too, had to be a terrible sin. Guiltily he snatched away his hand as though he had put it on a hot stove. People had a right to know about such an awful thing, he told himself. Forcefully he put his own problem aside and propelled himself down the crusted-over drift. The first serious erection of his life still paining him, Lonny hurried off to spread his tale.

There would be, he knew from experience, plenty of ears eager to hear what he had to say.

Chapter Four

The earth drummed hollow under the hooves of Everett Lockwood's horse, he pulled up as a solitary meadowlark braved the cold to warble its plaintive call. A treeful of crows answered in chorus. Scraggly patches of brown grass showed through the snow. Lockwood glanced at his companions, then pointed to a barely perceptible depression that showed the passage of his horse in the tall prairie grass.

"That ought to be a food cache. Indians down home used to bury food like that. Let's resupply ourselves and destroy the rest. Might be a few less Sioux here on the reservation come spring, eh?" He dismounted and motioned for a shovel.

"Dig right there," he instructed Clem Wells.

Wet, clayey soil made for hard digging. Clem worked up a sweat by the eighth shovelful. When he began to pant, Paul May took over.

"Let me dig at it. The heaviest thing you lift is a beer mug," the arrogant thug sneered.

A moaning wind scudded across the Pine Ridge Reservation. With it came the faint scent of wood smoke. There would be Indians near by, though Everett Lockwood gave it little thought. The pile of turned earth grew larger. A solid thump came with the next stab of the shovel.

"That's it. Clear the lid off and let's see what's inside," Lockwood enthused.

Eats Sparrow and Three Legs had been friends since earliest childhood. Now, in the Snow-on-Top seasons of their lives, they remained close. Each day, weather permitting, after they had greeted the Great Spirit and broken their fast, they took a long walk together. They would discuss the quality and quantity of the grass and speculate on the success of coming hunts, based on that. Or they would hold learned discourse—men didn't gossip—about the romantic peccadillos of the young men in camp. Sometimes they even talked about the white man. Then their words turned somber and they observed that the day was swift coming when there would be no room for the Sioux anywhere in the Great Spirit's world which He made for them. Why, they would wonder aloud, would the Maker of All Things do that, then bring the white man to take it all away from them?

Three Legs thought he knew. The *wasicun* were creatures made by Coyote. The old traditional trickster had designed them to try the patience of the Dakota. To test their faith. It was not a funny trick, Eats Sparrow was quick to point out. True, his companion admitted. Yet, Coyote had always been noted for a twisted sense of humor. Some day, *Sica* would have his plan discovered and the Great Spirit would blow it all away like the falling leaves as winter comes.

Their surprise was all the greater, that day, when they came upon the white men's horses and the whites gathered around one of the band's food caches. Jolted out of the complacency of their daily ritual, they hurried forward, tottering on old men's legs.

"You there," Three Legs called out in Lakota. "What are you doing?"

"Why are you digging up our food?" Eats Sparrow demanded in a quavering voice.

Everett Lockwood turned toward them with a big smile and the muzzle end of a .45 Colt revolver. The hammer fell and a slug spat in the direction of Eats Sparrow's chest. Hot lead splintered his sternum and blanketed him in darkness before he could cry out in pain.

Immediately, Three Legs veered his course and tried to scuttle to safety beyond a slight ridge formed by the bank of Ash Creek. Lockwood let him take three long strides before he brought his sixgun to shoulder level, eared back the hammer and let it drop.

Another cartridge exploded to life and the bullet hammered old Three Legs between the shoulder blades. It cracked his spine and erupted out the front of his chest, shattering his eagle bone breast plate. Jerking spasmotically, Three Legs fell to the ground and moaned his way into eternity.

"Damn, that was fast shootin'," Paul May declared in awe from within the pit.

"I was a little slow on the second shot. I wanted that old heathen bastard to think he might get away. What'd you find?"

"Nothin' but hog slop."

Ignoring May's remark, Everett had a look for himself. Right like he'd expected. Sausage-like bars of pemmican, strips of jerked buffalo and venison, and lots of closed parfleches of government issue parched corn. Not the most tasty of items, but good, solid iron rations for a harsh winter.

"Split up the best of that stuff and destroy the rest. Piss on it or whatever you want. Then we'd better be movin' out," Lockwood continued. "Someone coulda heard those shots. Best be long gone before anyone brings around the reservation police."

"Shouldn't we bury them?" Ralph asked his father.

"What for?"

"I, ah, don't know. Only, we do have the hole."

A grin brightened Everett Lockwood's face. "Why not? Be quick about it, though. And, gentlemen, that was only a little foretaste. Soon we'll have our sights on some real, wild Indians."

All of the snow had melted or been shoveled away from the big parade ground at Fort Snelling, headquarters of the Department of Dakota, across the river from Saint Paul, Minnesota. The crisp, staccato notes of *Officer's Call* seemed to still hang in the air. Major General Howard Phillips, the Department commander, stood with arms behind him, hands clasped, looking out over the large conference room, filled with his staff and the field commanders. The map behind him had two large pins, with red flags attached, stuck into it. One along the Union Pacific right-of-way and the other near the newly constructed Fort Keogh.

"Gentlemen, Colonel Nelson Miles is currently at Fort Keogh. His assignment, as I'm sure you know, has been to round up the straying Sioux and put them firmly and permanently onto the reservations. Until now, Washington has seen fit to interfere with this program on grounds of humanitarian reasons." General Phillips paused and winked broadly at the roomful of officers.

"I don't know about you, but I strongly distrust anything with a label like 'humanitarian reasons.'" Chuckles and some outright laughter filled the room. "We are not dealing with a group of mill girls who are striking for higher wages or better working conditions. We're not confronted by an angry contingent of the Women's Christian Temperance Union. Out here, we're facing the Sioux. And the Sioux, Buster, as I yesterday told a striped-pants Washington fairy, are some tough sons of bitches." He withheld further comment until he had walked to the front edge of the podium.

"Now, I don't imbibe spirits," General Phillips said with a straight face, then ignored the titters that ran around the conference room. "At least not in the quantities of a certain Union Army commander who was our former president. Not since, as some of my critics might imply, I discovered the invention of the funnel. Therefore, it is in total sobriety that I tell you that things are going to start to happen around here.

"There will be some changes of assignment, juggling of postings to out west, to cover for Miles. All of you will be affected in some manner."

"Sir, if the general pleases, sir, what will Colonel Miles be doing during this time?"

"To put it in plain words, Major Pepperidge, he'll be out kicking some Sioux ass. His recent dispatch, describing the massacre of a white family and orphaning of a ten year old boy has been sufficient to tip the balance in our favor. The massacre of a Union Pacific work crew four days ago certainly helped. Nelson is going to get his Indian campaign and we're going to be rid of the Sioux. At the end of this meeting, I shall draft a set of orders for Colonel Miles to head an expedition to round up the last of the recalcitrant Sioux and put them on the reservations. There are to be *no* exceptions."

A heartfelt cheer rose from the assembled officers.

"It is my opinion that Colonel Nelson Miles, and *only* Nelson Miles can pull this off. Particularly so during one of the harshest winters in memory. In order to make sure of success, I'm counting on each of you to do your part. I'm assigning a cavalry screen to Miles for his expedition, but no, not one from this headquarters. Now, following staff reports and routine assignments, you may be excused."

"Officers . . . At—ten-SHUN!" the adjutant bellowed.

Everyone shot upright from their chairs into uniform rigid posture and Major General Howard Phillips strutted jauntily out of the room.

Creaking bedsprings muffled the first knocks as Prudence Alden drove herself in a frenzy atop Eli

Holten. This was the fifth time today she had been impaled by his massive manhood. Oh, how she loved it. She could never, never get enough. Transported by the ecstasy generated by his churning vigor, she threw back her head and thrashed it from side to side, keening in delight. Goose bumps formed along her arms, heated thighs and up her back. Valiantly Eli tried to match her enthusiasm.

Two weeks of nearly endless bouts of loving had left him in a severely weakened condition. Not that they did nothing else, or that Prudence neglected nourishing him. To the contrary, she put out remarkable meals. To keep his strength up, she had informed the scout. For her, school was out until good weather returned, too few of the students could make it into town to attend in bad weather. So, outside of occasional shopping, cooking and tending to the house, she made herself readily and joyfully available for the magnificent bedroom romps she shared with Eli Holten.

"You're . . . so . . . good," Eli panted now. "So good you're . . . killing me."

"Keep up with me, keep going," Prudence grunted back. "There's plenty of sap in the old log."

"There's not much sap left in me, figuratively or literally, Pru. Seriously, we've got to slow down. Two or three times a night is enough."

"Not for me it isn't. Not for you, either."

"Pru! I . . . aaaaah! Aaaaaah! Aaaaaaaaaah!"

Prudence gave a mighty shudder and descended from her own warm release. A sound came from the front of the house. She stiffened and the muscles of her treasure trove did wonderful things to the scout's pulsing phallus.

"My God, someone's knocking at the door."

"Keep quiet and they'll go away," Eli suggested.

"I'm—I'm afraid we've made too much noise as it is."

"Open this door, Prudence Alden," the shrewish voice of Mrs. Addison Cramer rang through the room. "We heard you in there. I can't tell you how disgusting your goings-on sounded. Open up, I say!"

"Th-the school board. Oh, my, what . . . ?"

"Forget about them," Eli joked. "I thought you couldn't get enough loving."

"Not now," Prudence responded, her face a mask of confusion and fright. "Not with the school board pounding on my door. Get up. Get dressed. Get out of here!"

"Pru, Pru, calm down."

"You don't understand. A-a teacher's reputation and all is . . ."

Her sentence sliced off when the door slammed open and three women and a mousey male charged into the house. They came directly to the bedroom.

"In the name of Jesus, cover yourself, you shameless hussy!" Ophelia—Mrs. Addison—Cramer hissed.

"Oh, my. Oh my goodness," the flustered little gentleman nattered. "This is so, ah, shocking, Miss Alden."

"Get out of my house! By what right do you come storming in here like this?"

"We *are* the school board of Eagle Pass, you know," prim Mrs. Throckmorton Danbury snipped her words sparingly. "And it's a good thing that we've come when we did."

"I'm horrified," Ophelia declared in a shivery voice. "Absolutely horrified, and revolted," she added. "Yes, revolted, that a supposedly decent young woman, like you pretended to be, is actually entertaining a crude and vulgar frontier ruffian in your private quarters."

Eli had nearly completed dressing and tried to obscure himself in a corner, stung by the scathing tone of the self-righteous woman's voice.

"My private life is my own," Prudence began defensively.

"Not when you're teaching in our school," Madelaine Danbury snapped nastily. "Why, if it hadn't been for little Lonny Cramer, we would never have known of your shameful practices."

"Lonny? The school tattle-tale? What does he have to do with it?" Anger had begun to replace shock and embarrassment for Prudence.

"He happened to be passing by and, ah, accidentally observed your scandalous behavior."

"How? By crawling up a six-foot drift?" The import of that struck her like a fist and released more outrage. "I, ah, I suppose he did. I certainly wouldn't put it past him to be a window peeper."

"You're a fine one to be impugning the virtue of my son," Ophelia warbled in maternal defense.

"Such immoral conduct is not a fit example for our children," Priscilla Garner injected, in an attempt to return to the subject at hand.

Prudence had shrugged into her shift and now glared at her accusers with hot, glowing eyes. "Your precious children probably know a great deal more about clean, healthy sex than you think they do. More, I'm sure, than you yourselves."

"Why, that's . . . that's *libelous*!" Madelaine and Priscilla chorused.

"Prudence, I'm sorry," timid little Chester Bean squeaked. "The ladies on the board are quite correct. We cannot allow such carnal misconduct to blacken the reputation of our fine school. Your contract to teach in Eagle Pass is terminated as of this moment."

Prudence dissolved into tears, hands covering her face. And then Eli was there, strong arms around her shoulders, holding her tightly. For a long moment he glowered across her shaking shoulders at the self-righteous matrons of Eagle Pass, while they continued to shrilly heap imprecations on the shattered young woman.

Fury built at their injustice and his words came out a roar. "Shut your filthy, muck-spewing mouths! You've said quite too much already. You can thank your good fortune that I'll give you to the count of three to get the hell out of this house. After that, I'm not accountable for what I might do."

They departed in a clucking flurry, like fluttering old hens. Behind her, Eli lifted Prudence's tear-stained face.

"I'm sorry, Pru. It's my fault. Really it is."

"No it isn't. I-I-I," she gulped. "I got greedy. We didn't exercise enough caution. Ooooh, damnit all."

"There, that's better. More like my dear, sweet Prudence. Get mad at them, don't let those biddies drag you down."

"You'll help me, Eli, won't you?"

"Sure I will, sweetheart."

Meanwhile, little Lonny could no longer bear to watch the tender scene from his secure hiding place. Unable, over the past day and night, to abolish the burning rod that jutted from his groin, he found himself compelled to slip away to the privacy of the outhouse behind the school. No one, he reasoned, would find him there.

Inside the portion labeled "BOYS," Lonny removed a woolen mitten and fumbled open his clothing. He extricated his rigid member from within a thick swaddling of clothing. Wow! It had never been that big before. Shyly, glancing nervously over his shoulder, he applied a hand to the swollen organ, wrapping his fingers tightly around it. Then he began a slow, clumsy, inexperienced stroking.

How marvelous! "It" worked just fine. Lonny congratulated himself and sought to improve his technique. He'd often heard the other boys talking about doing "it" as a way to relieve the "itch," and had pretended to be as wisely experienced as they. Now he'd managed "it" for the first time. How great it felt!

After an experimental rearrangement of his grip, Lonny happily discovered that not only did doing "it" make his hot itch go away, but it made his organ tickle in a most pleasant manner. He'd have to consider doing "it" quite often in the future. With a contented sigh, he lowered himself to a sitting position on the wooden seat. Why was his mouth so dry? Why did he breathe so hard? He'd have to ask around to find out. And, most important of all, what was "it" called? Only "it?"

So absorbed in his delightful indulgence did Lonny become that he allowed his trousers and longjohn bottoms to slide down to his ankles. His wonderful manipulation transported him in imagination to a hundred different scenes. In each of which he, the mighty Lonny Cramer, equipped with a big, beautiful dingus like Eli Holten, made quick and sweet conquest of every pretty girl in his school. His solitary pleasure ended in a loud crash and a bright shaft of light as someone threw open the door to the outhouse.

Jumping with fright and sudden guilt, Lonnie looked upward to see the angry, reddened face of Eli Holten hovering above him. With one huge hand, the scout hauled the startled little boy off the rough wooden bench with its traditional two holes and bent Lonny's bare bottom over his knee.

"Haven't you anything else to do after ruining a kind, beautiful young woman's life than to come out here and jack off to celebrate? I have a good mind to stuff you head-first down one of those slop chutes. But this might do some good."

Swiftly, Eli applied a sound spanking, turning Lonny's buttocks a bright, cherry red. With each solid application of a big, calloused palm, Eli drove home another point.

"This is for being a sneak. This one is for being a rotten tattle-tale. This is for ruining Prudence Alden's life in Eagle Pass. She may never get a teaching job again, thanks to you. And this is for embarrassing me."

Lonny yowled, and wriggled, and howled until the chastisement ended. Abruptly Eli uprighted the crying lad and the scout's lips curled into a sarcastic sneer.

"Now you can go back to your personal reward for being such an effective snitch."

"B-b-but h-how can I?" Lonny wailed in desperation and pain. "Wh-when it's as limp and wrinkled as ever?"

"Let that be a lesson to you," the scout responded gruffly and stalked off.

He'd help locate Prudence in other quarters, get her settled in, Eli considered. Then maybe, just maybe, he could help make the hurt go away.

Chapter Five

Sparkling brightly and unseasonably hot, the sun burned down on Dakota Territory. A warm, southwest wind brushed over the prairie, dissolving the remaining swatches of white, as Eli Holten covered the last miles to Fort Rawlins. All in all it could be counted as a fine day. If one weren't Eli Holten. And if one didn't continue to feel partly responsible for the humiliation of Prudence Alden. Something *ugly* was going on in Eagle Pass. The mental midgets with their gigantic self-interpreted morality had moved in and were taking over, and . . . *civilizing* the town. Before long they would close down the sporting houses, put Mother Hubbards on the saloon girls and try to shut off the flow of booze. Maybe it had come time to move further west, the scout considered. At least, Prudence had been cared for.

Eli had found her a place to stay for a few days and

contributed to the small sum she had put aside. She could take the stage line to Pierre and the train on to somewhere to start a new life. Why, then, did he still feel guilty?

"Howdy, Mister Holten," the sentry at the main gate greeted him in a friendly manner.

"Mornin', Tom," Eli replied. He hoped he had the trooper's name right.

Bone-tired and sore, though it had been an easy ride, Eli went directly to the stables and cared for his horse. Then he crossed the compound to his quarters. There he kindled a fire to drive away the chill, stripped off his clothes, and washed with tepid water. By the time he finished, the coffee pot summoned him with a steaming aroma. He poured a cup and took a sip, then winced. Damnit! Pru made such a good cup of coffee. A couple of spoons of sugar would tame it, he thought resignedly. When he drained the last of the bitey brew he crawled between the covers and drifted off to sleep.

It seemed like he had barely closed his eyes when someone began to pound on his door. "Mister Holten, Mister Holten!"

"Yeah. I'm here. What is it?"

"The general's compliments, sir, and he would like you to join him in his office."

"Can't it wait until tomorrow?"

"The general said right away, sir."

"All right."

Holten shaved, dressed and tugged on his boots in less than five minutes. He donned his hat as he stepped out onto the street called officers row. Mud sucked at his heels as he strode over to the headquarters building.

A metal scraper by the bottom step cleaned most of the gumbo off his boots before he entered the office. The brigade sergeant major greeted him warmly.

"Good afternoon to ye, Mister Holten. Himself is waitin' for ye so ye can go right in."

"Thank you, Muldoon."

Holten rapped lightly on the door, turned the knob and entered Frank Corrington's office. He took notice of the significant brandy decanter and box of cigars first off. This would be another hard one right enough, Eli thought in resignation. The general waved him to a chair and pushed the cigars closer.

"Sit down, Eli. Have a cigar."

"What's it all about, Frank?"

"Well now, Eli, considering you're back from your, ah, leave, I thought I might fill you in on what's been happening in the department."

Oh shit! Does he know about Prudence?

"Can't that wait until officers' call in the morning?"

"Unfortunately, it can't. Let me pour you some brandy. As you know, Nelson Miles has been transferred into the department to gather up all the off-reservation Sioux. He has a regiment of infantry, the Ninth, and some artillery at Fort Keogh to perform the task. So far he hasn't accomplished a great deal because higher headquarters have chosen not to pursue the affair. Recently, an entire family out near Keogh were killed."

"I read about that in the newspaper."

"That incident, and the butchery of a train work crew, has tipped the balance in Miles' favor. Department headquarters has cut orders for him to take an expedition into the field at once. Yellowstone Kelly is chief of scouts for Miles and John Johnson is along, too."

"*Livereating* Johnson? Christ! If the Crow got wind of that, they might be willing to bury the hatchet with the Sioux for a chance to get at him."

"That feud is supposed to be smoothed over by now," Corrington said dryly. Everyone had heard of the legendary treaty, supposedly signed by the Crow nation with a single man, John Livereating Johnson.

"The essence is that Miles and the Ninth will take the field within a week."

"All that's of little interest or importance to me. Fort Keogh is at the far west end of the Department."

"Miles asked Department headquarters for a cavalry screen," Corrington went on. "In their infinite wisdom, our superiors at headquarters designated two companies of the Twelfth to form that screen."

"With me as their scout, I suppose?"

"I'm glad we agree on that."

"Frank! That was a question, not an offer to volunteer."

"I've decided on B and C Companies," Corrington continued, ignoring Eli's protest. "It should be an easy campaign. Indians settle down during the cold months. Everyone knows that."

"Yeah? Then what about that settler family you mentioned that got massacred not two weeks ago?"

"An exception to the rule," the general offered. "But one that got Miles moving at once. Something you should do also."

"Crap!"

"Have some more brandy."

"Bull crap!"

"You need to coordinate with Walter Brice and Arthur Phalan before today is over. You're to pull out tomorrow at first light."

"Frank, why are you doing this to me?"

"Because you're the best man I have."

Takin' care of cows in the winter was hard work. Cold, too, Billy Vanders added as he entered a large hay barn. Then, when a thaw like this came along, mud got all over everything. Why did old man Ellerby keep on only four hands from October until March? Everyone had to do double chores. Billy continued to savor his injustices as he climbed to the hay loft. He shivered slightly as he laid his shoulder into heaving open the big door over the corral. Bright sunlight set the world asparkle. Billy's gaze wandered out over the steaming brown backs of the hungry cattle to the far side of the corral.

There his eyes locked on the shiny, obsidian orbs of *Pisko*. Night Hawk sat his mount in the center of a curved line of Miniconjou warriors. To his right, *Tasa* clamped the braided horsehair rein of his favorite war pony under his thigh while he drew an arrow back almost to the sinew reinforced ash bow.

"Oh . . . my . . . God!" Billy spoke aloud in the weary voice of an old man.

When Red Buffalo released his hold, the projectile hummed mournfully through the space where Billy Vanders' chest had been before he dropped like a stone to the rough plank floor of the hay mow. More arrows, and a splatter of bullets, slammed into the barn wall. The flightier among the cattle began to bellow and mill about. Billy heard a loud, screeching crash and peeped over the doorsill.

Braided leather ropes extended between bare-legged braves and three corral posts. The uprights bent outward and the crossrails squealed in protest. A moment later the cattle bolted and charged clumsily out through the opening. All but the Sioux warriors attached to the posts swirled away and rode out of sight around the barn. Gunshots sounded from the direction of the bunkhouse and Billy curled into a protective ball.

He lay that way for a full fifteen minutes. Screams from dying men reached his ears and caused him to quail the more. He had no weapon and could never get to one now. Shouts and shots and the din of terrified animals roared in his ears. A moment later he smelled smoke and heard a steady crackling noise. Then came the tread of stealthy footsteps on the ladder bars.

Billy wanted to bawl like a baby and beg for his life. Instead, he looked around him in desperation and mumbled aloud a prayer for salvation. Then his glance lit upon an object unlikely, yet the only one he'd encountered so far, to be used as a weapon.

The work-worn handle of the hay fork felt reassuring in Billy's hands. He gripped it tightly and crouched near the top of the ladder. An anxious moment passed and the head of an Indian rose into view. By good fortune, he looked the other way. Swiftly Billy came upright, tightly holding the pitchfork. Satisfied, though cautious, the Miniconjou surged upward into the loft, one hand clutching a Winchester.

Screaming savagely, Billy Vanders drove the three tines of the fork into the soft belly of the warrior. A howl of sheer agony rose from the painted brave's chest and he dropped his weapon. Slowly the young Sioux leaned backward. Palms slippery with fear sweat, Billy could not stop the handle from sliding out of his grasp. He watched as his enemy dropped out of sight beyond the edge of the loft, the long-handled pitchfork wiggling in his rigid gut. Quickly the youthful cowhand snatched up the Winchester and checked the chamber. It held a round, but he had no idea how many more might be in the magazine.

During the next fifteen minutes, Billy valiantly defended his position from every attempt by the Miniconjou to drive him out. At last, his ammunition expended and flames leaping high through the barn, Billy abandoned his stronghold. With a mighty lunge, he jumped from the open door, caught a pulley rope and slid to the ground. He made it a good fifty feet before the first arrow caught him low in the back, pierced a kidney, and numbed his body with pain. In swift succession, three bullets slammed into his rib cage and another feathered shaft pinned his leg to the ground.

Through the dim shrouds of approaching death, Billy Vanders saw *Pisko* approaching him, a scalping knife in his hand.

For a people supposed to be immobile in winter, the

Sioux had been doing a hell of a lot of getting around, Nelson Miles thought as he sat at his desk and fumed. Three more settlers' places raided, burned to the ground. Twenty lives lost. He'd sent out patrols. All they had discovered were bloated white corpses. He'd double the size, mount them on mules for greater range and speed. Where the hell was the cavalry when he needed it?

"Major Hammond!" Miles raised his voice to summon his adjutant.

"Yes, sir?"

"Why haven't our patrols been finding any Indians?"

"I'm not sure, sir. Not even Mister Kelly has been able to make contact."

"Yellowstone Kelly is the best there is. What does he say is the reason?"

Hammond shrugged. "The infantry moves slowly. The weather. Maybe that the raids are being conducted by Cheyenne from further west, not the Sioux at all."

Miles squinted and brushed at his thick, black mustache. "That sounds like excuses instead of reasons. We could see the smoke from one of those attacks from the outer wall. Our only consolation is that whole villages of Sioux can't move this fast or secretly. I'd hate to have to report to Department headquarters that we've been outmaneuvered by a handful of renegade Sioux."

"I agree, Nelson. It would be ruinous. At least when the cavalry gets here . . ."

"When the cavalry gets here, we're taking this expedition out and we'll not come back until we find every last one of these renegades and drag them all kicking and screaming back to Pine Ridge."

Chapter Six

Rising like a monument out of the prairie, the two and a half story structure, with its crenelated roof and narrow, vertical windows resembled a medieval castle more than a ranch house. Built of native stone and thick pine logs, it could easily withstand an assault by all save modern artillery and mortars. Indians wouldn't have a chance. That's the way its owner, Grant Brockton planned it.

Even the out-buildings, connected by low, covered walkways, which resembled the spokes of a wheel, ended in curiously shaped barbettes and redoubts. The pleasant warming spell, during the first week of January, had exposed the complex layout from under its heavy layer of snow. A slim pole extended from the center of the tall central tower's roof. From it waved the American flag and, below that, a banner depicting Brockton's brand. Picked out in gold and blue, against a white field, the crown, ornamental bar and the letter B boldly proclaimed the owner to be in residence.

Grant Brockton enjoyed his baronial trappings. On the ground floor, the main hall had a flagstone floor, covered regularly with fresh straw and strewn with dried sage leaves and rose petals to provide a pleasant scent. It also boasted a walk-in fireplace for heat and cooking and enough trestle tables to seat two hundred. From the open beams, below the ceiling, hung ancient banners and standards, purporting to be the lineage of the clan Brockton. He had even imported a complete suit of armor to be displayed slightly behind and to one side of the large, high-backed chair where he held court.

At the present time, Brockton occupied that chair, with his foreman, Wayne Staples on his right and Everett Lockwood to his left. Some seventy men occupied places at the nearer tables. More than half their number had been summoned by Brockton, the remainder were members of the "Nebraska Rangers." Hard-working attendants bustled about to provide steaming platters of roasted meat and delicately cooked vegetables to the voracious assemblage. Brockton lifted a goblet and inclined its rim toward Lockwood.

"Your arrival here is most timely, sir. We had thought, since this is our land, to punish the savages alone. That others shared our intentions is heartening indeed. Now that we're settled at table, let us officially welcome you to the Crown-Bar-B."

Lockwood nodded gravely and considered his host. Brockton's use of the royal prerogative bothered Lockwood. Anyone with pretentions to nobility in a land of men proud to be free and equal, had to have his scuttle shy a few lumps of coal. Though he had to admit Brockton had the looks for the part. A couple of inches over six feet, he had big hands and broad shoulders. A long torso sat well atop powerful legs that fit proportionately. A thick cap of salt-and-pepper hair covered a large, long head and his straight, patrician nose provided the right amount of de-emphasis to his wide, thick-lipped mouth. In all, Brockton reminded Everett of the character of Prince John in Sir Walter Scott's *Ivanhoe*. His swift evaluation ended, Lockwood cleared his throat and made reply.

"We had hardly expected such a splendid reception in so remote a part of the Territory as this. In fact, my men and I thought we might be off to do battle alone. We saw visions of a few isolated homesteads, the settlers helpless in the face of increased depredations by the Sioux."

Brockton smiled, revealing large, white teeth. "We see that you are a romanticist. That speaks of nobility in a person. We, too, have enjoyed the writings of Scott. His heroes would have eagerly joined us in this crusade, eh?"

"Quite so." Shocked that Grant Brockton had seemingly plucked a thought directly from his mind, Everett Lockwood turned his attention to his meal.

Thick, shaggy eyebrows writhed like tortured caterpillars on the jutting ridge over Brockton's deep-set, flinty-colored eyes. He attacked a joint of meat that had been set on a platter before him, along with braised turnips, boiled onions and potatoes browned in pan drippings.

"Are you descended from one of the warrior clans?" Brockton waved the extricated leg bone from his joint of mutton at the banners above them.

"How's that?"

At fifty, Everett Lockwood thought of himself as "compact" and "solidly padded," rather than fat. Well along toward balding, his lank yellow hair grown long and combed in a manner that attempted to cover the shiny pate, he hardly considered himself to cut a martial figure. His service during the War of the Rebellion had been as a commissary officer for the Union Army.

"There are but a few superior families," Brockton explained, "scattered about the nations, who have produced the world's greatest leaders. The Caesars are one such. Even the heathen Orientals had examples, such as Ganghis Khan, his sons and grandsons. We are related to three such European families.

"During the Great War, we commanded a regiment of Sherman's foragers. We stripped the earth bare for miles' distance across our route of march to insure the Rebel scum could not reform and resupply behind us on our march to the sea."

Images of women and children, and their loyal darkies, hanging by their necks while crops and plantation buildings burned in the background leaped to Lockwood's mind. "I, ah, see. I don't think I'm cut of *that* cloth."

"Yet you are here on a noble quest, a leader, commanding his men as he should. And we say welcome to you. Now, then, to the contest at hand."

God, did he always talk in such a pompous manner? Everett Lockwood wondered. "The Sioux, you mean?"

"Precisely. There are far too many of the Sioux not on reservations. The Miniconjou in particular, but also Oglala, Hunkpapa and Teton. Their recent hostile acts give reason enough to field a force sufficient to quell them. We are prepared, with your help, to chase down any stray Sioux and deal with them as need be. How many live ones we deliver to the reservations is of no concern to us."

His fanatic hatred of Indians came to the fore and Lockwood responded vehemently. "Nor of mine."

"Then we are in agreement. Excellent. We know where there are a number of small encampments of Sioux. They are close to here. We can start with these."

Two days of steadily declining weather had passed since Eli Holten had bid goodbye to the train crew of the Platte River and Pacific Railroad. The two companies of cavalry and their horses had detrained out in the middle of nowhere and ridden northwest toward Fort Keogh. The scout rested now in the notch of a gentle swell and gazed off across the prairie toward a dark smudge that had to be the fort.

"Three hours, four at the most," Eli estimated aloud to Captain Phalan of B Company.

"Do you remember when we had to ride horses all this way?" The boyish, smiling officer asked.

"Do I! Funny, but the Sioux never seemed in much of a hurry in those days. We improve our transportation and the Sioux start moving faster. I wonder if it wouldn't have been better to leave things like they were?"

"Like it or not, Eli, we're a part of the modern world. And the modern demand is for speed."

Holten made a face. "Let's bring 'em on in, Art. We'll find out soon enough what we're up against."

Nelson Miles greeted them personally. He enthusiastically shook hands with the officers and Eli Holten, then adjourned with them to his office. Glasses of whiskey, small by comparison with General Corrington's generous brandy snifters, were passed around and everyone took a seat.

"Eli Holten, this is Luther Sage Kelly, Yellowstone Kelly. Kelly, Eli Holten."

Eli rose and extended a hand. "So you're *Wicasakala Cante Tinza*," Holten said warmly. "I'm most pleased to make your acquaintance."

Yellowstone Kelly grinned broadly and clamped a grip on Eli Holten's hand that threatened to grind the knuckles together. "You're not exactly unfamous yer-self, Holten."

"What's this *Wicasakala* business?" Miles inquired with a snap.

"It's what the Sioux call him, Colonel. Little Man with the Strong Heart. Didn't he ever tell you?"

Although small in stature, Kelly radiated a greatness few men would ever achieve. For all his aura of strength, he grinned shyly now and studied the toes of his boots.

"Never saw any reason for braggin' on myself, Holten, Colonel. T'Sioux stuck me with that moniker, all right, but I think Gen'ral Miles here deserves it more'n me." Kelly admitted, referring to Miles' brevet rank from the Union Army.

Although not a graduate of West Point, Miles had shown a brilliance and tenacity in combat that had earned him rapid promotion. When the war ended, he had been returned to a permanent rank of colonel. No one in his command, fiercely loyal to him to a man, would think of calling him by his proper rank. To all of them, save perhaps John Johnson, he was General Miles.

"Your modesty overwhelms me," Nelson Miles fumbled out. He'd never experienced such unbecoming reticence on the part of the man he'd named in official dispatches as, "a hero in war, a true American patriot in times of peace."

Eli Holten accepted the self-deprecation for what it truly meant among the elite class of frontier scouts. He retrieved his sore hand and snorted derisively.

"Chief Bullshit is more likely how it started off. If Kelly here hasn't been blowin' his own horn, he's not a true frontiersman."

"Awh, Holten, you've gone and ruined a good thing. I was buckin' for a softer bed an' my pick of assignments. Now I'll have to take pot luck. 'Sides, that was all down in the Department of the Platte."

"From whence we've been sent," Miles interrupted, "to corral your intransigent Sioux. As I'm sure you gentlemen are aware, Department headquarters has at last gotten off its collective duffs and cut orders mobilizing this expedition. There's plenty of hostiles out there, but more significantly, there's a large village of off-reservation Sioux near by. Now that you're here, I would like to set out at daybreak to round them up."

"If the colonel please, sir, we've only just arrived," Arthur Phalan injected, "as you say. We should meet your officers, coordinate our activities and study your general plan a bit before moving into the field."

"All of which I'm fully cognizant, Captain. For which, unfortunately, we'll take the next two days to accomplish. *Then* we shall sally forth against the wily tribesmen."

After the meeting, Yellowstone Kelly showed Eli Holten to the scouts' quarters. "You'll hardly get a dent in that bed, Holten. Ol' Piss and Vinegar's been snortin' to get started ever since we got here. Now he has his chance."

"What sort of a commander is Miles?" Eli asked, mentally picturing the calm brilliance of Frank Corrington in battle.

"The best. He never asks his men to do something he won't undertake. He never loses control and yells at someone in front of the others. He knows Injuns and how to get around 'em. Hell, we pacified all the Sioux in the Department of the Platte and sent 'em up here to the reservations. Half the time we didn't even have to fight the tricky devils. Miles outsmarted 'em. They got to callin' him Bear Coat, for his big woolly winter coat. He's more or less invented winter campaigns, when no one else would have any truck with 'em. Injuns don't like tryin' cold-stiffened bows or ice-coated strings against Springfields. Why, the Sioux get so disheartened when the soldiers march down on 'em, asshole deep in snow, that lots of them just give up."

"That sounds encouraging. I didn't exactly jump for joy when General Corrington ordered me out here."

"You just hide and watch, part'ner. Our only real problem is these hostiles that are raidin'. The rest will come along gentle as lambs. Those, we've gotta watch closely."

Chapter Seven

Sparks popped and whirled high into the night sky from the green wood placed on the big fire of buffalo chips. Smoke whipped to all points of the compass as a fretful breeze skipped through the village. The big ceremonial drum throbbed, sending deep, heartbeat tones out to reverberate off the distant hills and deep-cut canyon walls along the Tongue River. A sharper note came from the small two-headed drum carried by the leader of the *Kangi Yuha* warrior society.

In solemn mien, the warriors of the Raven Owners danced into the circle, following him, and a brave playing on an eagle wingbone whistle. At the rear of the procession came another drummer and a flute player. In the place of honor shuffled *Pisko*. He held aloft five willow hoop scalp stretchers with their grisly trophies. Next came *Tasa* with three. Each of the Raven Owners who had followed the war pipe with Night Hawk and Red Buffalo had at least one scalp to celebrate, most of them two. There would be feasting later and *Pisko* looked forward to it.

"*Wapiya hibu yelo*!" *Pisko* chanted, then repeated. "In a sacred manner I come. I have seen the enemy, I have seen his face. With my Black Feather club I have struck him, with my Black Feather club I have struck. I am not afraid. I have seen the enemy, I have seen his face. With my lance I have pierced him, with my lance I have pierced. I am not afraid."

On went his sing-song recitation until he had named every weapon used and recounted the taking of the scalps he held. Then *Tasa* took over, recounting his exploits. So it went until all the raiders had described their part in the attacks on whites. The dance became less stately then, as the remaining males over thirteen joined in. When the three rapid beats signaled the end, everyone went laughing and chattering to help themselves to the tempting, though scarce amount of food prepared for the feast.

Licking greasy fingers, *Pisko* rose to speak to the assembled warriors and the people of the Miniconjou village at about the time the moon slipped over to the western part of the sky. He wiped his face and smiled, turning with raised arms until even the small children fell silent.

"We avenged ourselves on those who intruded too far onto our lands. We've shown the white soldiers that we will stay free. These things are good. But they bring something that's not good." A mutter rose at his statement and Night Hawk waited for it to subside before going on.

"Many soldiers gather at the place of Bear Coat. Among them are pony soldiers from where the sun is born. My brothers and I have heard that they gather to come here, to take us all to the place of *Pine Ridge*." *Pisko* mouthed the English words like something vile to his taste.

"This we won't do. We would no longer be free. We would die at their *Pine Ridge*. I call on all warriors to take up the war pipe with me. Follow me in fighting the false men. They have no heart for battle when it is cold. We can't let them tame us. Come, join me."

"Night Hawk speaks brave words," old *Nitasunkecu* answered in a quavering voice. "For many seasons, I would have been first to stand at his side. I've seen the white soldiers in the hot seasons and in the cold. They always fight. We always lose. It's best if we hide from their faces. We must withdraw into the mountains and leave them to chase their tails. Your victories were not purchased cheaply. Men have died. Let's not have more die in a battle we cannot win. I have spoken."

"Takes-Your-Horse speaks wisely," *Pisko* responded. "I call for war, he offers peace. Both are good. Yet, is it not always a good day to die, *Nitasunkecu*?"

"It's as our people say," the old man responded in a surly tone.

"Who will go with me, then? Who will stay?"

Eager calls went around the big fireside. Takes-Your-Horse rose once more. "We can have peace and the young can make war. It has always been our way." Then he directed his words to Night Hawk. "You're not bound by my words, as you know, *Pisko*. If the soldiers truly come forth in the dead of winter, we must all make ourselves like the quail and hide from our enemy. Let our people think on it until the sun is reborn. Then we shall decide."

* * *

Soft and feathery, a white filigree covered every branch of sage brush, chokecherry, the reeds and grasses of the prairie. During the night a heavy frost had set in, the damp ground frozen stone-hard. On the northwest horizon dark clouds gathered and promised another snowfall. Rushed hoofbeats had a hollow, clopping sound, like wooden blocks pounded on a rock, as they approached the morning camp of the Nebraska Rangers and Grant Brockton's men. A squat, banty rooster of a man slid from the steaming back of his horse and reported to Brockton.

"Mister Grant, I come from Fort Keogh. The soldiers moved out yesterday to round up the Sioux."

"More likely a large patrol," Brockton opined.

"No, sir. The whole damned regiment's on the march, plus a couple of companies of cavalry. I counted real close like you said. They didn't take no artillery, so I figger they're plannin' on movin' fast. That steely-eyed bastard Miles was leadin' 'em out the gate."

"We'll thank you to speak more kindly of Nelson Miles. He's married to Bill Sherman's niece, Mary, and any man who has William Techumseh Sherman's approval is all right in our ledger." Having dressed his man down in what he saw as proper style, Brockton's mood changed. "Well then, this calls for some modification of our plan. Mister Lockwood, if you please?"

Everett Lockwood, accompanied by his son, Ralph, walked to where Grant Brockton lounged in a camp chair beside the fire. "What is it, Mister Brockton?"

"The army's in the field, at long last. Nelson Miles is a fire-eater. He'll not show mercy, but he will be fair.

Likely, he'll herd most of the Sioux onto reservations. Given time and men enough, that is. Perhaps we should confine our activities further west, to avoid encountering the soldiers. The military takes a dim view of civilians doing their job for them. A man has a right, an obligation, to protect what is his, yet the army calls us vigilantes."

"Where do you propose we go?"

"Out toward the Yellowstone country. There are Sioux and Cheyenne encampments the military has never seen. They'll talk out of the other sides of their mouths when we bring in a few of those, eh?"

"It sounds intriguing," Everett offered.

"It sounds like a lot of extra, unnecessary riding," Ralph put in.

Lockwood frowned at his son.

"The point is," Grant Brockton summed up. "We'll have a chance to rid the frontier of a lot of hostile Indians and open land for human settlement. No matter the army thinks it can do it better, we'll be heroes to the common people."

During the day's ride, Eli Holten had ample opportunity to consider the relationship between one man and another. The cause of his contemplation had been John Livereating Johnson. He was a huge, powerful man who seemed to always be spoiling for a fight. His reputation was such that some of the younger scouts outright feared him. In contrast to the clean-shaven faces of Luther Kelly and Eli Holten, John Johnson's personal appearance spoke of another, wilder, day and time.

He wore a ragged leather shirt and leggins, plainly made without beadwork, and stained shiny black with the grease and soot of innumerable cookfires. His wild hair had been frizzed and sun-faded and his unkempt beard bore heavy stains from chaw-spittle. His tobacco-eroded teeth had rotted to the gumline. Where Kelly quoted Milton and Sir Walter Scott, Johnson presented the image of an illiterate, unwashed, profane, roving-eyed, raucous left-over from the by-gone era of the fur trappers. If a person stood downwind, Johnson's gamey odor could knock one sprawling. Why Nelson Miles tolerated him, Eli could not understand. For the time being, the scout had other worries.

Throughout the day the cloud masses had continued to build and the temperature dropped alarmingly in mid-afternoon. An hour before camp time, the first dancing flakes started to fall. The wind increased. Snow began to adhere to anything it touched. It rapidly produced white mantles that covered the dark blue, wide-brimmed campaign hats the soldiers wore. Scarves appeared to cover the ears and cheeks of the cavalry troopers. The temperature plummeted to near zero.

Old timers told of it getting "too cold to snow." Their native wisdom clearly didn't apply this winter. Visibility had dropped to less than a quarter mile when Eli urged Captains Phalan and Brice to halt for the night. While the infantry moved slowly toward the spot, the cavalry made camp in lowering conditions.

Fires burned fitfully in the whipping wind, which had reached a velocity that produced moans even where no trees existed to tune the harmonics. Blinding volleys of snow obscured everything. A thin stand of box elder and another of scraggly lodgepole pine formed two irregular sides of a triangle where the camp lay, but did nothing to staunch the onslaught of a raging blue norther. Captain Brice carried a carefully cased, spirit thermometer, sent out by the War Department. Using it, he made detailed notations of temperature change to go with his other weather observations. For some unknown reason these reports seemed important to those in Washington. Shortly before sundown, he showed the instrument to Eli. The scarlet fluid indicated a shattering twenty below zero.

Such a frigid condition did little to cool the temper of Livereating Johnson. Huddled around their separate fire, the scouts discussed, as usual, their day's observations and pecularities. One of the younger men declared that the big Sioux encampment they sought could not lie too far away. This afternoon he had come upon fresh horse droppings. They had still been warm.

"Bull balls!" Livereating Johnson snapped. "Unless you was close enough to see the goddamned horse, those droppin's weren't hot. Not this afternoon they weren't."

"I saw them," Lars Lindstrom insisted. "I felt them."

"Yer own mount musta shit in yer hand for that to happen," Johnson sneered.

"A-are you calling me a liar?" Lars asked in an unsteady voice.

Johnson squinted his nearly colorless eyes and worked his thick lips around a generous chew of Union Leader. He spit juice in a long, brown stream that splattered on the young scout's boots, and came to his feet, fists balled.

"I'm callin' ya a iggerent son of a bitch." Johnson

eased back a bit and looked around at the others, turning with a swaggering step. "Now there, there. This pukin' mother's mistake either fights me to prove he's right or he admits he was bullshittin' like I knowed all along. What you say, huh? What you say to that, Sonny?"

Lars Lindstrom was a tall, heavy-muscled Swede, and no mean scrapper in his own right. His broad, smiling, Scandinavian face masked a hot temper and no small portion of courage. With a thrust of his thick arms he propelled himself upward, goaded by Johnson's taunts. It did him little good as Livereating delivered a vicious kick to Lars' chest, before the youth got to his feet, that sent the straw-haired Swede sprawling, nearly into the fire.

Winded and dazed, he managed to roll away from a deadly stomp aimed at his windpipe. His evasion gained him time to come upright, elbows cocked, clenched fists describing circles at his sides. Johnson rushed him again and Lindstrom side-stepped. When his opponent came even with him, Lars whipped a full powered punch to Johnson's right kidney.

Livereating sucked air in a thin whistle and propelled himself on around, grappling at Lindstrom's waist until he managed a back-breaking hug. Muscles bulged in Johnson's long arms as he tightened his grip, left wrist grasped firmly in his right hand. With apparently no strain, he lifted Lindstrom off the ground.

"Work on his face, Lars," a supporter advised.

Livereating had buried his face in his opponent's belly, rendering it invulnerable. In compensation, Lars began to pound on the top of Johnson's head. Lances of dizzying pain shot out from his lower back as Livereating contracted his arms like the coils of a boa constrictor. Lars found he could not breathe. He locked both hands together and slammed them down with all his remaining force.

Johnson grunted and his grip slackened slightly. Lars sucked in a deep, grateful breath and struck again. More pressure eased and he shoved away with a cry of relief. Although big, Livereating towered over Lars. He swayed for only a fraction of a second and came on again. Lars danced away, swung, ducked and shuffled off again.

"Stay still, you little asshole," Johnson growled. He didn't even pant.

"*Ja* sure," Lars reverted to his regional dialect. "So you can get those big arms around me again? Would it be that ya like boys to hug?"

"Ya dirty-minded shit, I'll squash ya like a bug!" Livereating howled.

Lars swung as Livereating charged, to find his arm caught and nearly yanked out of the socket when Johnson swung him with no more effort than flinging a cat by its tail. When his antagonist let go, Lars flew into the legs of the huddled scouts and sent several sprawling. Before he could extract himself, ham-like fists began to pound his face. Then they worked on his rib cage, sending shoots of fiery pain to his heart. Jerked free, Lars hurled toward the fire. He jinked away from that deadly end to wind up with Johnson astride him, pounding his body with blows so rapid he could not see the hands that delivered them. His vision grayed, dimmed and sank toward blackness.

"He's out of it, Livereatin'," a middle-aged scout

appealed. "Let him up."

"Up, hell. I ain't gonna quit 'till his soul squirts out his fuckin' ears."

"Yer killin' him," another protested.

"What the hell's that got to do with it? You heard what he said. You hear what he called me. He ain't got no goddamned right."

Returning from a meeting with the brass, Eli Holten came upon the fight at this point. He flung men aside to get to the contestants. His gaze took in the bloodied, torn features of Lars Lindstrom and he judged the scrappy young scout had less than a minute to live.

"Let him go, Johnson."

"Piss up a rope."

"Get off him or I'll crack a pistol barrel over your head," Eli commanded with deadly certainty.

Johnson released his left hand from the strangle-hold and swung it backhand so swiftly the scout saw only a blur. It hit his knee like a flying log and bowled him off his feet. Before he could roll over and come upright, Johnson scrambled off his first victim and kicked Eli in the back.

The scout splayed out on the ground and one gloved hand flopped in the fire. Johnson closed in and Eli bunched his legs, knees drawn. The double kick he released delivered all its power to Livereating's stomach. Air whooshed from the huge man and he bent forward, legs moving unsteadily. Holten regained his feet and slammed a hard right to the side of Johnson's head.

It felt like punching a stone wall. Pain shot up the scout's arm. Several men yelled encouragement but Eli heard it faintly. Johnson's leering face floated before him. He readied another blow and the lights went out. Eli rebounded from contact with the ground after Livereating's left-handed sneak punch. He shook his head in an attempt to clear it, knowing that each fraction of a second delay made it more difficult for him.

Johnson drove that point home with a moccasin toe under the chin. Only the superb condition of his body saved Eli from a broken neck. He rolled with the force and sprang shakily to his feet. Johnson looked like he hadn't exchanged two blows with a ten-year-old. A slight cut over his left eye slowly began to open and Eli decided to concentrate on that.

He endured punishing jabs to his ribs as he waded in for a mauling shot at the torn skin. Left-and-right, left-and-right, Eli drilled on the small wound. Flesh gave and a steady pour of blood developed. Livereating bellowed and stomped the ground, hurling his heavy arms at Holten's head. The scout managed to dodge one, only to have the other connect with the force of a runaway locomotive.

Staggered, the scene whirling around his balloon-like head, Eli reeled about a second before walking into another round-house that Johnson pulled up from his belt. Rocked back, Eli tried to lift his leaden arms into a defensive position. A grin split the whiskered lips of his opponent and Johnson lunged in again. Battered and bloody, Eli gulped air in a frantic attempt to straighten the universe. The gyrations slowed and he saw a big fist coming in time to dart his head to the side and avoid it. Desperate now, he grabbed Johnson's barrel-thick forearm with both hands and bit into flesh until a salty, metallic flow ran into his mouth.

"You baaaastard!" Johnson yowled. "Fight like a man!"

Eli released him and drove a backhand blow to Johnson's nose. "I am. Like a man in fear of his life."

"You'd better be," Johnson grunted. " 'Cause I'm gonna kill ya an' then finish that little twerp."

Don't run your mouth. It was one of the first rules of fighting Eli Holten had learned as a small boy. Let your fists do the talking. Eli recalled that lesson while Livereating started to add more to his challenge. Holten set his feet firmly and cut loose with the first of a one-two to the huge brutalizer's head.

Knuckles cracked off bone and silenced Livereating Johnson's words. He swayed from side to side in the fleeting moment before the second blow slammed home.

Livereating's mouth worked soundlessly and his eyes rolled upward for a second. He tottered like a beaver-girdled tree, then bent double. Eli clasped both hands and drove them downward on Johnson's exposed neck.

Livereating grunted and took two short, running steps. He gaped and gasped and shook his head groggily. Then he came erect and extended one hand, palm open.

"This chile' ain't seen many men could stay on their feet this long. Shake, 'cause we's just gonna have to be friends. We'd be too dangerous as enemies."

"What about Lars?" the scout asked belligerently.

"Awh, hell. Poor little guy never had a chance. I'll make it up to him later."

"I'm just glad he'll have a 'later,' " Eli returned as he took the giant's hand.

"What's the meaning of this disturbance?" Nelson

Miles' voice came from the darkness beyond the fire.

"Just a little knuckle drill," Yellowstone Kelly offered.

Miles stepped into the firelight. "Mister Holten? Mister Johnson? Is that essentially correct?"

"It is," Eli answered.

"Yup, Colonel."

Swiftly, Miles took in the circumstances and the degree of damage to each of the participants. While he stood in contemplation, Lars Lindstrom moaned, rolled on his side and vomited.

"Who, ah, accounted for him?"

"I did, Colonel," Johnson readily admitted.

"Very well then. Tomorrow morning, if this storm has ended, I'm detaching a company and a half of infantry to circle north and west. Their purpose is to block any escape by the off-reservation Sioux we're hunting. You will scout for that detail, Mister Johnson."

"Wha'ever you say, Colonel."

"That's all, then, gentlemen. Mister Holten, if you'll come with me."

Once out of earshot of the gathered scouts, Miles paused and pointed backward with his riding crop. "No matter how much I admire that man's aggressiveness against the Sioux, I find him an increasing bone of contention on this expedition."

"No explanations needed, Colonel. He would have killed that boy if I hadn't stepped in."

"You didn't do too damned well yourself, Holten."

"No, sir. I didn't. I gather it wasn't your original intention to send Johnson out with this reconnaissance in force?"

"Not at all. However, this way it should keep relative quiet in the main camp."

"That's something we could all use. I've a feeling there'll be fighting enough when we try to make the Sioux move onto the reservations," Eli remarked prophetically. Then added, "Good night, Colonel."

Chapter Eight

Tree limbs exploded like rifle shots as the temperature dove to a vicious thirty-eight below zero. A cloudless sky only aided rapid heat loss, for the tiny, bright coin of the sun, canted far over toward the southern horizon, held no discernible warmth. Hoofs crackled loudly through the thin layer of ice that had formed on the snow. Slowly the combined force of Grant Brockton and Everett Lockwood worked its way through a screening line of cottonwoods. In the fading light of late afternoon, they looked down into the broad valley formed by the widening action of the Musselshell River where it hurried northward to join the Missouri. Nestled in small circles, one clan touching the other to form the main hoop, stood the lodges of a Crow village. Screened by willows and low junipers, which formed an effective brake against snowdrifts, the site seemed idyllic and peaceful.

"That's Crows down there," Wayne Staples, Brockton's foreman advised. "And I've got a feeling we're on their reservation."

"What the hell difference does that make?" Everett Lockwood snapped. "An Indian's an Indian. We stir this bunch up and the army will be after them, too."

"If this is part of the reservation, we'll have the army after us," Staples returned.

"He's right, you know," Brockton added.

"My men scouted it out. There are few, if any, warriors in the village. We're going to attack regardless. It'll give the boys a chance to get blooded. You can join us or not as you wish."

Unaccustomed to others setting terms, Grant Brockton flushed a deep crimson, lips protruding into a hateful pout and his eyes locked in fiery anger on Everett Lockwood. The mood held an instant, then began to subside.

"B'God, we'll have to take to calling you Hotspur. We'll do it in two waves, then. If your men are so anxious to clash with the enemy, they may have the honor of leading out. First you go, sweep through the village firing at anything that moves. We'll come next, with our faithful chargers, about fifty yards behind you. That should overwhelm any possible resistance they can put up. We'll spill a little blood, then ride further north to catch the Sioux."

White Heron felt justifiably proud when he had been chosen for one of the five night guards. Just past his thirteenth summer, he would be the youngest of those who watched the pony herd. Red-orange streaks formed over the high canyon walls to the west, where cloud so thin as to be nearly invisible captured the rays of their Father the Sun as He went to His nightly rest. Pigeon-toed from a lifetime on horseback, White Heron strutted a bit as he draped his father's best braided rawhide rope over his winter-clad but bony chest, the coils resting against the right side of his neck, and joined the older boys. Tonight would be a special one, with added responsibility.

His father, along with many braves of the village, had gone to make meat. The unexpected warmth, followed by a swift snowfall forecast good hunting. Others of the warriors had gone to watch the eastern approaches favored by their old enemies, the Sioux, whom they had heard were stirred up again. White Heron wished he had been chosen to accompany these men, like his older brother, Flat Belly.

"In another summer you'll be old enough," his father had consoled him. Then he had tried to humor his son. "What would your uncle, Many Horses, do with two of you along? He'd be worn down to a tiny nub keeping up with you."

All the same, compared to the prospect of facing a Sioux war party, guarding the pony herd seemed dull. Until, of course, he set out to do just that. White Heron also brought along his fine, heavy new hunting bow and a quiver of precious metal-tipped arrows. Let anyone try to steal their horses.

"Who's that for?" croaked Bent Leg, an older boy with an unreliable voice that denoted the onset of the major change in his life.

"Anybody who gets in the way," White Heron told

him seriously.

Bent Leg hooted derisively. "Look at him!" he called to their companions. "White Heron is going to protect us all tonight."

Several boys, White Heron noticed, also carried their bows. "That's not fair!" he protested in a squeak.

His anguished complaint lost in a chorus of friendly jeers, White Heron went off to the station assigned him. At first he thought it to be an additional insult. Then, after a little consideration, he realized it made sense. The smallest, youngest boy should be the one closest to the village. He would be hardest to see by an approaching enemy, and could run swiftly to give the alarm in the event of trouble.

When exactly such a situation occurred, White Heron had to shake himself from a slight stupor to be certain he had not dreamed up the entire thing. No, he decided a moment later, it was entirely too real. Large men, white men with hairy faces, pounded toward the herd across the flats by the river bed.

In their hands they held shooting sticks, from which smoke and flame sprouted. Mechanically, without thinking through the process, White Heron drew an arrow and nocked it to the buffalo sinew string. Third Son, Bent Leg's younger brother suddenly lifted from the ground, a gout of red spurting from his mouth. White Heron heard the crack of rifle and revolver shots and realized that the worst possible of his wildest imaginings had come true. He drew his bow, took aim and loosed an arrow.

It flew swift and true, to sink deeply into the fatty part of a white man's belly. White Heron already had another projectile ready for release. From his right and some distance closer to the ponies and the whites, he dimly heard a voice calling his name.

"Go! Run swiftly and warn the village. There are eight hands of them."

White Heron quickly took aim at the big white man in the lead, with the greasy yellow locks and flowing hair under his nose. His thumb and fingers parted and the string twanged. White Heron didn't wait to see the result. He turned and raced toward the distant lodges.

He'd made only six running steps when something hit him hard between the shoulder blades. Numbness seeped outward a moment, before being followed by hot, savage agony and a whiteness that expanded from his brain and blanked out the sight and sound of fighting behind him.

With a shout of triumph, Everett Lockwood thundered down on the small boy he had shot. Whipping his attention to left and right he saw that none of the other herd guards had managed to alert the village. A lot of good it would do, he considered, the shots would warn them well enough. Indian ponies whinnied in fright and stampeded wildly around him. Good, if he could get his men to direct them, it would add to the confusion in the camp.

"That way," he directed. "Go around and head these horses toward the tipis."

Faintly, over the screaming of horses and thudding rattle of gunshots, Lockwood heard the drum of hoofs as Brockton's men made their charge. He nodded in satisfaction and turned his mount to help drive the herd toward the lodges. Something cracked noisily past his head and he swiveled it to look at the encampment.

Half a dozen men, older than might be expected for warriors, stood or knelt at the edge of the village, discharging their weapons in the direction of the attackers. Another bullet sang its deadly song over his head and Everett Lockwood decided to find another place in the line of battle. To his left he saw Ralph halt his prancing roan gelding and take careful aim. Hot gasses and burning particles of powder flashed at the muzzle of his son's rifle and one of the defenders staggered backward, hands over his belly. Blood streamed between the Crow brave's fingers.

Good shooting, Everett thought with pride. Ralph did well at such calm, distant shots. What bothered his father was a tendency to shun close-in encounters. Even as a little boy, Ralph had avoided fist fights among the lads his age. Even brief reflection on it gave Everett a niggling worry that Ralph might lack the essential courage to survive in a tough world. His concern vanished as the confused Crow ponies crashed into the outer ring of tipis. Two collapsed in a rumble and clatter, shrieking voices coming from within as the sharp, unshod hoofs of the animals pounded across the buffalo hide coverings.

"Go get 'em! Let's go get 'em," Everett shouted over the pandemonium.

Both Lockwoods, senior and junior, had read accounts of the slaughter of the Cheyenne by self-appointed Colonel Chivington and his Colorado Militia. The patently one-sided battle that followed reminded them of such an encounter. In the twenty minutes that followed, men, women and children died, many screaming for mercy and holding up infants swaddled in scraps of blanket or wrapped in soft deerskin robes. Methodically the lodges came down and flames flickered in their ruins. Total losses for the marauders amounted to three, with seven slightly wounded. Food bundles were ripped open and destroyed and only a handful of survivors remained to wail in grief and terror as the band of whites rode cheerfully away into the growing night.

All in all, Everett Lockwood and Grant Brockton considered it a job well done, even if it had not been a Sioux village. That could always come later.

Beneath a light gray overcast, a brisk northerly wind whipped up snow crystals to form a fog-like miasma in the air that limited visibility to less than five hundred yards. Eli Holten rode slightly below the rim of a ridge that followed along the east bank of the Tongue River. The rugged terrain made travel difficult and his caution heightened as the swirling white horizons closed in. It would snow again, he estimated, before nightfall. A swelling, rounded buttress protruded ahead from the nearly vertical wall of the defile. Eli dismounted, to scout ahead, before riding openly around such an obstruction. He hated nasty surprises.

Bent low, Eli approached the apex of the fan of fallen earth. Winchester in hand, he went to his belly and crawled the last twenty feet. He removed his hat and slowly raised his head above the convex curve. Nothing. He could see no further than before. A capricious fluke developed and, for a moment, the air cleared.

In that fleeting instant, Holten saw the tantalizing cone shape and eighteen slender lodge poles of a tipi not five hundred yards away. The wind shifted again and obscured his view. Teased by the vision, the scout decided to cross the river and find a better observation point.

He returned to where he had hobbled Sonny and walked the big stallion down to the water's edge, where ice crunched under foot for man and animal. Quickly, Holten led his mount across the shallow stream. A tense moment came on the far bank when Sonny slipped on the frozen ice and floundered noisily in the water.

Holten quickly led the animal free and crouched among the drooping, ice-coated limbs of a willow. After a frigid ten minute wait, he proceeded to where he felt he could see more clearly into the spreading vale beyond the escarpment. While he bided his time the sky darkened, reinforcing his prediction of snow. With the intensifying weather came a lessening of the wind.

Gradually the suspended particles precipitated out of the air. Holten's patience and forethought paid off as the increasing visibility revealed a cluster of lodges. Smoke drifted from them as the Sioux sheltered from the increasingly harsh weather. With the passage of another ten minutes, the atmosphere cleared at ground level so that an entire village came into the scout's view. Miniconjou, right enough, from the markings on the tipis Eli observed. He began a quick count.

His total surprised him. Fully sixty-seven lodges. A considerable force to reckon with. Rather than the traditional circular layout of a fair weather camp, the village had been set up in close clumpings, to take advantage of terrain and vegetation to provide snow and wind breaks. The dwellings had been placed far up on a shelf of rocky soil, to provide ample protection from early spring floods. Definitely the Miniconjou intended to remain a while. A thick sprinkling of white flakes descended and the scout took advantage of the obscuring effect to advance along the opposite shore to a point where he could see the far end of the camp.

Rich in horses, the animals still fat and sleek from summer grazing, the Miniconjou had staked out a sizable pasture for their pony herd. Holten attempted a count, only to give up in favor of an estimate due to the occasional swirls of snow caught up in fitful gusts. The result caused him to frown.

Based on the number of lodges, and the pony count, he estimated the likelihood of some one hundred fifty warriors. Most likely, it would be more. Given the number of older men, women who would fight and boys between ten and fifteen, it constituted a formidable force. Miles' infantry would be outnumbered nearly two to one. Eli shifted position to ease a cramped leg and devoted his attention to determining the size of the *akicita*—the camp police—and their state of alertness. After half an hour he was satisfied that, typically, no one wanted to remain out in such weather. The camp police had opted for the warmth and comfort of their warrior society ritual lodge, with occasional forays out to check on conditions. Few, if any, lifted their gaze to look beyond the furthest lodges.

Holten rose from his observations and led Sonny back along the path they had taken. Once clear of the echoing walls, he mounted and struck out at a fast pace for the column of infantry. Miles would swarm down on the village, no matter the odds, Holten considered grimly. He only hoped his advice would be appreciated and a blood-bath prevented. He'd covered half his route in such gloomy contemplation when the first fat, wet flakes turned to a swirling world of white. Worse, the scout acknowledged, was yet to come.

Chapter Nine

With a dedicated vengeance the storm raced down across the northern prairie. The heavy snowfall doubled in density by the time Eli Holten returned to Nelson Miles' camp. Moaning with the frightful abandon of a condemned soul already on the coals, the wind whipped up into a gale force. A regular Montana blizzard came forth, birthed full-grown and ravaging. The regular supply of heater stoves had been issued out and the fuel supply grown threateningly low before Eli entered the encampment and tended to his mount.

After a good rubdown, Holten rigged an over-large blanket over the back of his prized war horse, then hurried to report to the colonel. Snow had begun to pile up around the yellowish glowing gray shapes of the Sibley tents. Those men who did not receive stoves had buckets of shimmering coals to break the worst of the chill. Holten found that Miles had sacrificed his own comfort for that of his men. The scout warmed his icy fingers over the metal container of flickering pine knots and made his report.

"Damn! And we have to be pinned down here by this insufferable storm," Miles exploded in impatience. "We'll have to move at the earliest possible time."

"That'll be a day or two, Colonel," Eli returned dryly.

"Double damn that! Here, have some whiskey, Mister Holten. You must be frozen to the core."

"Thank you, Colonel. I sure am mite near to it. You hear from Kelly or Johnson as yet?"

"Yes, and no. Kelly and the others came in an hour ago. All signs they cut lead to the same general area where you described the Miniconjou encampment. This blizzard will have caught the contingent I sent with Johnson at about the point where they are supposed to turn west and cross to both banks of the Tongue. We'll not hear from them until the storm abates. Any idea how long this could hold us here?"

"A week, ten days at the worst. On the bright side, we could ride out of here by noon tomorrow. Depends on how much it snows and how bad it blows. They call this flat country, but high drifts can hide all sorts of unpleasant surprises."

"We haven't got a week or ten days," Miles came back.

"In weather like this, a man finds out he's got all the time in the world on his hands," the scout philosophized.

"That's just the trouble. In a week's time the men will be at each others' throats if we're snowbound in these tents. Thank God I got Johnson out of camp. Well, down that drink and have another shot. Then find yourself something to eat and a place to shelter."

"You make that sound a tempting proposal, Colonel.

Think I'll take advantage of it. Then I'll mosey around and see if I can scare up a card game."

Two days of poker exhausted Eli Holten's patience. Far from a professional, he still managed to play with a studied skill acquired through experience that found no match in the camp. Neither his fellow scouts nor the soldiers offered stiff competition. Thus, Holten found himself filled with eager anticipation when on the third morning some patches of pink-tinged blue revealed themselves shortly after sunrise. To his relief, the dark, bloated bellies of the snow clouds had moved on far to the east. The wind remained high, though and sent a particularly sharp chill through to everyone's bones.

"Think we can move out today?" Nelson Miles asked of his chief scout and Eli Holten.

"Wouldn't be a good idea, Gen'ral," Kelly responded slowly.

"Definitely not," Eli added. "And believe me, I'm not the least anxious to remain here another day."

"When?"

"At best, a couple of days," Kelly opined.

"But the Sioux . . ."

"They're not goin' anywhere after a blizzard like this," Eli injected.

"Holten's right," Yellowstone Kelly agreed. "Likely we can take up to a week and find 'em right there, like he saw 'em. Hell, Gen'ral, we could wait three months and they'd not have moved."

"I don't like it. This standing and waiting is detrimental to the welfare of the troops and accomplishes nothing toward our mission. We had enough of killing time at Keogh."

"So what do you reckon to do, Gen'ral?"

"Move out, Mister Kelly. Tomorrow, the next day at the latest, we'll strike camp and move to the Tongue."

Eli had to admire Nelson Miles for his determination and dedication to duty, yet he didn't like rushing into the unknown. The approaches they would use to the Sioux camp should be thoroughly scouted, depth of the snow determined and hazards uncovered. Yet, all he could do was offer suggestions.

"Country you know like your own hand can turn treacherous after a blizzard like the one we had," he informed Miles. "A strange stretch like this might cost us too much in men and equipment."

"You'd prefer we wait." Miles returned, a flat statement, not an inquiry.

"I'd prefer that the troops not move out until Kelly and the rest of us have an opportunity to thoroughly go over the ground between here and the village."

"How long?"

"Three, four days."

"We can't spare it. Make it two. We'll decamp on the third morning from now."

Susweca sat alone in her lodge at the center of the Miniconjou encampment on the Tongue. It had been twenty suns since the cramps and pain ended and she had left the *isnatipi*. Fire seemed to radiate in waves from her *san*. The old urge that Dragonfly had felt so strongly in the arms of *Pasu Tanka* returned with increased force each turning of her cycle. Although a childless widow, *Susweca* had seen but seventeen winters. In the prime of her passionate years, she had no man.

Not that several hadn't come forward. Fat old Big Horn and the adopted Cheyenne youth, Red Hair, in particular. Big Horn had been straightfoward enough. Come live in his lodge, he had demanded, and be his fourth wife because he preferred young girls to stocky, thick-bellied women of middle age. Red Hair's courtship had been much more charming.

"I was a stranger and alone and my Miniconjou brothers found me and took me in. A widow is like that, too. I know how it must be for you. Come, be my wife and we'll defeat loneliness together."

But, in his shy candor, he had admitted of having no experience with women. Dragonfly wanted a *man*. One who could thrill her and send her to the impossible heights of sheer joy she had experienced with her husband of so few seasons. She and Big Nose had been bonded together on the occasion of her sixteenth birthday. He had brought many ponies and gifts of succulent hump meat, tongue, and two large haunches of buffalo for the feast. That night, alone in the lodge they had borrowed until she could prepare a proper one, she had trembled at his touch. Nearly twice her age, Big Nose used all his experience to soothe her, arouse and thrill her. And then . . .

Ah, then had begun the most wonderful part of her short life. Fourteen moons later, Big Nose was dead, the victim of a frequent hunting accident. He had fallen from his horse in front of a wounded buffalo. Images of the wonderful things they had done together swam in *Susweca's* head, and one hand strayed to the burning, itching mound at the juncture of her legs.

Idly, as her fingers manipulated the sensitive flesh, she wondered; would it ever, ever be like that again?

"Five cases of frostbite overnight, Mister Brockton," Wayne Staples reported. "An' those fellers who got arrah-shot are festerin' something awful. If we don't get shut of those Crows attackin' us, we're gonna lose a lot of men."

"*That's* an astute observation," Brockton snapped. Then he moderated his temper. "Three attacks in as many days. Unusual for them to be so persistent."

"Not at all," Staples responded. "It was their village we sacked. The only thing we've got going for us is our numbers."

"Don't forget superior marksmanship," Everett Lockwood injected as he walked to the fire to get a cup of coffee. "It isn't one out of fifty of their bullets that hits a man or his horse. We're doing a great deal better. Keeps them at a distance."

"Except for an ambush like yesterday. They get in close enough to use bows, we're in trouble," the Brockton foreman responded.

"True enough, Staples. Sad, but true," his boss commented.

"What do you figger to do about it?" Staples looked from one leader to the other.

"Ride like hell until we're far enough in Sioux or Cheyenne country for the Crows to turn back," Lockwood suggested.

"I concur with that," Brockton came back readily.

It surprised Everett Lockwood. This was the first time he'd heard the affected rancher use the first person in referring to himself. Their misfortunes must be preying on him, Lockwood considered.

"Then we'd better get at it." Staples walked away in a bow-legged, limping sort of gait.

Lockwood hoisted his coffee cup in a toast. "Confusion to the enemy."

"Amen to that."

"Seriously, we have a problem that's not going to be easy to solve."

"Everett," Brockton said, surprising Lockwood again by the use of his first name. "That's a problem we've got to deal with, and quickly. The next time the Crow attack, if there is a next time, I think we should mount a counter-charge. It might upset their plans enough to discourage further attempts."

"I'm for anything that'll get us out of this fix."

"No offense, but you do recall that you were the one who insisted on destroying their village."

"Guilty as charged," Lockwood responded in an attempt to be light. "Well then, I'll tell my men. Ammunition is running low. That makes everyone a little jumpy. One good lick at the Crows ought to raise spirits."

"Corporal of the Guard! Outpost seven! Three warriors approaching."

"Are they Sioux?" Corporal Moynahan inquired.

"Don't think so. From their decorations and such they might be Crows."

"Send 'em on in."

Moynahan hurried to report to the Officer of the Day, who met with Colonel Miles and the three ranking scouts. His news interrupted the conference while everyone went to look at the visitors. Yellowstone Kelly greeted them in their language and inquired as to their purpose.

"Three days' ride to the west," Eli Holton translated for Colonel Miles, " 'white men attacked our village. Most of the warriors were gone and the whites destroyed the entire camp. Burned lodges, polluted food, killed the women, children and old people. Only a few are left.' He wants to know what the army will do about it."

Miles frowned in contemplation. "We'll identify them, of course, and round them up. First we have to deal with the Sioux."

"These must be the same men we heard about killing old people on the Pine Ridge reservation," Eli offered.

"Quite likely," Miles responded.

Yellowstone Kelly had completed the translation. It was obvious that the colonel's response didn't please the Crow warriors. Scowls darkened their faces and the spokesman grunted a short, harsh phrase.

"He says that for many years the Crow have been friendly to the white soldiers. 'In return, when we have trouble, we are told to wait,' " Eli translated. " 'Is this all that white friendship means?' "

"Tell him, ah . . ." Miles' voice faded out.

He bent and, using his swagger stick, drew a rough map in a smooth patch of snow. "This is where we are. There is a large Sioux village over here. We have come to take them away to the reservations to the east. Tell him that, Kelly. When we have these people captive, then I can send soldiers to arrest the bad white men."

For several long moments the Crows considered this.

A smile showed briefly on the face of the one in the middle. He spoke in quick, liquid syllables.

" 'It's good to have the cursed Cutthroats removed from this land. With them gone, our life will be better. Only . . . these white men take from us our wives and children. What sort of life do we have then?' "

Eli Holten's translation visibly moved Nelson Miles. "Damn. Some of the best scouts I've had were Crows. I don't want to let these people down. Try to make him understand that. And, ah, promise him that we will send troops after these renegade whites. That as soon as we have taken control of the Sioux encampment, within two days, we'll send men to help his people."

Kelly turned the words into Absaroka. Two of the scowls went away and the leader nodded solemnly. " 'It will be good because it's what you'll do.' Sorta like; it's not what we want but we'll have to live with it, Gen'ral. And, ah . . ." Kelly came up grinning after hearing the spokesman's next words.

"He asks can they come along and count *coup* on some Sioux?"

Now Miles produced a sincere, albeit relieved, smile. "Tell him he's more than welcome. There's coffee . . . and lots of sugar."

More flowing words came from the Crow leader. "He says that's fine with him, but a few Sioux scalps would be even better."

Chapter Ten

Another frigid morning dawned over the Miniconjou village. The cold seemed so intense that a person hesitated from moving rapidly for fear one might break off a limb. The ponies stood heads-down, in a tight knot, easily watched by the drowsy herd boys who had not yet been relieved.

Although well-bundled in buffalo robes, most of the lads ached from the deep chill, though none would admit it. Their cheerful morning calls set the camp dogs to barking. Shortly after sunrise, a brisk wind rose and whipped up a froth of snowflakes that turned familiar objects into indistinct gray shapes. Fresh herd watchers were sent out and the relieved night shift scampered to their lodges to warm themselves and fill their bellies with breakfast. Slowly the daily routine emerged. Mid-morning came and with it brought fateful change.

Black, furry shapes, like migrating bears or buffalo, appeared on the wide river flats opposite the village.

Swirling curtains of white caused them to flicker in and out of view. No one in the lodges had any awareness of their presence. Accordingly, the moving objects multiplied rapidly as they advanced. Not until they reached a position within half a dozen running steps of the outer tipis, did the dogs set up a strident yapping.

At once, larger, heavier figures burst through the trees and rushed toward the sheltering herd of horses. The heavy cavalry mounts plowed through chest-deep snow with relative ease and quickly formed a solid phalanx between the villagers and their precious ponies. Dragged out of their lethargy by the charging mounts, the herd boys yelled shrill alarm.

Shots crackled from a hundred Springfields and the pretend buffalo advanced on the village with fixed bayonets. Fear and confusion struck in advance of their approach. Children wailed and began to scurry about aimlessly. Women started to sob and howl. Several hot-blooded young men grabbed up weapons and rushed outside. The canine population, staked down by rawhide thongs, chorused nearly hysterical yelps and got underfoot. In her lonely tipi, panic struck at *Susweca*'s heart.

"What is it? What's happening?" she cried out several times before receiving an answer.

"It's the white soldiers that *Pisco* told us about," Sunflower, her chubby and usually jolly neighbor wailed.

"White men in our camp?" The idea astounded Dragonfly. "Such a thing cannot be," she protested.

Two bullets thwacked loudly through the taut hides of the small, handmade lodge, a foot above *Susweca*'s head. It added a frighteningly bizarre affirmation to

Sunflower's declaration. Dragonfly began to tremble.

Through the swirling banners of white, Col. Nelson Miles looked down on the Miniconjou village with a pair of field glasses. Even with the thick layers of his gloves, he could feel the cold of the metal barrels. He hoped his troops would be able to use their Springfields in such frigid conditions. Many soldiers professed an inability to handle cartridges when wearing gloves. On a day like this the brass cylinders would stick to bare flesh.

The end result would be men unable to use their weapons, except in self defense as a club or with the bayonet. Their advance went well, at least he could take satisfaction in that. His horse nickered fretfully and Miles broke off his study of the enveloping movement to glance along the line of cavalry that waited with him on the far side of the screening lines of trees from the village. The two companies would sweep through the pony herd and isolate the Sioux from their animals, completing the surround. Hopefully that would be before the Miniconjou could mount any sort of opposition.

Winter campaigning could be such fun, Miles thought in sour amusement. With every movement reduced to slow-motion, the terrain hidden and deceptive, the slightest error could result in disaster for one side or the other. And the Sioux had to know the ground better than his troops. Shoving aside the possibilities that line of reasoning opened, he put the field glasses to his eyes again.

There. All of the companies were in position, a long,

curving file, two ranks deep, around the open end of the village. A cold smile flickered a moment on Nelson Miles' lips. He turned partway in his saddle and spoke in a quiet tone.

"Captain Phalan's compliments and would he have the troops advance to the far side of the trees."

"Yes, sir," a young lieutenant responded.

A minute passed, seeming like a fleeting moment. Then came the muted commands. "B Company, C Company, forward at the walk . . . Hooo!"

New plumes of vapor formed at the muzzles of the heavy cavalry mounts and frost painted white the outer surfaces of the dark blue wool mufflers covering the faces of the troops. With muted thumps they negotiated their way through the tall, slender trunks.

"Pass the word to Captain Phalan. Have his trumpeter sound the *charge*," Miles commanded the moment the three ranks of soldiers cleared the trees.

Bright, crisp notes followed and the wave of mounted men swept toward the Miniconjou pony herd. Made ponderous by the deep snow, the advance lacked the usual awesome grace of a cavalry charge. So be it, Miles thought, committed now.

Lt. Charles Clarke thought he had a block of ice in his stomach. One far colder than his present surroundings. He had been newly posted to the Ninth Infantry only a month before this campaign. His normally watery, pale blue eyes now brimmed with moisture and he had the horrible feeling he might burst into tears right there in front of his men. Whatever could have possessed the War Department to have sent him to the frontier? With his family's position, his wealth and breeding, he should have been posted to the Diplomatic Service, or to one of the fashionable places like New York or Philadelphia. Instead, he found himself here, about to engage some decidedly hostile Indians, with the intention of herding them onto a reservation some two hundred miles east of this place. How could the army be so arbitrary and capricious?

Granted, he had not enjoyed a remarkably brilliant matriculation at the Academy. How could anyone find motivation to excel at West Point, with its gray uniforms, gray buildings and usually gray sky? Some few had, of course. Charles Clarke suspected them of using crib sheets like he had to get through examinations. But why not use any means at hand to get passing marks on dull examinations in dull courses about subjects one would never need in the real world? Strategy and tactics is what it came down to. Outsmart the instructors and win the coveted gold bar. Unbidden, Clarke's left hand strayed to his face, long, spatulate fingers rubbed his weak, slightly receding chin.

Naturally, his parents had not approved of his decision, Clarke's thoughts reminded him. "Shocking," his mother had called it. "Childish and irresponsible," his father labeled his determination to enter the United States Military Academy.

It took only a short time there for him to agree with them, though he would never admit it to anyone. His first disillusionment had come when he put on the uniform. His skinny, five foot ten frame, with sunken chest and narrow shoulders deprived him of the least bit of military bearing. He looked, as his only friend at the academy had put it, "like a little boy dressed up in his daddy's clothes." Yet none of those who knew him realized the real and most pressing reason for Charles' precipitous plunge into the military.

Maurine O'Day had become the town pump at the tender age of thirteen. What she had been giving away infrequently for a couple of years she then started bestowing only in exchange for small gifts, such as bits of jewelry, sweets or cash. She was also the daughter of Bridget O'Day, the Clarke family housekeeper who came daily to clean and "manage" for Mrs. Clarke. Falmouth Heights, Massachusetts, was a small town on the Cape Cod peninsula and, as small towns go, there was little for a young girl to get involved in. On summer days, when school was out, Maurine frequently accompanied her mother to the Clarke residence.

Nature being as it is, and the hot blood of adolescents being what it is, it didn't take long before then sixteen year old Charles found himself betwixt the shapely, readily yielding legs and up to the hilt inside the warm, moist, elastic channel of thirteen year old Maurine.

She certainly gave her best for whatever trinket was offered by her new swain. For his part, Charles had gleefully surrendered his virginity to her, a condition which he had lamented for several years, and enjoyed his pleasure to the fullest. The first time Maurine took Charles' achingly rigid organ into her mouth he experienced a momentary flash of terror.

Charles thought she might bite it off. To his delight he soon discovered she knew the "right" way to accomplish the act. Some four years earlier Charles had induced another girl to try and it had turned into a disaster of sharp teeth and tender flesh. With Maurine, Charles thought he had found paradise. Their thrice-weekly excursions into the fields of Eros continued into the fall, winter and on to the next summer. Then calamity struck.

How was he to know she could get pregnant? How, too, was he to know it was his child? Among the boys with whom Charles often went fishing down at the shore, the story went around that Maurine O'Day would fuck a snake if someone would hold it still for her. After all, hadn't she even put out to Tim Lassiter's ten-year-old brother? Scared the kid half to death until he realized what she was after. He hadn't stopped grinning since, and that was nearly a year ago. All the same, Maurine was in a family way and she insisted Charles was the father.

She could prove it too, she claimed, because she'd been saving herself just for him. What about the others? Charles had asked. In particular Tim Lassiter's kid brother, Bobby? There weren't any others, Maurine insisted, and Bobby Lassiter didn't count. He and a couple of his friends. They were safe, Maurine insisted, because she couldn't see Charles all the time and just had to have someone help her "scratch her itch." Little boys couldn't get her in trouble, so it wasn't the "real thing" like with her and Charles. Maurine wanted to get married, "before I get as big as a house." Charles wanted her to see the old woman who lived out on the edge of town.

Maurine wound up going to a nunnery and Charles went to West Point. That had been nearly five years ago. None of the parents ever knew the reasons. Then he ended up on the frontier. Perhaps he shouldn't have cheated on his exams. If he had failed his courses he wouldn't be in the army and he wouldn't be in Montana in the dead of winter chasing savage Sioux warriors.

Clear, sharp notes tumbled from a bugle.

Oh, God, we're going to attack, Lt. Charles Clarke thought in the first stage of blind panic.

Miniconjou women and children ran everywhere. Eli Holten sat astride his big Morgan stallion and watched the grim task of corralling them continue. Shouting angrily, a young Sioux mother, with a babe in her arms, spat at the soldier who shoved her roughly toward the containment area.

Picket ropes had been brought along and strung in the apex of the triangle to form a stockade. There troops armed with rifles and fixed bayonets prevented any escape. Already, some one hundred seventy women, old people and toddlers had been rounded up. Weeping bitterly, a Miniconjou squaw with five tykes stair-stepped downward from ten or so stumbled over the frozen ground. Suddenly her eldest produced a small knife and slashed a soldier's leg.

He got a butt plate in the mouth for his efforts, breaking all his teeth. The little lad fell to the ground bleeding terribly and howling in pain and terror. Holten kneed Sonny forward and the broad-chested Morgan bowled the angry trooper over.

"What the hell'd you do that for?" came a surly complaint.

"You had no call to butt-stroke the boy," Holten

growled.

"Th' little bastard cut me."

"If I catch you hurting a child again, I'll cut off your balls."

Holten dismounted and lifted the little boy in his arms. "I'll get help for him," he told the distraught mother in Lakota.

She clutched at his arm and her eyes mirrored her gratitude. Holten strode away toward the regimental surgeon, reminding himself that this wasn't the Twelfth and he had no authority over these men. As he passed a small tipi, he heard a shrill scream from inside.

It held a note of something other than mere surprise or offense. Holten went quickly to investigate. Ducking low he carried the whimpering child into the lodge with him. There, in a frozen tableau, he saw a young infantry lieutenant with his hand on the pert breast of a young Sioux woman. Carefully the scout let the Miniconjou boy down on his own feet.

"At least you concealed your conduct from the eyes of your men, Lieutenant," Holten told him in an acid tone. "We're supposed to remove these people to the reservation, not rape them."

"This is no concern of yours, Scout. Besides, she offered herself to me. Bold as brass these Indian chippies are."

"He says you invited him to touch you," Holten rattled off in Lakota.

"He lies," she hissed.

Holten scowled and nodded his head sharply. "It's not nice to call an officer and a gentleman a liar and a rapist, so I'll simply tell you to get the hell out of here, Lieutenant."

"You have no authority over me," Lt. Charles Clarke choked out.

"That's quite true. Yet, as chief scout of a cavalry regiment I have rank and pay equivalent to a major. Who's the courtmartial board going to believe? Me or a shavetail fresh out here from West Point?"

Without a word, Lieutenant Clarke left the lodge, his lips pursed in a petulant manner. Eli Holten turned to the girl.

"I am called *Susweca*."

"Dragonfly," Holten repeated the name. "I like that. It's a pretty name. I am called Tall Bear by the Oglala."

"I thought . . . your accent is . . ."

"I lived for many years among the lodges of the Oglala. Two Horns was my adopted father."

Susweca's eyes grew big and round. "Then you are the one called Hol-ten. You are said to be a mighty fighter and a friend to the Dakota."

"I try to be, when I can." At *Susweca*'s frown, he added, "Both, I mean. A good fighter and a friend to the Dakota. Sometimes that's not possible."

"You were not at the Greasy Grass."

"No. And I'm glad. My father's people were and they fought Yellow Hair. Had I ridden with the soldiers, I would have been torn to pieces. Part of me would have been on each side."

"You would have died."

"Yes, most surely."

Her tone softened and *Susweca* had a glow in her eyes that suggested more than casual concern. "I wouldn't have liked it if you did."

"I, er, ah, I don't think I would have either."

Susweca giggled. Quite a looker, Holten decided now

he had time to examine her. Young, though, and still in trim shape. Her breasts, though not large, stood out pert and firm. Trim ankles. A smooth, glowing complexion. Nice teeth, small and bright. She took good care of her hair, he observed.

"Am I violating another man's rights by protecting you?"

"No. I am a widow." Another trill of laughter came from her generous, full-lipped mouth. "Not all widows are old, gray and toothless. My husband was killed during a buffalo hunt."

"A beautiful young woman like you should not be alone for long."

"I won't be. Not when the right man comes along."

Her tone and expression told Eli that *he* was that "right man."

"I, ah, must take care of the boy. Will we meet again?"

"I hope so," *Susweca* told him with a level gaze.

Chapter Eleven

"Hammond, see that Captains Brand and Mason have these Sioux organized for a morning departure," Col. Nelson Miles told his adjutant.

"Yes, sir," Major Hammond responded. "Will they be riding their ponies, General?"

"No. They can walk, just like our infantry. We'll need enough horses to haul their lodges. Pick a detail to remain behind and kill the rest after we have these Miniconjou out of sight."

"It's a shame to kill so many helpless animals, sir," Hammond observed. "Why not mount as many of our men as we can?"

"That's a good idea, Hammond. Only it would take two days to break these Indian ponies to new riders. We haven't the time to spare."

"Some of the troops are well experienced with horses, sir. You'd be surprised how quickly they could bring these mustangs to heel," Hammond countered, still loathe to carry out the alternative.

A brief smile creased the corners of Miles' mouth. "All right, Jim, if that's the way you want it. But they had better make it fast. Start this afternoon if you want."

"Yes, sir," Hammond enthused with relief.

"Oh, ah, send Kelly and Holten to me, will you?"

"Right away."

Eli Holten arrived first. "How does it look to you, Mister Holten?" Miles asked.

"I don't like it much, sir. There are too few men of fighting age in this village. I think our raiding hostiles are from this band and they're still out there somewhere."

"Hummm." Miles tugged at one end of his long, full mustache. "We'll go after them next. I've ordered that we pull out first thing tomorrow. In the meantime, I want you and Kelly to talk to the Sioux. Explain that we don't want to hurt them. That we're only taking them to the reservation."

"Their answer will be that the Red Cloud treaty promised them this land for as long as the grass grew and the waters ran."

"We could build dams to stop the rivers and burn the grass, I suppose."

"Indians don't see things that way, sir. It's been a sore point since Custer and his surveyors found gold in the Black Hills. More and more white men have come pouring into land that a solemn treaty preserved as theirs for eternity. Over the last few years the Indians have become inconvenient for the miners, farmers and ranchers who have flocked out here."

"What about Custer."

"As I said, the Indians are an inconvenience. Treaty or no treaty, the whites want them gone. We broke the treaty, not the Sioux. When Terry tried to enforce the wishes of the newcomers, Custer got killed. I'll try,

Colonel, but I won't guarantee anything."

Scant color remained on the western horizon when Grant Brockton gave the order to saddle up. Grateful to be moving, doing anything that might promise a respite from the numbing cold, the mixed lot of ranch hands and Nebraska Rangers made short work of their preparations. Brockton stood to one side, with Lockwood, listening to a report from Ephram Sprague.

"Ten lodges. They're Sioux right enough. And all settlin' in for the night."

"How many warriors?" Everett Lockwood inquired.

"Didn't see but three or so. Mostly older people and a few brats. This should be easy."

"I'll believe that after we finish up," Lockwood stated flatly.

Their losses had been heavier than the Valentine merchant had expected. Most of the fifteen casualties had been wounded, or injured in some mishap, fortunately. Had the death toll been that high, he and Brockton wouldn't have anyone to command except themselves. Everett could see rabbit behind the eyes of a lot of their men. It didn't please him. A nice, easy raid would lift morale. He pressed his scout for more details.

"How large is their pony herd?"

Sprague shrugged. "Around forty horses. Not much of a herd at all. An' there aren't any ponies ground-hitched at tipi doors. All of the lodges are tucked up close to a south-facing bluff to cut down on the cold wind."

"Then we can hit them from only three sides?"

Brockton asked.

"That's right."

"What if we put men on the top of that bluff to roll rocks and fire bundles down on them?" Brockton speculated aloud.

"It's a long damned ride to get up there, if you'll pardon me sayin' it, Mister Brockton. I'm not talkin' a matter of an hour or so, either. We'd have to hang around here a couple of days while a way up there was found."

"In that case, we'd better go with what we've got," Everett Lockwood urged.

"We'll divide our force then, swing around to strike from all three directions."

"Those Sioux ain't gonna have a chance," Ephram Sprague enthused.

And they didn't.

Hoofbeats, muffled by the snow, sounded their warning too late for all but five Teton men to snatch up weapons any offer and show of resistance. Two of them died before they fired a shot. There seemed to be white men everywhere. Lodges burst into flame, women and children screamed in terror. The gathering darkness grew bright. Bends Bow, the aged civil chief, summoned his grandson in the middle of the pandemonium.

"Look to yourself," he informed the thirteen year old Squirrel. "Take care not to be seen by the enemy. Go to the horses, select a swift one and ride for all you can. Warn the other camps close to us and try to find help."

"I want to fight, Grandfather," the boy protested.

"You can fight later, with warriors who will avenge this. You can't be of any good here, so go quickly while you have the chance."

The old man and the stripling youth embraced warmly and parted company. Encumbered though he was by heavy winter clothing, the boy managed to evade the blood-lusting gaze of the marauders. He selected a strong mount, smooth of limb, with bunched muscles in his haunches. Squirrel led the nervous animal half a mile from the scene of slaughter, then mounted and sped away toward the east. In the village fighting continued.

"Over there," Paul May shouted. "Don't let 'em get away."

Two of the raiders responded with blasts from their Winchesters. A gray-haired woman and tottering old man jolted forward and fell to the ground, pierced by .44-40 slugs. Laughing wildly, May turned his attention to a girl of fifteen or so whom he had snatched up and dumped over his saddle in front of him. Eyes aglow with lust, he reached out and patted her small, round bottom. Like an avenging bolt from heaven, an arrow whispered mournfully past his ear and he jerked his mount aside.

"Where is he? Which one shot at me?" Paul called out, fear cracking his voice.

For the moment, his assailant escaped detection. Paul hoisted his captive's elkhide dress and revealed her bare buttocks. He began to roughly caress the bronze flesh when a big hand grabbed his shoulder and yanked him part way around.

"There's no time for that," Grant Brockton snapped. "Let her go or shoot her where she is." His full lips curled in distaste. "Rutting with these creatures is like having your way with a beast of the field. In our book it's an act of bestiality. Be done!"

"Awh, what the hell . . ." Paul May started to protest. He cut off his words quickly enough when the large, black hole at the muzzle of Grant Brockton's Colt .45 centered on his chest.

"Do as you are told, you lout," Brockton growled.

Paul twitched his shoulders nervously, drew his knife and slit the girl's throat before pushing her off his horse. Brockton headed away to organize the final sweep of destruction. Behind him Paul May's face turned ugly with suppressed fury.

"There'll be another time," he promised darkly.

The bright, twinkling encrustations that crowded the black velvet above seemed near enough to reach out and touch as Eli Holten scratched lightly beside the door flap to the small lodge in the Broken Reed clan circle. A soft voice bade him enter.

A low fire lighted the interior. At its side a cast-iron trade kettle simmered slowly, the fragrant aroma of buffalo stew rose invitingly. *Susweca* sat in a graceful pose, feet and legs tucked under the hem of her beaded elkhide dress. She had combed out her hair so that it glowed richly in thick black braids. A shy smile lifted the corners of her mouth.

"It's only a small stew," she offered by way of apology. "There's been no hunting since the last storm and the meat is getting a little old."

"No reason to apologize to me, Dragonfly," Eli responded, as he removed his heavy coat. "A few wild onions and some red peppers will cure that."

Susweca's eyes widened. "Oh! You are a cook then?"

Eli made a wry face. "Not exactly. At least to hear others talk about my efforts."

They both laughed and Eli seated himself where she indicated. She produced a bowl and filled it, then handed it to him with grave formality. A buffalo horn spoon followed. Eli tasted, chewed, nodded and smiled, then dug in with a will. He'd not eaten since early that morning. The growling protest of a too-long ignored stomach caused them both to laugh again.

"I've not cooked for a man for so long," Dragonfly said with downcast eyes.

"There's something terribly wrong about that. You could cook for me any time."

"What I need is someone to fix meals for all the time. Someone who'll . . . who'll make me a woman again."

Her boldness made Eli wonder for a moment if perhaps the horny young lieutenant might not have had a bit of truth on his side. But then he doubted it. They hadn't time to exchange names, let alone bring up the topic of carnal desires. Particularly so, Eli reminded himself, when Clarke certainly didn't speak Lakota. Some fry-bread, made earlier on the fire outside, appeared before him and he sopped up spicy juice with a piece while he did in the bowl of stew. *Susweca* covered her mouth with small, slim fingers.

"I shouldn't take on like that. It's not proper for a woman to . . ."

"Would you rather I not know how you feel? Would it be proper for us both to be longing for the same thing and hurting for not realizing it?"

Color rushed to her face and her heart fluttered. Could it be? Were the words of Tall Bear straight? She saw the glow in his eyes and the soft accents of growing desire in his expression. Oh, yes. Yes, he did feel that way toward her. A humming giddiness spread through her body.

Eli remained silent for a while and accepted a second bowl. This he ate more slowly, his attention remaining on *Susweca*. Color rushed to her cheeks, brightening them and her eyes sparkled. Encouraged, *Susweca* asked the boldest question a Sioux woman could ever imagine.

"Where will you put your blankets tonight?"

Eli Holten reached out and touched her lightly on the shoulder. "Anywhere you'd like me to, *Susweca*."

Suddenly flustered and nervous, *Susweca* fairly bolted to the back side of the lodge and fluffed up a pile of buffalo robes. "Oh, here, here with mine," she blurted breathlessly. For a moment she thought she would swoon. "I would be ever . . . ever so honored."

"It's *I* who'd be honored," Eli said simply. Arousal lay only seconds away, the scout realized from the expanding tightness in his groin.

He'd come here with the intention in mind, only to find Dragonfly even more eager than himself to sample the sweetness of love. She fairly trembled and her anxiety gave her an even more girl-like appearance. Each movement of her sweet lips, each shy glance, the way she wrinkled her small nose, enflamed the scout further. He had eaten his fill and satisfied the demands of his body, yet he found himself consumed with another sort of hunger.

"I could not stay with you," he cautioned. "My feet are in the camp of the white soldiers."

Ghostly ripples of sadness crossed her face. "I know this. Tonight though, and for many nights as we travel to the place called Pine Ridge, we can be . . . can pretend to be man and wife. Say that's so. Please, Tall Bear."

"I couldn't say it better than you did. Nor truer."

She came into his arms then, grasping him tightly around the neck. Eli held her firmly and their lips met in a thrilling shock. *Susweca* groaned, as though suffering from some terrible burden. She shivered as Eli's tongue probed into her mouth and the sound changed to a mew of contentment. His big, rough hand found her left breast and squeezed gently.

"It's so wonderful," she gasped when their embrace ended. "I'd almost forgotten how delicious it can be."

She kissed him on the nose, then the lips. Her small hands searched downward until she encountered the rigid evidence of his involvement. Awed by its apparent great size, she flew at the buttons, opening the flap fly of his trousers. With the coy inquisitiveness a girl brings with her to her first encounter with a male, she explored within.

Her warm, moist touch sent a jolt of sheer delight through Eli's body. She encircled his rigid manhood with both hands and squeezed gently, sliding up and down in a tentative manner. Then she drew his fleshly lance into the open. Her eyes grew round and solemn. The pink tip of her tongue wet her lips.

"O-o-h, so big."

"Take . . . take off your dress," Eli whispered into her ear.

Quickly she complied, while he slid out of his shirt and trousers. *Susweca* glowed with health and youth. Her faintly bronze skin had a sheen and smoothness unblemished by any flaw. She rose on her knees and bent toward the scout. Eli drew her to him and his joy leaped at the contact of their naked flesh. Once more *Susweca* took his rigid organ in a two-hand grip and began to gently manipulate it. As she did, she bent lower and lower.

Her thick, soft braids brushed Eli's belly and then fire and ice erupted from the sensitive tip of his engorged phallus as she flicked over it with her tongue.

"Aaaah, yes. *Ceazin, ceazin*," Eli panted as *Susweca* closed her tender lips over his fiery knob. "*Wasteste*."

With one hand he kneaded a firm breast, while the other cupped her swollen mound. Tightness encased him as he sought out the hard little node at the top of her portal. *Susweca* cooed in delight. She edged closer and took him deeper into her warm mouth.

Wildness surged through her slender figure as Eli created endless jolts of bliss for her love-starved body. Tonight, she thought ecstatically, the earth would move and the stars would fall from the sky. A bolt of purest euphoria blazed through her and she happily welcomed the first fulfilling climax she had experienced in a year's time.

Eli lay back on the buffalo robes and gently patted the top of *Susweca's* head. "Turn around and get on top," he suggested.

Eager as a child with a new toy, she complied. She could not contain the squeal of ecstasy when he buried his quick tongue between her fevered portals. Her legs trembled and waved in the air. Seized by a sudden frenzy she began to gulp and slurp as she applied herself to his turgid lance in an effort to bring about his own explosion.

When he reached the critical point, she too hurtled

off the precipice. Slowly reason and the real world returned. They lay in a tangle, spent, though easy to arouse again.

"I don't . . . I've never . . ."

"You were perfect," Eli assured her.

"You were wonderful," *Susweca* responded dreamily. "Did you feel it?"

"Feel what?"

"The earth shifted beneath us."

Eli chuckled softly. "Yes, I suppose it did. Want to try to make it move again?"

"Oh, yes!"

Eli applied himself to achieving the erect state again, kissing *Susweca* at every sensitive point on her body. She squirmed with an overload of pleasant sensations by the time he separated her legs and situated himself between them. Slowly he brought his fiery lance into contact with the leafy fronds that pouted pinkly from her hairless mound. A short thrust and he had cleaved her. *Susweca* uttered a little squeak of anticipation and reached for his firm, flat buttocks. He obliged her by inserting more, straining slightly at the tightness that gripped him like a vise. One more prodigious effort and they were fully joined.

Dragonfly moaned and whimpered as Eli impaled her over and over, driving in a smooth, increasing rhythm. Their senses reeled and the heady odor of their lovemaking permeated the lodge. The honeyed elixir she exuded eased in part the smallness of her passage so that the scout could plunge fully within, drawing back tantalizingly, only to thrust with increased power. Shrill, strident cries announced the arrival of *Susweca's* climax.

She shivered over the gulf and slid happily down to start over again. Eli's steady efforts mounted his own incline to bliss and the unending pressure of her clinging walls wracked him with euphoria. At long last they cried out together and dissolved into sweet oblivion.

Outside the lodge, a dark, bulky figure bent closely, hearing the joyful sounds of their accomplishment and burning with impotent rage. Lt. Charles Clarke flamed with jealousy. Acid bile consumed his stomach and he cramped with unassuaged passion. Silently he cursed Eli Holten. He knew absolutely that the Indian girl preferred him to the coarse, brutish scout. Why then, why had she surrendered so easily?

Consumed by his acrid torment, he vehemently vowed to make Eli Holten pay for this betrayal.

Chapter Twelve

Heads bowed and silent, the Sioux women trudged along across the snow-splotched prairie. Usually shrill and playful on the march, the children also maintained a solemn mien. Only the eerie wail of an axle in much need of grease broke the quiet. The supply column, along with two platoons of cavalry, had been detailed to supervise the captives. Ahead of them marched the infantry, with nearly half their number astride captured Miniconjou ponies. The generally fractious animals behaved remarkably well, having been ridden to weariness by the experienced men during the past day. A number of soldiers so favored by having a mount didn't consider it all that great a privilege.

They had no saddles, except for the hide-bound wooden war saddles of the Sioux. Blankets, packs and rifles banged against their bodies on the rare occasions they called upon their stiff-legged little steeds for speed greater than a walk. It soon made the stoutest among them long for the ground-devouring pace afoot that they had learned in the infantry. The idea of mounting infantry for rapid deployment against hostile acts caught on with their commander, though.

Nelson Miles watched his ersatz-cavalry with considerable interest and appreciation. Infantry, it had long been argued, could move further in a day with fewer supplies and support equipment than cavalry. That might be so, but mounted troops moved faster. They were not fighting a European style army in the field. The Sioux and Cheyenne didn't know the meaning of infantry tactics.

They fought on horseback. They also escaped that way in the event of serious pursuit. The best infantryman on his best day could not outrun a Sioux war pony. If ever he would succeed at this assignment, Miles considered, it would be through mobility and speed.

"Hell, even if we had to put them on mules . . ." Miles blurted aloud.

"A, ah, what, sir?" Jim Hammond, the adjutant inquired.

"Oh, uh, nothing, Jim. I was arguing with myself. It's this mounted infantry thing. I think it'll work out fine for frontier service."

"You know how hard-headed the big brass are about unorthodox change," Jim challenged.

"Oh, yes, indeed. What say we go about doing it, round up the Sioux quickly that way and then tell them about it?"

"You've never lacked in impetuosity, Nelson. But then, you weren't a Point man, were you?" Unconsciously Jim Hammond felt the West Point signet ring beneath his riding glove.

"I never considered it as a criteria for innovative thinking, Jim," Miles answered coolly.

Over the years since the War Between the States,

Nelson Miles had frequent opportunity to smart over his reduction in rank from his brevet as a brigadier general. He should have made his star back before now. He had entered service as a junior officer in a volunteer regiment and rapidly rose in rank under federal service. Then came the onset of peace and the parsimonious cutbacks by Congress. Nearly thirteen years as a colonel. Well enough then, he resigned himself, when one considered the number of men who had already retired at that rank or left the service full of bitterness at being repeatedly passed over.

He'd hold in there and do his job and never complain . . . until in their infinite wisdom, his superiors elevated him to the rank for which he felt himself so ideally suited. The pathway to a general's stars lay through repeated, and spectacular, victories. The only enemy about were the Indians. So, he would become the best Indian fighter alive, west of the Mississippi. A growing nation needed more land.

At least that's what the land speculators and railroad entrepreneurs stridently bleated on their flyers and broadsides. "From coast to coast!" had become a trite phrase through endless repetition in handbills. And only the few worn down, degraded Indians stood in the way of such glorious progress. Never mind that they had been promised the land, albeit in smaller portions each time, in endless treaties which the cynical politicians had not the slightest intention of honoring. Perhaps that scout from the Twelfth, Holten, had the right of it.

Who could be counted the worse thief? The teenaged Sioux boy who stole a couple of horses from the Pawnee, Arapaho or Crow? Or the white man who stole a whole continent from its red possessors? Fine Indian fighter he'd make thinking that way, Miles chided himself. Back to business before he started talking to himself again.

"Jim, my compliments to the company commanders and we'll make camp early today. Also have any of the scouts not on detail to forge ahead and try for some fresh meat. We've a lot of mouths to feed."

"You've a painful truth to face there, Nelson. How many more Sioux can we afford to round up at one time?"

"Not a great deal, I'll grant you. For now it's going to be beans and bacon for everyone unless the scouts can jump a few buffalo."

Tight-lipped, *Pisko* looked across the abandoned valley. The chill, incessant wind fluttered the twin eagle feathers he had tucked into his tightly braided hair. The discovery had shocked him, taken from him his sense of place and security. Like his life-long companion, *Tasa*, he had known no other home, no kin or clan than those of this village. Now only the bare ground of frequently used paths marked any previous occupancy.

"The white soldiers?" *Tasa* asked.

"Who else? I feel as though it were my fault. We, all of us here, spoke for staying and fighting. We'd have shown ourselves better men if we had listened to *Nitasunkecu*."

"Now what?"

"We find them. We're strong, more so, perhaps than the soldiers. Our people will listen when we call to them. Attacked by us, and from within, the soldiers can't prevent our escape."

Tasa placed a hand on his friend's shoulder, hardly felt through the thick buffalo robe *Pisko* wore. "Then what, my friend?"

Pisko stared long and hard at the ground. Humiliation, born of the words he must speak, burned his cheeks. "We must run. Hide. Let the soldiers wear themselves out in the cold and go back to where they came from."

"I had thought that . . ."

"What, friend *Tasa*?"

"The whites, the ones who aren't blue-suits, who attack Dakota villages. I thought we might turn on them and destroy them."

A slow nod from *Pisko* revealed the conflict within the war leader's mind. "I'd like that, too. But the safety of our people comes first. We'll ride now, day and night, until we find them and get them away from the soldiers. Then we ride south into the high mountains. After that, we can fall on those carrion birds who fight women and children. Not even the army, Bear Coat Miles in particular, can complain about killing them."

To Eli Holten, his present situation seemed like he had at last settled down to a homelife of his own. Had *Susweca* any children around the lodge, he would see the illusion as complete. In a way it mildly disturbed him. Yet the benefits could not be denied.

"Back ribs and some hump meat!" Eli exclaimed happily as he settled down to his evening meal. "How did you manage that?"

"I did it for my man," *Susweca* told him in a quiet voice. "I fought like a mountain cat with the other women. It's cold and you work hard every day. You need the good meat."

"You keep me warm enough," Holten responded between bites.

Shyly, *Susweca* reached over the corner of the fire and touched Eli's cheek. A strong wave of mutual desire and genuine affection swept over them. It felt good like this, the scout reflected, to come home to something besides a cold stove and an empty coffee pot. A touch of sadness colored his feelings when he acknowledged that it couldn't go on. Once at Pine Ridge, *Susweca* would remain behind, while he went on with his duties for the army. It could be no other way. The men who married Indian women were, for the most part, loners. They established small trading posts or carelessly maintained farms, or lived with the tribes. They, and most particularly their wives, were not welcome in "polite society," nor on military posts.

Delightful though it may be, this interlude with Dragonfly would have to end. When it came to the doing, however, Eli always found another time to be more auspicious. Yet that would come only too soon.

"You are somewhere far away," *Susweca* observed with a frown. "What troubles your heart, Tall Bear?"

"Uh, nothing. No, that's not so. We've not heard from the detachment sent out to the north. The warriors from your camp are still out there somewhere. Some bad white men are attacking isolated groups of Sioux. I have much to worry me."

Concern wrote itself on *Susweca's* lovely features. She crossed the dividing line of the fire pit and huddled at

Eli's side. A warm, moist hand lay on his cheek. Her breath, sweet and vital, touched his ear as she spoke.

"You've done enough for one day. Take off your clothes and let me rub your back the way you like so much."

His meal finished, Eli grinned at her as he removed his buckskin shirt and trousers, slid from his fur-lined, high-top moccasins and out of his warm longjohns. He lay on his belly on a pile of buffalo robes and *Susweca* came to him a minute later with a large horn spoon of warm, pleasantly scented oil.

This she dribbled onto his back and then removed her own clothing. Then she began to work at the tension hardened muscles. Slowly the rigid fibers relaxed at her touch, kneaded and pounded to supple repose. *Susweca* straddled him while she labored and her warm body sent electric shocks through Eli's long, corded frame. Her steamy mound pressed against his buttocks as she leaned far forward to manipulate his shoulders and slid tantalizingly along the back of one thigh as she moved lower.

Soft grunts and little sighs of contentment escaped from deep in the scout's chest as she erased the strain that had held him tightly all day. When she had finished with his calves, *Susweca* swatted him playfully on one glowing buttock.

"Turn over."

Eli languidly complied, revealing his partly aroused phallus. It swayed in a drooping arc and rapidly extended to full rigidity when *Susweca* moved to his side and started to massage his chest, working lower with each circular stroke. Across his hard, ridged belly she went, exerting a deft touch that pleasantly chilled and warmed in turn. His thighs, pale white from lack of exposure to the sun, trembled slightly at her touch. She worked on, seemingly oblivious to his excited state, until she had carefully bent and articulated each toe. Then, with a cry of delight, she straddled him once more and sank down upon his burning lance.

By gradual increments it pierced her, sliding in the tight passage now heated and moistly welcoming. Tiny white teeth bit at *Susweca's* lower lip as she concentrated on consuming this mighty rod of fleshy iron. A tremor deep in her belly brought forth a groan. Her quick smile destroyed any notion that he might have hurt her. With a mighty shudder she took the last of him.

She bent forward now, drawing the hard, stingingly sensitive nipples of her breasts across his chest. Goose bumps formed for Eli and he reached out to grasp her under her firm young breasts. His thumbs began to rub.

"Aaah! Oh, yes, Tall Bear. Good, so very good," *Susweca* panted.

"*Waste, wasteste*," Holten repeated her praise.

Eli's hips rose in counterpoint, matching the energetic young Miniconjou thrust for thrust. Always he felt the incredible tightness, the elastic yielding as he penetrated to the ultimate depths. A warm pink glow spread outward, balloon-like, to engulf them both.

Sounds of their love-making filled the lodge. The fire burnt low, flickered, receded into a mound of glowing coals. Outside the tipi, Lt. Charles Clarke shook with suppressed fury. Every gasp, groan or squeal of delight that reached his ears came like a knife in his heart. *It was all so wrong!*

She didn't love Eli Holten, Clarke's mind railed at

him. "She loves me," he murmured under his breath.

"Ayyyyyiiii! N-now . . . oh . . . now, Eli . . . NOW!" *Susweca* cried out as she reached her first pinnacle.

You're not hearing this, his blindly jealous mind screamed at him. She's saying "No," and trying to fight him off.

"Oh! Oooh, oooh, again. More . . . more . . . HARDER!" the Miniconjou maid called out.

Despite the icy weather, sweat beaded Lieutenant Clarke's forehead. His hands trembled and his groin ached from a painful erection that strained the front of his trousers. Tears welled in Clarke's eyes. It wasn't fair! He fell in love the moment he saw her. She had encouraged him with her big green-tinged eyes. Tensions heightened his senses and the slippery, rustling sounds of the love contest thundered in his ears. A keening crescendo heralded their mutual completion, so prolonged and unabashedly erotic that, unbidden, a hot, wet expulsion flooded Clarke's longjohns.

Severe pain doubled him over and he soundlessly cursed Eli Holten. He'd make Holten pay, he vowed. He'd destroy the lecherous civilian scout, he grimly determined as he stumbled away toward the most distant picket line.

Inside the lodge, nostrils filled with the heady scent of their amorous engagement, Eli withdrew from *Susweca's* firmly gripping passage and, kissing her, slid from beneath the kneeling girl. On his knees he worked his way behind her and drew near. He spread her coppery buttocks and slipped his still-rigid organ far between her thighs.

With the aid of one hand, he directed the tingling tip

against the pouting lips of her cleft and entered once more her golden purse. Grasping her flared hips, Eli pulled her backward until he entered to the furthest possible extent.

"Oh, Tall Bear, I love you more with every beat of my heart."

"And I, you," Eli vowed as he slid slowly outward and thrust forward with an eager will.

Chapter Thirteen

"No. If it happened at that time, I haven't any idea how the horses could have strayed from a picket rope, Colonel," Eli Holten told Nelson Miles the next morning.

"Did you check the cavalry mounts last night, Mister Holten?"

"Yes, I did. Only that was a good two hours before the time you quoted."

"Hummm. That's odd. The Officer of the Day was quite firm on the time he saw you at the picket line."

"He must have read his watch wrong. Who was it?"

"Lieutenant Clarke. He said he was positive. You were there at nine o'clock and no one else came close to the horses after that."

Eli lifted a length of braided hemp from the small field desk in Colonel Miles' tent. "From the condition of this, I'd say it had been cut, Colonel."

Miles flushed. "I'd seen that."

"What reason would I have for cutting that rope?"

"What reason would Clarke have for lying?"

Holten thought for only a moment and recalled the scene he had witnessed the day the Sioux encampment had been taken. "Perhaps to discredit me."

"What do you mean?"

Quickly Eli outlined the incident. Then he added, "Although I didn't report it at the time, it might be sticking in Clarke's craw. He could be trying to create enough doubt in your mind that if I ever did bring the subject up it would not be given full weight."

"Clarke tried to force himself on this, ah, girl?"

"Yes, sir."

"The same one that you've, ah, been so friendly with of late?"

"As a matter of fact, yes."

"I'm not dealing with a squabble over a woman, am I? You two aren't using me as a means to, er, contend for her affections by any chance?"

"Not on my part," the scout answered hotly.

Such a suspicion would never have risen in Frank Corrington's mind. But then, Nelson Miles hadn't known him as long or as closely as the general. Eli's mind sought some means of convincing Miles without losing his temper in the process. A hail from the regimental sergeant major interrupted the tense confrontation.

"Messenger, sir, from Fort Keogh."

"Send him in, Sergeant Major."

"Right away, General."

With swift, gulping words, still panting from his last long run, the messenger delivered information about the latest attacks by the unknown white force on Sioux encampments to the west of their position. When he finished, Miles dismissed him and slammed a fist into his other palm.

"Damnit, I haven't enough to contend with. I had thought that this would die down once the word got around that the regiment was in the field. Now it looks like I'm going to have to handle it somehow before we can get on with the assignment. The simplest way would be to send a troop of cavalry to round up these nitwits."

"They're violating treaties, breaking several other laws and killing a lot of innocent people," Eli Holten injected. "Somewhere in there, I think a swift trial and a noose would be in order for every one of them."

"All of them?" Miles countered. "Going soft on Indians, Mister Holten?"

"Hell no. Only, if we expect to see the Sioux obeying the law in the future we'd damned well better show them that the law will be equally enforced for *every person* who violates it. I think you'd discover that hanging a few killers of Sioux women and children would have a salutary effect on our captives here. I'm willing to bet you'd be able to find a goodly number who would be more than happy to go along and hunt down these self-appointed avengers."

"No doubt," Miles answered dryly. "I want to take this up with the staff, my senior troop leaders, you and Mister Kelly immediately after the noon meal stop."

"I'll be there, Colonel."

Holten left to ride forward and check on the trail and the scouts who had departed at sunrise. In his wake, Lt. Charles Clarke looked on with ill-concealed animosity, and a long-fingered hand to his weak chin. A speculative gleam slowly crept into his eyes.

Half of the men were reeling drunk. The punitive force led by Grant Brockton and Everett Lockwood had come upon the small trading post shortly before mid-day. It had taken the ill-disciplined Nebraska avengers only fifteen minutes to uncover the small cache of contraband whiskey that the reprobate who owned the place used in trading with the Sioux. The awesomely potent liquor, concocted of raw alcohol, cayenne pepper, burnt sugar and a little rat poison, took its toll rapidly. The result far from pleased the leaders.

"It'll be two days before they get over this," Brockton said with disgust.

"The boys needed to let off a little steam, but this is going too far," Lockwood agreed. "It's a wonder they aren't dying from it."

Several of the self-proclaimed Rangers had complained of stomach cramps and most had vomited more than once. The hearty few who kept their feet staggered around in stuporous condition, hands clasped to their bellies and vacuous expressions on their faces. Even those who had abstained from the treacherous booze soon found reason for complaint.

"That pickled pork he's sellin' has green fur on it thick enough to shave with a dull axe," one of Brockton's men complained a while later.

"You can bet he don't eat this himself," yet another remarked, waving a thick plate of jerky. "I'll bet he makes this jerked meat outta the hide."

"We gonna let him get away with this, Mister Lockwood?" Clem Wells asked plaintively. "He must have his good stores hid out somewhere. Ain't white nor Christian to treat us folks like this."

For a moment, Everett Lockwood recalled the weekly torchlight meetings at Valentine. The men in hoods, many with sheets draped over them like Roman togas, weapons ready at hand, gathered under the trees outside town. By the light of the flaming brands, they raised angry voices to denounce this or that injustice in the community or surrounding farmland. Once the darkies had been run out, the Rangers turned their attention to backsliders among their own kind.

Some of their actions had been just. Abe Waters, for instance, who received a horsewhipping for savagely beating his wife and children. Or the medicine drummer who had come through with a new elixir made with swamp water that had given everyone who used it a bad case of the trots. He'd been rounded up, tarred and feathered and run out of the county. And there'd been Howard Barry, the mousy clerk in the harness shop, who had a hanker for small boys.

The Rangers dragged him from his one-room cottage one night and took him out to an abandoned homestead. There they clamped him by his penis between two planks of a corn crib and set the contents afire. Provided a rusty razor, Barry had been left with the choice of burning to death or performing a rather radical and excessive circumcision to free himself. Granted, most of these examples had been severely criticized by the county sheriff and some of the do-gooders in town had urged an investigation, comparing the Rangers with the infamous Knights of the White Camellia down in the South. Everett Lockwood had found himself in disagreement with his followers on more than one occasion.

Despite those previous differences, Lockwood felt that the proprietor of this reeking den of offal deserved a sound lesson in business ethics. "Wouldn't it seem likely that you fellows owe it to unsuspecting wayfarers who pass by here in the future to expose this errant creature's perfidy?"

"Y'mean," Paul May began with blank-faced ignorance, "that the Rangers oughtta take a hand?"

"How astute of you, Paul. I'd suggest it be a heavy one."

"There he is now," burly Sergeant Pallisier growled.

"Goddamned Squaw-man," Private Carson spat. "Way I hear it from the lieutenant, he'll get us all killed if he has his way."

"We oughtta fix him good," snarled a thick-waisted corporal.

Eli Holten, the subject of their conspiratorial abuse, had ridden into the supply column bivouac half an hour before sundown. He reported to Captain Dunning regarding the condition of the trail and that a message had come to Miles that the two companies to their north, one cavalry, one infantry, had apprehended some thirty-five Sioux and were sending them under guard to join the rest.

"Just what I need. More damned Sioux," Capt. Richard Denning responded. "Has the general reached any decision as to what will be done about the whites raiding west of us? Whatever he comes up with is bound to affect my command."

"Nothing so far. The staff meeting determined that a detachment should be sent at once. Who's going hasn't been announced," the scout informed him.

"Well and good. Mark what I say, Holten, it'll wind up being another pain in the ass for me. Well, go get something to eat and have a good night's sleep. That's about all any of us can do for the time being."

"I'll do that, Captain. And I'll be out early in the morning. Colonel Miles is going to move the infantry ahead at a faster pace to try catching any more stragglers, so you'll be on your own for a few days."

"Marvelous. Simply marvelous. Good night Holten."

Their brief, sour conversation ended, Eli Holten now stood outside the dust-stained Sibley and straightened his hat. His keen gaze, always sweeping the area around him, took in the knot of soldiers who that moment broke their huddle and moved purposefully in his direction. The scout sensed the tension that crackled from one trooper to the other. For no ready reason, he recognized himself as the center of their agitation.

"Holten! We know about you and that filthy squaw," their spokesman snapped out when some ten paces separated the angry soldiers from the scout.

Eli had no desire to exchange hot words with these men, nor to see the incident brought forward to a worse conclusion. He raised a hand, as though signaling for a halt.

"Sergeant Pallisier, isn't it? Well, Sergeant, you'd be well advised to see these men disperse smartly before there is real trouble. As to my involvement with *Susweca*, that's no concern of yours."

"It is when our lives are at stake," Corporal Tanner injected.

"Yeah, yeah. We know all about it," a mutter of

voices joined in.

"I'm afraid you know nothing about anything," Holten rejoindered. "Whoever's been stuffing your heads with this nonsense is as full of shit as a Christmas goose."

"We know about the plot, that's enough," Private Carson snarled.

"Which plot?"

"To have the Sioux kill us while we sleep and destroy the supplies, then slink off into the night and attack the rest of the regiment."

"That's ridiculous."

"You lived with the Sioux a long time before you became a scout, didn't you?" Sergeant Pallisier accused.

"That has no bearing . . ."

"We say it does," Corporal Tanner yelled, advancing three steps.

"Hold it right there, Corporal. Use some reason, men," Eli attempted after his command.

Angered and inflamed, the men weren't listening. Two more advanced to stand beside Tanner. Pallisier balled his fists and pushed his way between them. Realizing he would be unable to talk his way out of it, Eli Holten made ready for a one-sided battle. He slipped a pair of thin leather gloves on his hands and took two paces toward his challengers. Whiteness exploded inside his head, followed by a blossom of red and then numbing blackness.

His knees went slack and he fell to the ground, a dark, greasy smear of blood mixed with the thick yellow locks on the back of his head. Over him stood Lt. Charles Clarke, his revolver held by the cylinder and frame, club-like. A red smear glistened on the butt and a wisp of blond hair clung to the backstrap.

"You men drag him away," Clarke commanded. "Confine him in a wagon. When he comes around tell him he's under arrest for collaboration with the enemy and attempted mutiny."

Chapter Fourteen

Sharp and clear on the icy air, an early snowbird's plaintive call chirped as a harbinger of dawn. Atop the low ridge to the west of the army encampment, an answering note sounded. *Pisko* nodded in acknowledgement of the man-made signal and a slight lifting of his lips revealed his approval. Everything was in readiness. The thick, orange crescent that swelled on the eastern horizon brought better illumination of his enemies below.

With it he began to see the nature of unexpected activity. Cook fires had been lighted earlier, betraying the movements of an abnormal number of men. Now the pony-soldiers moved to their lines of horses and began to saddle them. The camp was a long affair, the part that interested him most being nearest to where he lay observing. While he watched, the pony-soldiers rode off to the southwest, along with many of the blue-legs riding captured Miniconjou ponies. Then the remaining blue-legs marched off. The rolling-wood lodges remained in place. With them, the people of his band, captives now, like the ponies ridden by the enemy. This unexpected change in the routine encouraged *Pisko*. With the soldiers scattered in two directions it would make his task easier.

Pisko had been reinforced only the day before by a number of Teton warriors, and some Brule braves who had come to aid their brothers. Likewise, the remaining

Miniconjou bands had rallied to their support, sending all of the fighting men they could spare. His scouts had reported on the soldiers' routine and he felt confident that now his strength was enough to carry out a rescue of the prisoners. This change in the morning order of things suggested to him a new plan.

"See that everyone remains out of sight," he whispered to Red Hair, the adopted Cheyenne youth who lay at his side, peering through the brown grass. "We wait until the blue-suits all go away. When they're too far to return in time, we will act."

A white slice of smile split Red Hair's face. "The rolling-wood lodges are slow. We'll have no trouble freeing our people."

"That's true, Red Hair, but we must be careful. Our people will have no ponies. We'll have to cut the rabbit-ears free from the harness and double up many women and children with our warriors. Then we ride south, into the tall mountains, where the soldiers will never come."

"It's a good plan," Elk Tail remarked from *Pisko's* left.

"We'll have only one chance to make it work," *Pisko* cautioned. "Make sure all the men know."

Not until mid-day did the wagons start on their slow trek behind the advancing infantry. Nelson Miles had changed his strategy, based on his increased mobility, and sought to make round-ups of off-reservation Sioux quickly with sweeps of mounted troops, who would then assume the role of escorts for any captured to the main supply camp where the former hostiles were guarded.

Eli Holten had learned of this second hand, through

the remarks of the surly corporal who had brought him some breakfast. Now he gazed out at a monotony of blue, bordered by the tail gate and an arc of once-white canvas, stretched tightly on the hickory bows. For the first time in a long while, the scout had no place to go and nothing to do.

Both wrists secured by manacles, looped through the spokes of a spare wheel, Holten rode uncomfortably in the box of a heavy army supply wagon. His head still throbbed from the blow he'd suffered at Lieutenant Clarke's hands. Small consolation that Captain Dunning had visited him after he'd regained consciousness and expressed the opinion that he didn't believe the charges. For now that didn't affect the scout's condition in any way. At least the wheels of several wagons had been greased, he acknowledged in a sour mood.

Once they were rolling that would only serve to add to the eerie quiet. Once more the usual noisy chatter of a tribe on the move remained absent. Only an occasional word spoken to caution a child or ask for water came from the downtrodden Sioux as the women rustled silently about the business of packing. The platoon of cavalry moved past to serve as an advance screen, one of the horses breaking wind noisily. The troops assigned to the supply column apparently found nothing worth commenting on. Hell, Eli thought, there was no reason for that.

He recalled a song he had learned as a youth of fourteen, living in the village of Two Horns. Some voyaging Cherokees had taught it to the Oglala and they had kept it for its beauty. It was sung, according to the journeyers, on the Trail of Tears, when the Cherokee had been removed from their homeland in the east to Indian Territory. Eli recognized the tune, *Amazing Grace*, and oddly, for the Sioux, they had kept the Cherokee words. A faint, fleeting smile creased the scout's face as he began to sing in a clear, resonant baritone.

"*U-ne la nv, hi u we-tsi.*"

First one, then another woman's voice rose from outside his prison. "*I ga gu yv he-yi.*"

Grinning widely, his eyes moist, Eli increased his volume. "*Hna quo tso sv wi yu lo se, I ga gu yv ho-nv.*"

"Stop that singing! Stop it at once!" Lt. Charles Clarke shouted from the left side of Holten's wagon.

"Oh, hell, Lieutenant," Holten called out in a taunting voice. "They're only singing a hymn."

"They're blaspheming! These heathens are making a mockery of our Christian faith! Make them stop this instant."

"What'er you going to do, Lieutenant, sir? Are you going to shoot the lot of them?"

"Move out!" sounded faintly in the distance, followed by the crack of Private Carson's whip as Eli's wagon lurched forward.

Clarke jabbed the round knobs of his blunt military spurs into the flanks of his mount and moved in closer to the wagon. His voice broke in shards of unreasoning anger.

"And you're the one who started it. It's only further proof of your conspiracy with these hostiles. I'll report this incident to General Miles."

"Oh, I'm sure you will, Lieutenant, sir. *A sa no-yi u ne tse-yi, I yu no du le-nu,*" Holten sang brightly.

In chorus the whole of the Miniconjou captives added their voices. "*Ta-le ne dv tse lu tse li, u dv ne-yu ne tsv.*"

"Stop it, damn you!" Clarke shrieked, his grip on his nerves shattered.

He started to roughly rein his horse away from the wagon, intent on immediately reporting this incident to Captain Dunning. His plan changed abruptly when an arrow zipped moaningly in front of his chest and buried its metal tip in one of the thick side boards of the wagon box. Nearly unhorsed, Clarke cried out in panicked alarm.

"Indians! We're under attack!"

Pisko waited until the soldiers began to move into a great fan-shaped sprawl across the prairie. Many miles separated the fighting elements from the supply column when he gave the signal. His followers, more now than seventy-five strong, crested the ridge and loosed a volley of arrows, then began the bounding, sliding descent.

Tasa released the first arrow, and watched with disappointment as it missed its target, the soldier-chief near the wagons. Quickly a hailstorm of barbed missiles followed his effort from the three-deep ranks of the vengeful Sioux. Swiftly the charging warriors closed the distance between them and the confused soldiers. *Pisko* rose in his short stirrups and shouted a taunting challenge.

"*Hu ihpeya wicayapo!*"

"*Hau-hau! Huka hey! Huka hey!*" the vanguard yelled in approval.

Rifles opened up on both sides. A poorly aimed bullet struck a mule. The animal leaped into the air, forefeet pawing, then fell in its traces, squalling and kicking its life away. The wagon came to a crashing halt.

The warriors had drawn closer now. *Pisko* watched as the enemy began to turn the careening vehicles into a half-circle. Blue-legs ran among the scattering Miniconjou. They began to herd the people within the confines of their makeshift barricade. From ahead of the beleaguered column, the cavalry troops came racing back. One fast slash will have to free them, he estimated. If that didn't work, they would have to try another way.

Eli Holten reacted to Lt. Charles Clarke's startled cry and the thud of the arrow in the most natural of ways. That brought instant pain to his bound wrists and his head. Suppressing a groan, he leaned back against the wagon wheel once more. The driver whipped up his team and the bouncing, jolting wagon lashed its prisoner back and forth as the speed increased. Rifle fire began from both sides and Holten shouted over the rumble of the lurching vehicle.

"Let me out of these. That attack can be stopped."

"Not by you," the surly Private Carson growled from the driver's seat. "You prob'ly caused it anyway."

Men and animals vied for raising a din. The shrieks and wails of the Sioux women and children added to the pandemonium. Arrows pierced the canvas wagon top and the sound of gunfire grew closer. With a final jolt, the wagon stopped.

"Form as skirmishers!" Captain Dunning ordered, his voice coming from close beside the wagon Holten rode.

"Captain Dunning, let me out of here, I can help," Holten tried again.

He received no answer for his efforts. Unshod hoofs pounded the frozen ground close at hand and Holten instinctively ducked low to avoid any stray projectiles that might find a home in his flesh. Carson, who had been wielding a Springfield with cool competence, suddenly uttered a sharp grunt, flung his arms wide and toppled from the seat ahead of where Eli sat chained to the spare wagon wheel.

"First rank, kneel. Second rank, take aim," Sergeant Bascomb commanded levelly. "First rank . . . Fire!"

A ragged volley got off in a long smear of greasy powder smoke. "Second rank . . . Fire!"

Rifles crashed again and the Sioux wheeled away from the deadly spew of lead. Although he could not see the action, Eli's experience let him visualize the effect. For once the frozen ground had an advantage. No dust would obscure the scene of battle, the scout considered. marksmanship would be greatly improved as a result. Off to the right came the strident sounds of hand-to-hand engagement. The fierce contest ended abruptly as the attackers scattered.

"They'll come back!" First Sergeant Davis yelled. "Stand fast, men."

From a distance, the Sioux continued to fire into the defensive position. Men yelled and horses neighed frantically. Once more hoofs pounded over the solid earth. Individual war cries could be discerned among the general whoops and yells. Someone among the enlisted infantry threw back his head and responded in kind with an eerie, bone-chilling rendition of the Rebel yell.

"Yiiiiiii-aaaaaaaah-hooooooo!"

It came again, picked up by other throats. The right

flank, apparently the weaker, came into close contact once more. Holten listened with growing anxiety to the sounds of the struggle. Then he heard the high-pitched voice of Lieutenant Clarke, broken by terror and uncertainty.

"Fall back! Fall back and regroup!"

"What's going on out there?" Holten called out.

"It's the Cap'n, Mister Holten," Lane Davis shouted. "He's been done for. Lieutenant Clarke's in charge and he ain't in control of himself, let alone any of us."

"Get me out of here, First Sergeant," Eli commanded, aware of the speaker by his voice.

"Can't rightly do that, Mister Holten."

"You'd damned well better if you want to get out of this alive."

"Someone's gotta take charge," Corporal Moynahan, Eli's former accuser observed plaintively. "Clarke's afraid of Holten. He'll back down if we stand by the scout."

Eli could not resist the opportunity. "Thank you for your vote of confidence, Corporal Moynahan."

"I ain't changed my mind that much, Holten," Moynahan growled as he climbed into the wagon, a set of keys in one hand. "It's just that I want to save my ass. They say you're a fighter. Now's your chance to prove it."

"My arms are numb, Corporal. While I get fixed, have the cavalry escort pull off to one side."

"Then what?"

"I'll figure that out by the time it's done."

Moynahan shrugged. He freed Eli and jumped lightly out over the tail gate. The scout followed. First Sergeant Davis handed Eli his weapons.

"Now you've got to stop that yellow-belly Clarke before he has us runnin' for our lives and leavin' our kit behind us, along with our Sioux charges."

"Colonel Miles would take a dim view of that," Eli said dryly.

"I'm sure that he would," Davis allowed with a grin. "He's not going to like what we've got to say about our dandy little lieutenant, either."

"Where's my horse?'

"Over yonder there, by the farrier's rig, sir."

Mounted on Sonny, Eli trotted to where Clarke dithered and appealed to the defenders to retreat. Holten looked down disdainfully at the terrified officer, his lip curled, then eased his big Remington .44 from its soft leather scabbard and laid its muzzle casually across the saddle horn.

"Stop that cowardly nonsense and get these men organized to stand off another charge, Lieutenant."

Holten's deep, commanding voice froze Lieutenant Clarke for a long, crucial second. The men who had been so ready to flee paused, their attention turned on the scout. Clarke chose the wrong course for his response.

"What are you doing out of confinement, Holten?"

"That doesn't matter. What are you doing about standing off that raiding party?"

"We're withdrawing in the direction of the infantry, of course."

"No you're not," Holten growled. "You are relieved of your command, Lieutenant Clarke. You men, form up in companies," Eli went on before Clarke could respond. "Three ranks deep. Sergeant Davis, take charge. Volley fire, but hold it until they're under fifty yards."

"I've got it, Mister Holten."

"You can't do this!" Clarke wailed.

"I've already done so." Holten turned away and trotted to where the cavalry platoon waited under command of Lt. Dwight Random. "Lieutenant, we're going to hit the Sioux flank right after they come under fire by the infantry. Be ready to ride hard and make every shot count."

"This is more like it, Mister Holten. General Corrington would've had that prick Clarke shot for what he pulled."

"The general's not here, Random. So we do what we can. Ready now."

"You're going with us?"

"Hell yes, I don't want to stay around where Clarke can put a bullet in my back."

"The, ah, Sioux might have an idea or two along that line, sir."

Holten grinned. "*They* at least *are* the enemy."

At fifty yards, Davis ordered the first volley. The three ranks fired together with withering effect on men and animals. Rapidly the troops reloaded and continued to blast into the front of the advancing hostiles. Random raised his arm and swung it forward to signal the advance.

"At the gallop . . . forward . . . yoooo!"

Pisko saw them coming and ordered his followers to whirl away and ride out of range. The cavalry followed. Springfield carbines barked and three of the Sioux fell from their mounts. Eli let the chase continue for three hundred yards, then suggested they break off.

"You never know when there's more out there."

The counter-offensive worked well enough, though.

Pisko called his *blotahunka* together for a quick counsel. Grim-faced they climbed the backside of the ridge, out of range of the besieged army position.

"They fight better than we thought," Fat Bull, eldest of the war party advisers observed.

"We can come back," *Pisko* countered. "They are weaker now. Later, if we're out of sight, they'll forget and grow lax. Then we strike once more."

"Some of us should have called to our people to break away and follow us," Hip suggested.

"Yes. We can do that now."

"Look, blue-legs on that rise. They come to help their brothers," Fat Bull declared.

Pisko frowned. "There are too many. We must plan again."

"They will not give us the chance."

"Then we'll make our own," *Pisko* declared confidently.

Chapter Fifteen

Powder smoke wafted away on the brisk, chill wind. Silence and a degree of order returned to the besieged supply column. Two wounded animals were dispatched, punctuating the quiet with dull, flat discharges. The Miniconjou women and children looked with bright-eyed hope toward the rolling plains beyond the wagons.

Their avenue of escape to the southward had been closed off by the return of the cavalry detachment assigned to the slow-moving vehicles. Dispatch riders had been sent off to the infantry and cavalry columns. The newer troops relaxed from the pressure of battle, some seeking coffee and food, which were not yet prepared. Those who had experience of previous Indian attacks did not relax. Tension radiated from them as they went calmly about their duties, for they knew they could expect another assault whenever the hostiles decided upon it. The return to relative normalcy created problems for First Sergeant Davis.

"You will return command of this unit to me at once, First Sergeant. Do you understand?" Charles Clarke demanded huffily.

"I'm right sorry, sir, but I can't do that, Lieutenant, sir."

"That's a direct order, Sergeant Davis, given in the presence of the enemy. You will obey it or suffer the consequences!" Clarke's voice cracked with the intensity of his agitation.

"Can't do it, sir. I take my orders from acting-Major Holten, sir."

"Holten be damned! I'll have you charged with aiding in his escape from confinement. Your career is at stake here, Davis," Clarke warned darkly. "I'll have your stripes and you'll be busting up rocks at Leavenworth if you don't do as I say."

"I see, sir. If I may ask, sir, what if I did back you in taking command? What would your first order be, sir?"

"Why, to fall back toward the infantry, of course."

"And get us all killed," Davis observed. "With all due respect, sir, to hell with that. Mist . . . er, Major Holten kept the hair on our heads, when what you propose would get us wiped out in one lick. So, when he says you're in charge again, I'll back you whole-heartedly. Until then . . ." Davis shrugged and walked away.

"Here they come boys." a soldier sang out.

More than seventy strong, the warriors thundered over the frozen sod in a long line that turned sinuously to form a circle around the besieged whites and their prisoners. Hampered by the presence of their own people, they dared not fire, except along the northwest facing barricade of wagons. Unrestrained by this, the soldiers divided at First Sergeant Davis' command and discharged volley after volley into the ring of hostiles.

Col. Nelson Miles' face clouded with anger. The hostiles he sought had turned on him and were now attacking the supply column. Well and good. They would soon learn the folly of such a maneuver.

"Major Hammond," Miles summoned in a loud voice. "Have the men relieve themselves of their field packs. Pile them up by company and assign a detail to guard them. The troops will then form in a column of fours and we'll return to lift the siege."

"This is not a criticism, Nelson, but how can we reach them in time to affect the relief?"

Through his thunderous expression, Miles cracked a brief smile. "By running, Jim. We'll run like the devil himself chased us."

"It's more than three miles," Hammond reminded his commander.

"The soldiers of this command have run five miles a day more than once," Miles reminded his adjutant. "Even in these goddamned cardboard boots the Commissary General keeps sending us."

"That was in good weather, Nelson."

"Then we pretend this is a pleasant spring day and run like hell."

"As you wish, General."

"And, Jim, we don't want anyone falling out. When we get there we want to scare the be-Jesus out of those hostiles."

Pisko turned out of the deadly ring of warriors to stare incredulously at the strange apparition that approached at a fast, steady pace. Soldiers ran over the uneven prairie toward the weak defenses which his followers attacked. At an unheard order the advancing troops halted. Bright slivers rippled in the air and the unintelligible words of a command reached his ears.

"Prepare to fix bayonets . . . Fix bayo—nets!"

Icy apprehension gripped *Pisko* for a moment as he sensed the importance of this movement. The soldiers made lances of their rifles. They would give no quarter. A quick glance at the circling warriors told him that none of the others realized the danger. He must act quickly.

"Load and lock one round! Rifles at the ready . . . forward at the trot . . . Hoooo!"

Pisko spun his war pony and sprinted to where he could get the attention of his followers. He whooped loudly and gestured toward the charging enemy. Curvetting their horses in a nearly perfect drill, the Sioux broke off their engagement of the stranded wagons and sprinted away to safety. Behind them a shouted command spread the long blue worm into a broad-fronted skirmish line. Laughing, *Pisko* and *Tasa* sat on a low knoll and watched as the troops streamed into the area defended by their companions. In a high, clear voice, *Pisko* began to taunt the soldiers.

"You are women! Your hearts hold no fire for fighting! Come out and test your courage against us!"

The vast, snow-dotted land swallowed his words.

"People of the Miniconjou, hear me! Watch for my signal. When the time comes, slip away into the night. Free yourselves from your captors. We will be here, watching. We will fight again."

Yellowstone Kelly translated the distorted, slightly muffled words to Col. Nelson Miles. When he'd heard the last, Miles snorted in derision and smashed one fist into the opposite palm.

"Damn. If we'd had the cavalry and my mounted infantry here we could have scooped up the lot of them. Jim," he went on to his adjutant, "find out which of my officers organized this defense. He deserves a commendation. From what Kelly tells me we didn't lose a single captive, and only four men wounded."

"Right away, sir."

Only three short minutes passed before Major Hammond returned with a splutteringly angry Lieutenant Clarke. So engrossed in the injustice he had suffered that he barely remembered to salute, Lieutenant Clarke launched immediately into a harangue against Eli Holten.

"He incited the captives to riot, sir. Then he signaled for the attack. Worse, when I attempted to get the troops to fall back on the infantry, he escaped confinement with the collusion of Sergeants Davis and Pallisier and tried to disrupt my command."

"Oh, did he now? This is Eli Holten you're referring to, Lieutenant?"

"Yes, sir. I thought I had made that clear."

"How did he go about disrupting your command?"

"H-he tried to relieve me, sir. Put command in the hands of First Sergeant Davis, sir."

"Ummmm. Then the defense was actually conducted by Mister Holten and First Sergeant Davis, eh?"

"I . . . well, you see, sir . . . I, ah, they—they j-just t-took over . . ."

"A good thing they did," Miles thundered. "Had I been here, I would have done the same. Running from mounted Indians is not only an act of cowardice, sir, but suicide. You could have lost every man in the column and we'd have had to round up the Sioux all over again. Consider yourself fortunate that someone had the sense to know what to do and acted accordingly. Hammond, send for Holten and First Sergeant Davis."

"But . . . what about me, sir? What about the insubordination, the humiliation, and the m-mutiny, sir?"

Nearly colorless eyes bored icily into Lieutenant Clarke's forehead. "There *was* no mutiny, sir. Nor any insubordination from what you've told me. As to humiliation, you've brought that on yourself. Lieutenant Clarke, you're lucky to be alive to receive the reprimand, which I shall personally write into your record. Don't press it with your continued childish complaints. You are dismissed."

Shoulders slumped, face screwed into an expression of malicious spite, Lieutenant Clarke stalked away from his commanding officer. Impotent rage and bitter envy boiled within him and his brain churned with a little boy's vicious fantasies of revenge. Somehow he would find a way to hurt Eli Holten beyond repair or reprieve. And when he did, how sweet, how very sweet the taste of victory.

"General sir, you wished to see us, sir?" Davis rapped out formally, along with a sharp, parade ground salute, when he and Holten came to where Colonel Miles stood.

"That I did, First Sergeant, you and Mister Holten. I understand I have you two to thank for saving this column from disaster. Tell me what happened."

Simply and directly, leaving nothing out, First Sergeant Davis recounted the happenings of the morning. When he finished, Eli Holten answered a few pointed questions from Nelson Miles, detailing his own conduct. When he concluded, to the commander's satisfaction, Miles smiled broadly at the scout.

"I'm glad you both performed as you did. Charlie Clarke is young and a fool. He's had no experience with Indian fighting, yet he surely learned that a column of moving wagons cannot defend itself. Somehow, I don't feel that gets to the heart of this. What about the manner of your arrest in the first place?"

In a calm, quiet tone, Eli recounted the incident.

"That's odd. Lieutenant Clarke had reported to me that you had deliberately provoked an incident with the soldiers involved."

"No, sir. Ask Sergeant Pallisier. He still has suspicions of my loyalty, but he did free my hands and let me out of the wagon when the attack started. As a result, I think you can get an unbiased account from him." Holten took a deep breath, considering the advisability to continue.

"I don't wish to go over old ground, Colonel, but in my own defense, I feel it necessary to point out that in every incident of misconduct cited by you, Lieutenant Clarke has been the complaining witness. I think I might be safe in assuming that his version of his conduct, and ours, during the attack by the Sioux differed considerably from what Sergeant Davis and I conveyed to you?"

"Uh . . . yes. Yes, you can be sure of that."

"You spoke before of a rivalry over a woman, sir.

Might I suggest it goes deeper than that?"

"I hate to think of such a possibility, but you could be right. Suppose . . . suppose we give Lieutenant Clarke a little more rope? If, say in your absence, Clarke concocts additional calumnies against you . . ."

"That rope might turn into a noose," Holten concluded for the commander. "What do you have in mind, sir?"

"We have our hostiles at hand. All we need do is catch them. In the meanwhile, there's still these troublesome white marauders to deal with. Say that I detail a company of your Twelfth to go after the vigilantes, with you to scout for them? That should give time for the air to clear."

"I would think so, sir. One way or the other. When should we be ready to leave?"

"After the noon meal, if it can be done that quickly."

"No problem there, sir."

Lt. Charles Clarke, a smug smirk spreading on his face, watched Eli Holten and the men of Arthur Phalan's B Company of the Twelfth ride out of camp. By that time, shortly after one-thirty in the afternoon, C Company and the mounted infantry had returned at the summons of the dispatch rider sent off when the supply column came under attack. Word spread quickly through the ranks that the colonel had changed his plans. The mounted infantry would be used to protect the captives and the invaluable supplies, while C Company of the Twelfth would concentrate on containing the mobile hostiles within easy range of apprehension when the time was right. Meanwhile, Holten and B Company would deal with the whites who had been stirring up trouble faster than the army could manage to suppress it.

"Well and good," Clarke muttered to himself. "Now we shall see, my fine civilian bastard. Now we'll find out what you're made of when you learn I've hung the horns on you."

Clarke set out the moment the supply column got underway. On horseback, he worked his way among the captive Sioux. Here and there he'd give an impatient nudge of his mount's chest to a slowly moving oldster, or snarl at a child. Constantly his eyes searched out a familiar figure. How clearly he remembered each line and curve, the thrilling up-turn of a small, proud breast. Urgency ignited into burning lust as he at last located *Susweca* and guided his steed in her direction.

Dragonfly saw him coming and cut away diagonally from his approach. Eyes lowered, a shawl pulled tightly around her shoulders, she sought to become invisible in the sea of black braids and copper skins. Clarke pressed on, the discomfort of a rigid erection a goad to his flaming desire. Inexorably he closed the gap. His roan gelding snorted and snuffled at her shoulder.

Despite herself, *Susweca* looked up, eyes big and liquid with dread, mouth down-turned with loathing, regardless of her timidity. His unwholesome leer exposed big, horsey teeth. To her, his long unwashed body exuded a repulsive odor of pork and cabbage. Her stomach gave a momentary lurch and she feared that she might shame herself as she had been doing each morning of late.

Her time of *isnati* had come, but the blood didn't flow. Then, a few days ago, the vomiting had begun. One old, wise woman among the Miniconjou had listened with wrinkled brow and nodding head, then cackled with delight.

"You carry a child, dear girl. The child of Tall Bear of the Oglala. It is a time to be happy."

And so she had. Until now, with this loathesome blue-leg casting lustful eyes on her. Could the mere sight of this vile creature cause harm to the life she knew she carried within? Would there be any effect on the quickening speck that would become the man-child of Tall Bear? In desperation, *Susweca* stifled a sob and tried to escape this confrontation. Lt. Charles Clarke was having none of that.

"Now don't take on like that, sweet-thing," Clarke purred. "You'n me, we'ge going to have a whole lot of fun while that bastard Holten is gone."

"Keep away from me," *Susweca* hissed in Lakota. "I am Tall Bear's woman."

"Well, she's got a voice after all. Rather pretty for a savage at that. I've got another way I want you to use your mouth," Clarke persisted. "But you'll find out all about that tonight. Just keep the door-flap open for me, what say?"

"I don't know your words," *Susweca* replied in her language, "but I know your kind. You are dog dung, filth not worth drying for a fire. When Tall Bear returns, he will cut out your heart. For now, go away! Leave me alone!"

Charles Clarke bent low and tweaked *Susweca's* cheek. Mustering all her courage and determination, she swung an arm and struck his bloated, obscene face stingingly with an open palm.

"Oh, a little fire there, is it? I like that. No matter," Clarke replied in self-delusion. He patted the bulge at his crotch and fairly chortled as he assured her, "Your mood will change tonight when you see what I've got here for you. You think about it, honey. We're going to have lots of fun."

Chapter Sixteen

"It's an ill wind that doesn't blow someone good," Capt. Arthur Phalan grumbled tritely to Eli Holten.

He spoke of the scout's discovery during the latest approach of bad weather. It came howling out of the north to coat the sky with low-flying, dark gray clouds that released millions of large, wet flakes that whirled and danced in the frigid air. A laggardly dawn had brought no increase in temperature and, as the morning wore on, the storm gathered and it grew steadily colder. The cavalry column had made good time the previous afternoon.

Headed westward, Eli Holten and Randy Thorne had marked a clear trail as they forged ahead of the troops. They crossed the icy Musselshell River and continued on to its major tributary, where the night camp was established. The two scouts forded the stream at daybreak and advanced only some ten miles when the numbing cold descended on the prairie, along with near zero visibility as the snowfall quickly followed. In the process, though, they had come upon the recently burned ruins of a small Sioux encampment. It was these charred lodges and bloated bodies to which Captain Phalan referred.

"You say not more than two days?"

"That's right, Captain," Eli answered. "There's ample marks of shod hoofs and a clear indication of the direction the killers took when they left here."

"Where are they headed?"

"I'm no expert on this part of the territory, Art, no more than you. But, if I were to take a wild guess, I'd say they decided to move on to the mountains. I figure somewhere in the Big Snowy Mountains or the Northern Rockies. If this storm hadn't come up we could have caught up to them in a day and a half."

"Yes. Damn this. And it's getting colder. Any chance of our moving on today?"

"Not much. I have a compass and over there, that dark ridge and the prominent peak you see . . . that's Greathouse Peak if I'm not mistaken. It's a good forty, fifty miles away. We can guide on it and still keep in the general direction taken by the marauders."

"We'll do that, then, Eli. We need to make all the distance we can before this gets worse."

Conditions worsened faster than expected. Less than two miles had been covered when the raging blizzard enclosed them in a whirling white world in which a man could not see the trooper in front of him. The column halted and the soldiers went grumblingly to the task of erecting their shelters. At least, Eli thought, it couldn't get much colder until the storm abated and the cloud cover lifted. If that were to happen during the night, there'd be hell to pay.

The leading edge of the storm struck the supply column in mid-afternoon. Quickly the Sioux lodges and the army's Sibley tents went up and before the snowfall became a tumult, the scant fuel available had been gathered. A numbed quiet lowered over the camp. By the time darkness came, a foot of snow had accumulated around each shelter. Lt. Charles Clarke saw the conditions as ideal for his plans.

Contrary to his lofty confidence, he had been soundly rebuffed by the Sioux girl the night before. Railing at him in her barbarous language she had hurled a small pot of scalding water at him when he'd tried to enter her tipi. His face burning in humiliation at the taunting laughter of the Miniconjou who had witnessed his rout, he had made a hasty retreat. Tonight, he vowed, would be different.

He chose to wait until the troops had settled down and sleep had come to their captives. The storm had blown over and bright, unnaturally magnified stars winked in the frigid blackness above as he ventured out of his tent. Sub-zero cold stung his cheeks and he imagined he could feel the scant warmth being sucked upward into the void. Clarke's feet crunched and squeaked as they compressed the heavy, wet snow that lay on the frozen ground. He possessed little skill at silent movement and the uncertain surface deprived him of exercising even that.

"She'll give herself to me tonight, I know she will," he muttered, his exhalations plumed white around his head.

Unerringly, he directed himself to where she had set up her small lodge. This time he had come prepared. The keen edge of his sheath knife slit the bindings of the door flap and he entered the warm interior of the lodge in a rush. Neatly banked coals gave off a ruddy glow that provided Clarke with sufficient illumination to locate the huddled mound that would be the object of his lust. He crossed to *Susweca* in a rush and knelt beside the pile of buffalo robes.

Quickly, stealthily, Clarke removed his coat, uniform tunic and shirt. He shook from the intensity of his desire. His hand might have been palsied as he hesitantly reached out to draw back the coverings. *Susweca* made a small mewing sound and rolled partway toward the outer wall. Startled, Clarke drew back and fumbled with the buttons of his trousers. With the clumsy efforts of the inexperienced, he managed to expose his genitals.

Cold night air did nothing to reduce the heat that generated from his rigid shaft. With one hand he began to stroke it gently, as he had often done as a small boy. His resolve restored by the familiar, he reached out of a sudden and threw back the soft buffalo robe covers.

His heart nearly stopped when he saw *Susweca* lying naked among the furs. Her pert young breasts swelled upward toward him—in invitation, Clarke imagined it. He trembled so violently he nearly missed when he bent to cover her mouth with one hard, long-fingered hand and prevent the scream he saw building deep in her chest. Forcefully he scrambled atop her suddenly writhing figure and used his knees to pry apart her thighs.

"Don't fight. You love me," he murmured to the terrified girl. "Yes, you do. You love me and no one else. Tonight I make you mine. Oh, you'll like it, yes you will."

In a frenzy of passion, Charles Clarke tried to drive his pulsating phallus into her cleft. *Susweca* clawed at his back. Red ribbons appeared on Clarke's pallid flesh and hot pain flared. He balled one fist and smashed it into her contorted face.

"You bitch! You hurt me."

Again he thrust against her and felt a consuming warmth and tightness surround his turgid penis. Another powerful effort had him almost fully encased. Wildly he slammed against her and drove his overstimulated organ to the hilt. Slowly he began to withdraw.

Only to explode despite his best efforts to prevent the premature climax.

She had caused it, his unbalanced personality screamed. She did it to humiliate him, to rob him of his masculinity. Only virgin little boys erupted on their initial penetration, Charles thought in disgust. Angered and excited beyond control, Charles began to rip and tear into her. Blood lubricated her tight passage and eased his efforts. His second commencement took only a bit longer.

With a stifled howl of intense sensation, Charles sent another splash of vital sap into her savaged canal. *Susweca* strained against him and shut her eyes in an effort to remove forever the horror of his brutal assault.

"Wiggle for me," Charles demanded. "Wiggle you little Indian slut!"

Using both hands now, Charles began to beat at her face. A red mist rose in his mind, to obscure his vision, and his hearing blocked out the sounds of his savagery. Shock robbed *Susweca* of the ability to cry for help. Only bitter sobs and soft, helpless moans escaped from her battered lips. Tears streamed from the corners of her eyes. Crazed by the intensity of his passion, blind to the ferocious animal nature that dominated him, Lieutenant Clarke humped and ground himself against the helpless Miniconjou girl.

Three minutes passed in oblivion, then five . . . six

. . . ten. With a wail of bitter frustration, Lieutenant Clarke felt himself go limp, his friction-burned flesh wrinkling and shriveling, without the least sign of an approach of nirvana. Withered to a small fraction of its former, rampaging self his penis was easily expelled by a slight muscular contraction on the part of his victim.

Undone, he started to shiver in the cold. As though in a dream he began to dress himself and tidy his uniform. All the while, strange though it seemed to him, he could not bring himself to look at the battered young woman who lay in the bloody ruin of her sleeping robes. Without a word, he slipped from the lodge and stole off into the night like a cowardly sneak-thief.

Dawn crept like a gray-clad footpad across the subzero prairie. Within its pewter cloak it bore a calm that allowed the air to clear and distant objects become stark and bold on the horizon. Bundled up in a fleece-lined coat, a thick buffalo vest over it, Eli Holten took a measurement of the accumulation of snow. It registered a fraction over a foot and a half.

"If it warms some we can get underway by midmorning," the scout informed Captain Phalan. "If it stays like this, or gets worse we won't be going anywhere."

"The same applies to the men we're after, fortunately," Phalan responded, never one to give thought to the dark side. "A big, hearty breakfast is in order, I do believe. I ordered biscuits, ham slices and eggs from the officers mess sergeant. You'll join us, won't you, Eli?"

"With an offer like that, who could refuse?"

Lieutenant Random, his face a study in concern,

approached them. "sir, some of the men on guard mount complain of frost bite."

"Small wonder," Phalan returned. "Is the field surgeon treating them?"

"Yes, sir. There's more, sir. As a whole, the troops seem disinclined to move about this morning."

"Well then, we'll get their asses stirring. Sergeant Donnovan," Phalan called.

First Sergeant Patrick Liam Donnovan snapped upright from his bent position over the coffee pot. "Yes, sir!"

"Tell the men to get moving, First Sergeant. I want the company in formation in five minutes or we'll pour that coffee on the ground."

"Heaven forbid it . . . uh, beggin' yer pardon, sir, I'll see to it right away. 'Twould be a sin to see such a lovely brew goin' to waste, if I may say so, sir. They'll be out an' about, with faces shinin', in no time, sir."

Holten suppressed a grin. "Why is it that coffee—even on a blistering hot day—has such an allure?"

"Beyond me to say, Eli," Phalan responded.

"It's more than the taste, or the aroma," Holten continued, wrapped up in his philosophical examination of the aromatic beverage. "Or both combined. There's a feeling of, ah, closeness among a group of people sipping coffee together. It's one of the binders of social propriety."

"I presume this all has a relevant application to our present situation," Captain Phalan charged firmly.

"What? Oh, yes, of course it does." Eli drew himself up in best rhetorical style. "Simply put, I'd certainly appreciate a cup before you get around to dumping it out, if that's what you're going to do."

"Get outta here, Eli!"

"I intend to. After breakfast I'm going out with Randy, push ahead a way and see how badly drifted it is."

To everyone's satisfaction, the sun continued to warm the earth. Water dripped from ice-coated branches and the white mantle that hugged the ground slagged in on itself fast enough to be discerned by the human eye. Holten and his fellow scout struck off toward the distant purple line of mountains. They found the way easier than expected. The prospect heightened their chances of closing ground on the gang of whites they sought.

"Randy, head back and bring the column up to this point," Eli instructed. "I'll give a look around to the north and south of here. Might be we'll encounter something."

Caught in the open by the blizzard, the Nebraska Rangers and Grant Brockton's men had been driven back on their westward course. They had sheltered through the worst of the storm in a deep creek bed, where willows and driftwood provided sufficient material for a meager fire. They had survived at a terrible cost to men and animals.

"These horses ain't good for much longer," Ephram Sprague observed to Paul May as they saddled up the morning following the storm.

"We shoulda brought feed and supplies, tents maybe," May suggested.

"Couldn't travel fast that way. The idea was to hit and run."

"We've been doin' a lot of runnin," May made sour

observation.

"I accept the blame for that," Everett Lockwood volunteered as he walked to where they worked. "I had no idea those Crow warriors would be so persistent in hunting us down. For a few days there I have to admit I didn't know where we were. Those are the Big Snowies to the west of us. We're right about where we should be. I've talked it over with Grant Brockton and we're agreed. We'll be turning more to the north now and then swing back east.

"That way we'll miss the soldiers and be able to get home without anyone bein' the wiser. Should be back in Valentine within a week."

"That's good news," Clem Wells injected as he led his horse to the picket rope. "Mister Lockwood, I've been out takin' a look around. There ain't nothin' but a lot of snow any way you go. We didn't reckon on something like this. The sooner we head for home the happier most of the boys are gonna be."

"I appreciate that, Clem and that's exactly what we're going to do. Get yourself some grub and we'll head out shortly."

"To the north?"

"You've got it. There's a good trail up that way according to Grant Brockton."

"You'll find a lot of loose snow up that way, too," Clem informed his leader. "It's just waitin' for a good wind to come up."

B company caught up to Eli Holten shortly after noon. The wind had come up again, sharp-edged and persistent, gusting occasionally to thirty or forty miles per hour. Wherever these capricious whorls appeared, they lifted powdery flakes into the air and obscured everything for several hundred yards. Eli had his brow puckered and he spoke hesitantly to Captain Phalan.

"There's movement out there a way. With all this blowing snow I'm not sure what it is. Could be more hostile Sioux. Then again, it might be the men we're after."

"Nothing for it but to ride ahead and find out," Phalan suggested.

Half an hour later, B Company disappeared into a gigantic whirlwind of icy crystals. They stung and wet the men and animals, clung to eyelashes and brows and obscured vision in every direction. Dismounted, the troops led their horses forward, one hand holding the tail of the creature ahead. The miniature tornado lasted for several long, tense minutes, then resolved into a hazy state that lingered a while longer. Suddenly, as though the air could no longer support them, the snowflakes tumbled to the ground.

Directly ahead, the soldiers of B Company found themselves face-to-face with the Indian-hating whites they had come to apprehend. Surprised, both parties stood their ground and glowered.

Chapter Seventeen

Tendrils of smoke rose from more low-to-the-ground lodges than ever before. Soaring confidence lifted *Pisko*'s heart as he gazed across the large encampment from the rim of the valley. Word had gone far and the result he now counted on his fingers. Five times two hands and seven tipis crowded the narrow vale in the Big Smoky Mountains. Constant probes by the mounted blue-legs had forced him to withdraw.

For two days he smarted from the heavy sense of failure. Then new warriors began to come to his standard. Singly, in pairs and small bands, they brought their short lodges for protection from the awesome weather, their weapons and high hopes. It had come time at last, *Pisko* decided, to organize a final battle to free their people. To that end, he touched his heels lightly to his pony's flanks and negotiated the narrow path to the camp.

"*Tasa*, *Napetanka*, Red Hair, Elk Tail, come!" *Pisko* called out as he rode through the rings of lodges. "Bear Fat of the Teton, Kills-His-Enemy of the Oglala, we're holding a war council."

Eleven leaders, representing some ninety-seven warriors, filled to overflowing *Pisko*'s small tipi. The warmth from the fire and the closely crowded bodies eased the pains from old wounds for many who joined the parlay.

Excitement generated of itself as *Pisko* laid out his suggestion.

"The soldiers are too strong for us to attack them in the open. Instead of us going to them, I propose that we have them come to us."

"Yes, yes," Big Hands spoke out. "An ambush. That's the best idea I've heard since we started out to punish the whites."

"*Napetanka*, you see into my head," *Pisko* told him jokingly. "An ambush is exactly what I had in mind. The question is, where?"

Discussion ranged around the fire pit circle. Red Buffalo gathered the most supporters with his plan to trap the soldiers on a river bank. *Pisko* weighed the idea carefully before commenting.

"*Tasa*, that's a favorite trick of the white soldiers and works quite well. It would work for us, except for one thing. The rivers are freezing over now. Many are solid enough to cross on horseback. We'd not find them trapped as you laid out, rather able to escape, swing wide and attack us from behind by crossing and recrossing the river. We need a solid obstruction."

"No place is more solid than a mountain."

Every face in the lodge turned toward the adopted Cheyenne youth, Red Hair. A broad smile bloomed suddenly on *Pisko*'s face.

"Your tongue has been given great wisdom, Red Hair," the Miniconjou warrior leader complimented. "Speak on."

Suddenly off balance in such an august gathering, Red Hair looked from one advisor to the other. His throat worked and at last he found words.

"Well, I . . . that is, it's reasonable isn't it? We do

something to make the soldiers ride into these mountains without thinking of a possible ambush. Get them angry. Then, in the right place . . . we fall on them."

Fall on them. The words stuck in *Pisko*'s mind.

Paul May drew first. Although generally considered to be a few buttons shy, no one could fault Paul's reflexes, reaction speed, or gunhandling ability. Weak sunlight glinted off the barrel of his Colt .45 as he brought it free of leather and point-shot at Eli Holten.

Sped along by a sizable load of black powder, the 240 grain lead slug ripped into the thick outer clothing the scout wore. Reduced in velocity, and deflected by two each alternating layers of thick, compact hair and leather, it smashed bruisingly into Holten's ribs and burnt a gouge in flesh from front to rear around his left side. The impact nearly unhorsed him.

Sonny reared and flashed out with his forefeet, instantly transformed into a warhorse. The diversion, though Sonny's attack failed to reach anyone, served to allow Eli to unholster his own sidearm.

Holten's hefty Remington .44 bellowed into the icy air. Lead smashed into the forehead of a jittery horse in front of the scout and Grant Brockton pitched free of the saddle.

"Sidearms!" Captain Phalan shouted. "Draw sidearms!"

"Get me a horse!" Brockton bellowed.

"Jesus did you see that draw?" Jim Bench exclaimed. "That scout feller's faster even than Paul."

"Hell with that," Ephram Sprague blurted. "Let's get some cover."

Several of the more experienced troopers ignored the command to draw their revolvers. Their Springfield carbines boomed loudly, the usual sharp edge of the detonations dulled slightly by the snow cover. Sixguns popped along both lines of contenders. A trooper expelled a gout of blood from his mouth a moment before he whisked out of Eli's sight on his panicked mount. Holten steadied his aim and shot one of Brockton's followers between the eyes.

"As skirmishers . . . Forward . . . yoooo!" Phalan commanded.

The two lines crashed together and a wild melee ensued.

Off to one flank, Ralph Lockwood watched the hand-to-hand contest with eyes that rapidly grew wider and rounder. His cheeks paled and he found himself in desperate need to relieve the pressure of his bladder. A bullet cracked past close to his right ear and he eliminated the necessity to urinate. The warm wetness spread down from his crotch, staining both legs of his trousers. In flour-sack hood and white cape Ralph could be brave enough. Here, caught in the mad swirl of a deadly battle, he lost all control. His throat began to churn and his lips writhed in an effort to give voice to his terror. At last a single moaning sound erupted and he feverishly put spurs to his horse's flanks.

"No-o-o-o-o-o!" Ralph wailed as he sought to flee the scene of slaughter.

Three other men saw him and broke off to join in the escape. Eli Holten observed the defection and directed Sonny in that direction. He quickly closed on the last of the deserters and Eli clubbed the man from his saddle with the butt of his Remington. Three more to go.

Eli rode down another of the Nebraska Rangers as Everett Lockwood took notice of his son's cowardice. Shame flamed the elder Lockwood's cheeks as he set off to bring his errant son back to the fight. First he would deal with the man in the buffalo vest.

The crack of the bullet reached Eli's ears at the same instant his hat flew from his head. He glanced around and saw a compact, balding man closing rapidly. Before the marauder could fire again, Eli sent a fast shot in his direction.

Everett Lockwood ducked away from the slug's path and pressed on. Everett's thick-lipped, perpetually puckered mouth flared with color so that to Eli it resembled a red, wet anus. By his count the scout had emptied his revolver so he returned it to its holster and pulled free his Winchester. Eli turned Sonny sideways and halted him by pressure of his knees. He took careful aim and squeezed off a .44-40 round.

Utter astonishment registered on Everett Lockwood's face as the hot metal projectile slipped through his pursed lips, shattered a few teeth and plowed downward through his tongue. He lost all expression a fraction of a second later when the scout's bullet disintegrated the top-most vertebra and dislodged Lockwood's head from his spine. The corpse continued to ride for a while, passing Eli before toppling to the ground almost at Ralph Lockwood's feet.

"Fa-a-ather!" the younger Lockwood wailed.

"Give it up now, or you'll get the same," Holten growled.

Ralph Lockwood looked at the scout and the Winchester in his hands and raised his arms. Slowly he bowed his head and began to sob. The clean-up took only a short while longer. The superior training and tactics of the cavalry troops easily prevailed over the undisciplined resistance of the instigators of the Sioux bloodbath. Within five minutes the survivors were herded together and disarmed.

"Put them in chains and we head back to the column," Captain Arthur Phalan commanded. "So, Eli, a job well done."

"I agree, Art. With them out of the picture the rest should go easily. There's one of them, that young man over there, who's a bone coward. He'll take some special watching. No telling what he might do when desperation sets in."

How heavy is my shame, *Susweca* lamented, sunk in misery. She should have used her knife, should have fought more. Tears stung the cuts and bruises on her face, which she hid with the folds of a blanket. The stains of her degradation were plain on her dress. That filthy beast in the blue suit had left his seed within her, had tainted beyond saving the precious life she carried for Tall Bear. As though from a distance, *Susweca* thought she heard the soft notes of a Sioux courting flute.

So sad. Never again would those beautiful sounds tease her ear. Nor would she ever see the small one who would have made Tall Bear so proud. Life was a mystery that lived in a mystery. No man could claim to unravel the twisted ball of hair-fine sinew that the Great Spirit caused to behave as he willed. For a while she had believed that truly Tall Bear would become her man. He would take what pleasure he wished from her person and from the babe that would brighten their lodge. Her life had been lived and came to this end. What more, what else could she do? *Susweca* waited while the camp quieted for the night. The day had been agony. She could not face her people, she could not face the soldiers. The ache in her heart for Tall Bear nearly overwhelmed her.

Because of it, she feared for a moment that she could not do it. Then the hateful image of the leering, lustful face of the blue-leg soldier chief returned and she gathered courage. The knife filled her hand. Why hadn't she used it the night before? Its tip touched the flesh at the inside of her wrist. A large bowl of hot water waited. It would cool as her life did. Only a little pressure . . . and . . . now!

Flute-song haunted her ebbing memories as she placed the gushing wrist in the water. Farewell lonesome flute player. Farewell Tall Bear. Farewell . . .

Chapter Eighteen

Had the regimental band been brought along, the mid-day air, heavy with the odor of cookfires, would have shimmered with shrilling brass and clashing cymbals. Eli Holten and Capt. Arthur Phalan led in chains Grant Brockton and Ralph Lockwood, along with eighteen of their followers. The troops entered the large encampment in high spirits. They had accomplished their mission with minimal loss in killed or wounded. Since these whites had fired on federal troops and soldiers had died, it was a surety that they would hang. Curiously, considering that these men had been responsible for the murder of many Sioux, Eli Holten noticed that some of the women captives began to wail and turned their faces aside as he rode past. Once the white prisoners had been accommodated, Eli sought an explanation.

He found Nelson Miles to be strangely hesitant also. "Well, ah, Holten, there was a, ah . . . One of the Sioux women, er-ah, that is, the, ah, young woman you were, ah, acquainted with . . . well, she, ah, took her life the other night."

"What!" Eli shouted in pained consternation. "*Susweca* dead? Why? How?"

"Yes, she's dead. I'm sorry. As to why, we don't know. She, ah, opened the veins in her wrist and just, ah, slipped away."

Grief, cold and leaden, burdened the scout. He shook his head in a futile attempt to deny the whole, terrible incident. She couldn't have. She had no reason. *Susweca*, young, healthy and beautiful. No. It couldn't be. His mouth went dry and he had to work up moisture to speak. Even then, he croaked miserably.

"Where . . . where is she?"

"Back along our trail. The Sioux took care of her yesterday."

"Ph-Phalan can handle the report on our capture of the marauders. I, uh, I want to go there, be with her for a little while."

"I, er, understand, Holten. Dammit, it grieves me, too, to have to be the one to tell you."

Something stirred in Eli's sorrow-numbed memory. It brought to life a faint unease and a nagging suspicion. "There's something not being said here. I don't know what it is, but this just isn't right. With your permission, I'd like to talk to the Miniconjou, find out if they know anything."

"Wouldn't they have gotten word to me if they did?"

"Not necessarily, Colonel. You're the white chief who captured them, remember? That doesn't place you at the top of their list of most trusted people. There's—there's something not being brought out here. I know it. *Susweca* had no reason at all for . . . for killing herself. I'll find out if I ask the right questions."

Miles sympathized and likewise desired to know more. "Go ahead, with my blessing. I hope you'll be satisfied with what you learn."

"Nothing can satisfy me with *Susweca* gone," the scout said sadly.

"You must seek your answer among the blue-legs," *Nitasunkecu* told Eli cryptically.

"Haven't you anything else you can tell me, Steals-Your-Horse?"

"I'm a prisoner. I know little of what goes on among the white soldiers."

"But you hear things," Holten pressed.

After a long moment's pause, *Nitasunkecu* nodded gravely. "I would ask *Huyasapa* if I wanted to know more," the civil chief remarked shortly.

"Thank you, Grandfather, I will."

Holten found Blackbird preparing her three gangling youngsters for the afternoon's march. The eldest, a boy of eleven, looked skinny even in his heavy winter clothing. A big-eyed girl of nine studied the tall, lean scout solemnly as he asked questions. Hair-Face, explosively energetic at eight, ran about them giving an imitation of a buffalo hunt.

"The Great Spirit smiles on you to have two such fine sons as these," Holten began diplomatically.

"Yes. And a husband who is out there planning to free us from the white soldiers."

No doubt where she stood, Eli thought. "He is brave, but the soldiers are many. Life on the reservation would not be so bad."

"You are here about the girl, *Susweca*."

"Uh, yes, I am."

"She was your woman, so you have a right to know."

"What is it I should know?"

"She was shamed and degraded by one of the blue-leg chiefs."

"How do you mean?" Eli demanded, though a sinking sensation inside told him he already knew the answer.

"The young one with greasy yellow locks, the *unkee-sunka* whom she once ran off with boiling water."

Despite his deep sorrow, the image created by these words brought a smile of pride and amusement to the scout's lips. It also brought to mind only one person whom the Sioux might call dog shit. Lt. Charles Clarke. Fury galloped in Eli's chest and he reined it back to get more proof.

"The one who was a coward when your husband and the warriors attacked?"

Blackbird smiled and nodded eager assent. "Yes, that's the one."

"What happened?" Holten asked in a strangled voice.

"He came back. It was in the dead of night, *Susweca* told me. He beat her in the face with his hands, forced her. She became a spoiled woman, one who had betrayed her man. You were her man and she loved you."

"It wasn't her fault," Eli cried in anguish. "We could have gotten over it."

"She carried your child. It was . . . it was washed in the seed of that *unkee-sunka*. She could not live with that shame and with her debasing as well."

"Oh . . . my . . . God!" Holten cried in anguish "Cla-a-r-r-r-ke! I'll have your ass for this!"

With a great effort, Holten recovered his emotions

and thanked *Huyasapa* for the information. Then he set out to find Lt. Charles Clarke.

"It's not fair at all," Ralph Lockwood complained pettishly to Grant Brockton. "What's more, it's not right in the least. After all, we were only fighting Indians. They should thank us, not lock us up like common criminals."

"You'll find there's little fair in this world," Brockton answered in a tired voice. "We also fired on the soldiers. At least some of those half-wits your father brought along got it started. Had it not been for that we might have a rosier future to contemplate."

"What are you getting at?"

"I have little doubt that you and I, along with about half of the men with us will be hanged for that little stupidity."

Ralph paled and his voice quavered. "You can't be serious."

Bored with this cowardly, petulant, spoiled brat, Brockton had to throttle the desire to snarl at him. "I mean exactly that. Which is the reason we have to plan for an escape. I'd rather be a fugitive, prowling the mountains for food and shelter, than swung on a rope at Fort Keogh."

"But they can't! I mean, we're American citizens and all . . . *can they*?"

"Oh, yes. Because we *are* American citizens and in armed conflict with the army, a representative of the government. Had we been foreigners, we might be imprisoned for a while, certainly deported. As it is, all we have to look ahead to is a gallows."

Tears welled in Ralph's eyes and, for a moment, Grant thought the kid might begin to bawl. Ralph fought at it and conquered his natural inclination. "All right. What do you want me to do to help?"

A tiny flicker of admiration mellowed Brockton's attitude toward young Lockwood. Perhaps, just perhaps, they had a chance.

Lt. Charles Clarke had led a patrol of mounted infantry out in a sweep around the area in search of the Miniconjou warriors and their allies who had been dogging the column for so many days. He returned secretly relieved, though outwardly disappointed, that they had not located any sign of the hostiles. He dismissed his men and started walking his horse toward the picket line along officer's row. From there he'd go make his report to Colonel Miles. He made about twenty steps when a heavy hand landed on his shoulder and spun him around.

"You miserable son of a bitch!" Eli Holten hissed in the fraction of an instant before he drove a big, hard fist into Charles Clarke's face.

A rear tooth splintered and bone gave slightly in Clarke's cheek. He went down in an ungainly pratt-fall to the sticky gumbo mud.

"I'm going to kill you, Clarke."

"Stop it! Stop at once. Wha-wha-what's this all about?"

"You rotten prick," Holten growled as he moved in on the sitting form of his enemy. "You might as well have killed her yourself."

Puzzlement and pain washed from Clarke's face.

"Oh, you mean that Sioux fluff? Hardly something worth getting all dirty over. Now, let me get up and I'll promise to forget about this whole incident."

"You'll carry it to your grave, you stinking bastard. Do you know what the Miniconjou call you? Dog Shit. Yeah, it sort of fits, doesn't it? Something so vile smelling and ugly that a Sioux won't even dirty his moccasin to kick it out of the way. Yeah, *Unkee-Sunka*—Dog Shit Clarke."

"Here now, be reasonable. Sure, I regret that she did something so drastic. After all, she was such a good lay."

Holten's boot toe rammed into Clarke's chest. It drove the young lieutenant backward to wallow in more mud.

"Get up! I'm going to take you apart with my bare hands."

"See here, Holten," Clarke spluttered. "I'll summon the provost marshal and have you confined."

"You won't have the chance. Now stand on your legs and fight a little. You're making it too easy."

"You're being ridiculous," Clarke protested as he raised himself to a kneeling position. "Such a fuss over a squaw is hardly gentlemanly. However, if you insist, I'll give you satisfaction in a civilized manner. An affair of honor, shall we call it?"

Holten radiated intense hatred and his nostrils quivered as he examined this proposition. "Any way you want it, Clarke. Because from now on you're a dead man."

Clarke came to his feet, wiping mud from his hands onto a frost-white linen handkerchief. "As I'm the abused party, I have choice of weapons. Say . . . cavalry sabers?"

Hardly a weapon Eli could be considered fully familiar with, he shrugged at the offer. "To the death."

"When and where?"

"Any time you want, any place."

"My, we're anxious aren't we?"

"Don't simper at me, you whore's son," Holten snarled. "Sunup tomorrow? Three miles from camp, at that lightning-blasted cottonwood?"

"Good enough. My seconds and I will be waiting your pleasure."

Holten despised a show of hollow bravado in others, yet his inner anguish would not throttle a final, caustic remark. "If you've got balls enough to show up, you're fucking dead, Clarke."

Charles Clarke's mocking laughter followed Eli across the open space to the supply column cookfires. His rage in check for the moment, Holten accepted a cup of coffee and stared malignantly back at the tall, slender form of his enemy as Clarke went about discharging his final duty for the day. Eli's thoughts turned toward the duel.

He'd need at least one second. An armed witness to insure no foul play. For a moment Eli considered ignoring the rules and simply blowing out Clarke's goddamned brains with his Remington. The idea had a certain appeal. No, he rejected, he couldn't do that. Whoever Clarke involved as his seconds would be innocent of the crimes Clarke had precipitated. Even so, if he cheated and blasted Clarke, he'd have to gun down the lieutenant's seconds also.

Christ! Why had he agreed to sabers? They didn't use bullets and couldn't be plied like a Bowie knife. He'd gotten his ass in a rather tight crack this time.

"Buy ye a drink, Mister Holten?" Regimental Sergeant Major Fione Quinlan had walked up unseen during Eli's reverie. His words broke the brooding spell.

"Well now, Sergeant Major, don't be telling me you've stashed a bottle somewhere?"

Quinlan beamed. "Sure an' I have. Right in me regimental administrative field locker. Ah, far medicinal purposes only, ye understand." His voice became confidential, almost conspiratorial, and he nodded toward where Lieutenant Clarke disappeared into Colonel Miles' tent. "Between you an' me, anyone fixin' to remove such a nasty piece of business from the world deserves a good snort or two beforehand, he does."

Holten produced the first sincere grin he'd managed since hearing of *Susweca*'s fate. "Why, bless you, Sergeant Major, and I'll be proud to take you up on that. Lead the way."

"Beggin' yer pardon, sir, but you will be doin' him up right proper, won't ye? I mean zggghhhiiittt! Slit 'im from tongue to bellows, eh?"

"The word travels fast in the infantry, I see," Holten observed. "Wherever did you hear about any, ah, affair of honor between Lieutenant Clarke and myself?"

They walked apart from all others in the camp. Quinlan smirked at Holten's question and threw out his chest. "Oh, there's a little yard bird that flits about singin' in the ears of those with the need to know. There's little love lost between Clarke an' the other officers, sir. More'n a few were for treatin' him to the Boston Bounce, once they learned what'd he'd gone an' done."

"Boston . . . Bounce? What's that?"

"It's a dance done in mid-air, sir, while bein' supported by a hemp necktie," Quinlan responded with a straight face. "Are ye yet aware that yer own Captain Phalan an' our young Lieutenant Hildebrand have let it be known that they'd be honored to serve as yer seconds?"

"Well, I'll be damned."

"Accept it as a gesture of respect, Mister Holten, as ye should the wee drop o' the auld sod I'll be pourin' ye."

Eli forced his voice into the lilt of his benefactor. "An' grateful I'll be far the both."

Chapter Nineteen

Nine men gathered at the old burned-out cottonwood in the icy orange light of dawn. Great plumes of white jetted from their mouths and the nostrils of their mounts. It might appear that they were characters in one of Thomas Nast's political cartoons, with ink-drawn balloons to contain their words.

"Is there no means by which we can satisfactorily end this affair without bloodshed?" Captains Mason and Brice—who had been pressed into service as judges—inquired of both belligerents.

"Y-yes, there is," Lieutenant Clarke responded shakily, hope coming alive. "I demand a full and complete apology from Mister Holten, also compensation for my wounded dignity and damaged clothing."

"Nope," Eli Holten answered. "I came here to kill that son of a bitch and I have every intention of doing it."

"Very well, gentlemen," Captain Mason said regretfully. "This is to be a contest to the death?"

"Damn' right it is," Eli spat.

"Uh, n-no, er-ah, yes," Clarke quavered.

His intestines seethed. Although fully confident he could best this frontier lout with a saber, Charles Clarke knew a moment of utter, blind panic. He, too, could die here, or be maimed for life. He could even lose a limb. Dueling, after all, was prohibited to officers of the army and navy, outlawed in fact in every state. He had to come out of it unscratched or face possible court martial and dismissal from the service. Such a disgrace would be impossible to bear. Now time, which had dragged so painfully slowly through the night, seemed to rush past him. If only . . .

"Will the respective seconds please come forward and inspect the weapons?" Captain Brice requested in a somber tone.

That accomplished, he turned to the principals. "Remove your coats, please. You may select the blade of your choice. At the command of Captain Mason, you will face each other and assume the *en garde* position. At my command, you will commence the engagement, which shall continue until one of you falls mortally wounded. And may the best man win. Select, please."

Holten and Clark each took a saber.

"Atten—tion! Salute your opponent. *En garde!*"

Arm extended to full length, his linen handkerchief resting on the crossed blade tips, Capt. Harley Mason drew a deep breath. "*Engage*!" At the command he let the kerchief fall.

Instantly, young Clarke went on the offensive. He made a strong beat in *second*, started a false lunge in *prime*, then reversed and swung a vicious horizontal stroke at Holten's unprotected neck. Clumsily, the scout executed a *moulinet* and jumped back a step.

Off balance, he barely managed to parry an immediate attack in *sept*. Clarke's blade tip caught in the bunched cloth of Holten's borrowed linen shirt. It ripped open a great gouge and a thin, red line appeared on the scout's side, below the ribs. Eli winced and slammed downward at Charles' blade in an attempt to disarm him.

A powerful wrist and long, strong fingers prevented Clarke from losing his saber. He performed a smooth disengage and thrust directly at Eli's sternum. Holten parried easily, batted aside two more probes and smashed the flat of his blade into the side of Clarke's head.

Staggered by the powerful blow, Charles Clarke reeled backward, his guard down. Holten came after him, tip sagging slightly, droplets of sweat forming on his forehead despite the cold. He walked into a classic deception that found him fully extended in a lunge when Clarke's saber flashed downward and the keen edge bit into flesh in the upper part of Eli's thick forearm.

Searing heat radiated from the wound as Holten jerked away, and his right hand opened reflexively. He managed to catch the falling sword lefthanded before Clarke's overhand follow-through could descend and split his skull. Sparks flew from the impact of steel on steel. Driven to his knees, Eli fought helplessly to prevent his certain death.

"Only . . . a . . . matter . . . of time," Clarke panted.

Foreleg flashing, Clarke closed the gap once more and executed a series of lightning-quick flicks of the tip. One sliced open the skin over Eli's left cheekbone and another created a long, dripping cut under his chin. The realization that Clarke toyed with him washed over Eli like the water of an icy stream.

Revitalized by desperation and the persistent burn for revenge, Holten fought back skillessly. He had no strategy, didn't understand the finer points of how to use the saber, felt his stamina oozing out of him with his flowing blood, yet he battled furiously, albeit ineptly. What he lacked in technique, he made up for with strength and fast reflexes.

A slash, aimed at his exposed left side, ended in a clang of metal as the scout locked his handguard against that of his opponent. Although pallid from inner fear and a bit green around the lips, Lieutenant Clarke grinned wolfishly. Extended in a full lunge, Clarke nevertheless snapped his leading leg forward in a swift kick toward Holten's crotch.

Eli jumped back, disengaged his saber, and let the off-balance Clarke fall face first in the mud. Before he could scramble upright, Eli came at him, blade swishing in a downward, horizontal stroke. Eyes wild in desperation, the young lieutenant made a clumsy parry that left a rent in his shirt and a thin line of blood welling in the cut over his left shoulder blade. Holten pressed his advantage.

Again Clarke raised the heavy saber in time to prevent the top of his skull from being removed. With all his strength, he heaved Holten backward and regained his feet. Gasping for air, he exerted all his skill.

Clarke's blade blurred in a whirlwind series of attacks, right-left-right-top-left, mixing *moulinets* with *capolettes*, and ending in a metal-screeching *passe de deux*. Confounded by the masterful sword work, Holten gave ground. When he came chest-to-chest with his opponent, as they changed places in the *passe de deux*, an inspiration came to him.

Instead of resisting the force, Eli gave with it. He found himself with his opponent's unprotected back exposed to his naked steel. A wail of horror escaped from Lieutenant Clarke as he desperately attempted to reverse himself and bring his saber into a defensive position.

Too late!

The blunt tip of Eli Holten's saber rested under Lieutenant Charles Clarke's chin. One short upward slice and the young officer would die, his throat slit from ear to ear.

"That will be quite enough, both of you." The stern voice of Col. Nelson Miles shattered the tense silence that held as the contestants looked closely at leering death.

"Mister Holten," Miles' voice crackled again. "Put down the saber, if you please, sir. Now you, Lieutenant. Thank you both. Suppose someone gives me a complete explanation of this? Considering that duelling is in direct violation of army regulations and decidedly against the civilian law, I'm moved to a certain curiosity. Well?"

"Perhaps sir, it should come from a third party," Captain Mason suggested.

"Very well, proceed," Miles commanded.

Tightly, to the best of his ability, Captain Mason filled in the details leading up to the duel. Nelson Miles' incredulity grew with each remark. At last he could contain his astonishment no further.

"This is the young woman who killed herself?" he blurted out.

"The same, sir."

Fire from the inferno blazed in Col. Nelson Miles' eyes as he glowered at Lt. Charles Clarke. "Is all this true? That—that you are responsible for this woman taking her life?"

"Absolutely not, sir. I-I, uh, she, ah, may have done

herself in, but it wasn't because of me. She-she threw herself at me, flirted shamelessly and taunted me until the, ah, flesh weakened. I, ah, may have, ah, had knowledge of her, sir, but it was of her doing."

"You lying, self-serving son of a bitch," Holten growled. "I should have cut your throat while I had the chance."

"Enough, Mister Holten," Miles snapped.

"It's not 'enough,' goddamnit! He raped her, Colonel. He beat her black-and-blue, forced himself on her and left her in disgrace. *Susweca* saw herself as shamed before her people, shamed in her own eyes and, God help her, shamed to me. Sh-she carried my child. And this bastard killed them both as surely as if he had wielded the knife."

Raging inwardly now, Miles turned on Lieutenant Clarke. "I saw her body, Lieutenant. As I recall, she had been rather soundly battered. At the time it was passed off as her having fought with some other Sioux women. That report was made by you, I believe. Now I'd like to hear the whole truth."

All at once the burden became too much for Lt. Charles Clarke to bear. Torn within by the guilty knowledge of his calumny against Eli Holton, of his dishonorable conduct with the Sioux girl, and still shaken by his close encounter with death, his resources ran out. His features crumpled into the pinched, wrinkly expression of a small child about to cry. And, like a guilty little boy, he took refuge in self-serving evasions.

"No. No, it's not true. She loved me. I swear she did. She coaxed me into her tipi, suggested we do all sorts of things, made lewd advances, and begged me to show her what a man was really like."

Eli Holten's groan of anguish preceded only by a fraction of a second his hard fist. Bunched knuckles struck Lieutenant Clarke below his right eye and sent him reeling. Sergeant Major Quinlan and Lieutenant Hildebrand restrained the scout from further assault.

"She couldn't even speak English, you bastard!" Eli shouted.

"Captain Mason," Miles commanded in a stony voice. "Place Lieutenant Clarke under arrest. Have him confined in chains with the other prisoners. For the time being, the charges will be: rape, accessory to murder, promoting a duel in violation of regulations, dereliction of duty and conduct unbecoming an officer."

"And Mister Holten, sir?"

Miles turned toward the scout. His expression softened slightly though his voice remained gruff. "Eli, although I personally think you were a fool to accept Clarke's suggestion of a duel, I can't blame you. All things considered, it must have taken enormous restraint not to have simply shot him on sight."

Eli grinned ruefully. "The thought did occur, Colonel. In fact, I was in the process of killing him with my bare hands when this duel came up. Seemed like a good idea at the time."

"From the looks of you, you've had better ones. Sergeant Major, I assume that your role in this was as attending physician. I suggest you relinquish that duty to our surgeon, Major Bateman, and have him attend to Mister Holten's injuries at once. Oh, and he might take a look at Lieutenant Clarke, too. When he, ah, has time."

"You can't get away with that! I'm hurt, I'm wounded." Lieutenant Clarke's eyes suddenly went wild with madness and he railed in a grating voice. "I'll get you all! I'll make every one of you pay for this!"

"When?" Nelson Miles snapped. "After your court martial? After you get out of Leavenworth?"

"Yes! Yes, if it has to be that way!"

Eli Holton patted the walnut butt grips of his Remington, which Captain Mason had returned to him, and leered expectantly at Lt. Charles Clarke.

"I'll be waiting . . . Dog shit."

"What have we here?" Ralph Lockwood asked sneeringly when a sobbing Lt. Charles Clarke was placed in one of the wagons containing the white prisoners. "Our pretty-boy lieutenant must have stubbed his toe."

Despite his dishonor and defeat, Clarke still possessed a fiery temper. "Keep out of my affairs or you'll regret it."

"Oh, my, he bites," Paul May taunted.

"He's been cut up some," Ephram Sprague observed. "Now who'd do that?"

"Yeah? Who carved you like a Christmas goose?" Ralph asked, brave enough in the face of someone more demeaned than himself.

"It—it's that bastard Holten. And the general went along with it."

"Two of a kind, if you ask me," Ephram Sprague remarked. "What you figure to do about it?"

Helplessness overwhelmed Clarke again. "What *can* I do?" He raised up manacled hands in a pitiful gesture of defeat.

Grant Brockton had been following the conversation with little interest until this point. Now he worked himself closer and laid a consoling hand on the young officer's shoulder.

"You could work on a way of getting away from here. That is if you are really in trouble with the army?"

Clarke cringed from the touch and his face broke into that all-too-familiar expression of a child on the verge of tears. "I'm in trouble all right. All because of that scout bastard and a damned Indian slut."

"Maybe you'd better tell us all about it," Brockton suggested.

Charles Clarke unburdened his soul. In a highly colorful version, he revealed the tragic romance, which existed in his imagination, between himself and *Susweca*. In his rendition, it was Holten who had raped and degraded her and caused her death. Then . . .

". . . then, when I stood up for her honor, the coward grudgingly met me in a duel. I nearly had him. I did! Until . . . until Colonel Miles showed up and deliberately distracted me. Quick as that, Holten cut me four times and nearly slit my throat before Miles had him dragged off me."

"That . . . that's touching. Sounds just like one of them meller-dramas."

"Shut up, Paul," Ralph snarled at Paul May.

Ralph had been deeply moved. The events, as portrayed by Charles Clarke, sounded so much like his own life, as he saw it. Surely, this fine young officer had been betrayed and deserted by his own kind. And Holten was indeed a villianous bastard. He'd been the one who killed Ralph's father right before his eyes. It was easy to see one such as he walked rough-shod over the feelings of an innocent young girl and drove her to the ultimate sacrifice, then besmirched the good name of her beloved.

"Frankly, I don't believe half of that, the way you tell it," Grant Brockton growled. "But I don't care if you're a hundred percent full of shit. You're in the same jackpot with us now, Sonny. You want out, you do what we say, got that?"

"Uh . . ." Charles Clarke gave long pause to consider this.

His career was ruined, of that much he could be sure. He might face time in the federal prison at Leavenworth. How ghastly. What a blow to the family. No matter what he decided to do from now on, none of that could be changed. So, he might as well run with this outlaw pack.

"I, uh, think I can, ah, do that. Yes, sir. I'll do whatever you say. And, for this escape you seem to be planning, I might be able to be of some help."

Chapter Twenty

Weathered pine logs, some fourteen feet tall, sharpened on the top ends, had been sunk into the ground to form a circular stockade. Rammed earth walls added to its appearance of strength. Called Haven because that's what it often represented to distressed immigrants along the trail, the stockade had survived since the Gold Rush days. A small community of six houses, a saloon-and-trading post, and a blacksmith's had grown up around it. Even through the terrible times following the Custer Massacre, Haven had survived the excesses of the Sioux. Thirty people called Haven home and believed they lived in peace.

At least until *Pisko* and his Sioux war party swarmed across the high plains and unleashed death and destruction.

Bullets split the air and arrows sought their marks, while horses, mules and two sway-backed milk cows made crazed animal noises. The warriors came fast, too fast for Absalom Brandywine to close the high gates. Men, women and children ran in fright, many looking back with horror-filled eyes at the ululating braves who rode down on them. Wood splintered in the buildings outside the stockade. Half a dozen of the adult male population died in less than thirty seconds. At last Ab Brandywine got one of the brass wall guns loaded with langrage and it boomed authoritatively as it sent out a shower of broken horse shoes, bent nails and rusty nuts.

This demoralizing event caused the Sioux to draw off to what protection the surrounding buildings might afford. Curious, like all Indians, they began to explore the incomprehensible world of the white man. Several appeared in doorways, clad in bloomers or ruffle-fronted dresses. Three displayed the latest fashion in bonnets. Hoots of triumph came from those who had invaded the saloon.

Raw, burning whiskey of questionable origin and content, began to flow freely as the braves dunked beer mugs, dippers and dirty hands into the breached top of a cask of the potent spirit. Two young bucks yipped gleefully when they unraveled the mystery of the long handle on the draught mechanism and showered each other with cellar-cooled beer. Others rifled the trade goods and helped themselves to large quantities of coffee beans, sugar, flour and salt. Still others, of a more practical bent, scooped up great quantities of jerked meat, tins of beef and pork, a crock of hominy and two barrels of pickles.

"Sour! Sour!" one cried delightedly as he crunched into a long, fat dill.

"Where they make salt rain?" his companion asked as he tasted of a finger he had dipped into the pickling brine.

Outside, the wall gun boomed again. A solid round-shot smacked through the front of the trading post. Several Miniconjou ducked away from its moaning passage. One curious youngster had to see for himself. He reached out boldly and placed a finger, which he lost, in the path of the clearly visible, low-velocity projectile. Then the three pound ball smacked into the ornate backbar and disintegrated the saloon mirror.

Outraged at the unprecedented removal of his left index finger, the young brave yelled to his friends to join him in silencing the offending gun. The attack resumed. While the warriors streamed toward the poorly defended fort, several remained behind to put to the torch all of the buildings. Then they too yipped and yowled their war cries and joined in the final destruction.

Only weeping women and children were spared. Every last man died by bullet, arrow or tomahawk. Then *Pisko* and *Tasa* ordered the survivors gathered into a bunch. Through Red Hair, who spoke some English, he gruffly gave them orders.

" 'Go from here. This is no longer your lodge. Go toward the place where the sun is born,' ah, he means to go east. 'There you'll find the white soldiers. Blue-legs who fight for Bear Coat Miles. Tell them that Night Hawk does not slay women and children. Tell Bear Coat that we don't make war like the bad whites. Tell him that we want our women back, our old people, our children. We live in peace, why does he make war?' "

"H-how can w-we d-d-do this?" one frightened recently made widow asked.

"You can walk," Red Hair told her, then added a giggle at the image of white folks moving about without their rolling-wood lodges. "Night Hawk commands it," he tacked on to give weight to his order.

"Now just a darned minute," a gray-haired, stern-faced matron demanded, hands on hips. "We ain't movin' till we say words over our menfolk."

"What's she want?" *Pisko* asked as he bent low to

whisper to Red Hair.

"They want to mourn their dead, Night Hawk."

"Huh! It is proper, as we do ours. They'll have to hurry."

"I'll tell them that."

To the demoralized whites, he announced, "Night Hawk says you may bury your dead and mourn them as is proper. But you must hurry. Before the sun reaches the top of the sky, you have to be on your way to Bear Coat Miles."

"Post Number Four! Riders comin' in!" came a crisp call shortly before the evening meal was to be served.

Activity stirred in Nelson Miles' camp as the figures grew larger, revealing a variety of clothing, flapping mufflers and floppy hats. At the head of the small column, Livereating Johnson waved his rifle in the air as a signal and hallooed loud enough to startle some of the mules.

"It appears our Mister Johnson is back," Miles said dryly to his staff officers.

Several produced expressions of curiosity. None indicated pleasure. Johnson and his scouts entered the camp at a slow trot, picketed their horses and then walked boisterously to the colonel's tent. All but Johnson and a young frontiersman named Stroud remained outside.

"It's colder'n a witch's tit, Colonel," Johnson said by way of greeting.

"I gather you've completed your circuit," Miles replied, ignoring the colorful remark.

"That we have. There ain't nary a single hostile out

there what hasn't joined up with Night Hawk. All the little bands have strung together. We saw marks and we saw some castoff junk. No Sioux, though."

"Any idea where they've gone?" Miles inquired, the fingers of one hand stroking his long, black mustache.

"Yep. All the drag marks an' snow breaks point toward the Big Snowy Mountains. Oh, an' we come across some burned out homesteads, killed off cattle. The pattern of raids points toward the Big Snowies too. Way I figger, that's where them damn' heathens'll be."

"It couldn't be much plainer," Miles retorted.

"Lessen of course they wanted us to think that and head off in the wrong direction," Johnson added.

"What's the chances of that?"

"Somewhere twixt slim an' none. This ain't the sort of weather to be playin' games. Those boys have gone into the mountains. I'd stake everything on that."

"I see. Thank you, Mister Johnson. You and your men find some food and get settled in. We'll break camp first thing in the morning and head for the Big Snowy Mountains."

Eli Holten sat beside the heating stove in one of the four-man tents assigned to the scouts. He stared blankly at the cherry-red side of the squat, round iron firebox. The sudden end to the duel, Clarke's arrest and confinement left him with a gnawing emptiness. *Susweca* was gone. He would never see her again. Never hear her tinkling laugh nor enjoy the fiery passion she could generate. Gone, too, was the child he'd never had. He should be able to shrug it off, he told himself angrily.

Such niceties as a home and family responsibilities

weren't for him. Hadn't he made that decision long ago? Yet . . .

The tent flap scraped open. "Share a jug with a lonely so'jer, Mister Holten?"

First Sergeant Patrick Liam Donnovan of B Company stood in the doorway, a crockery jug of Monongahela rye hooked on one thick finger. Behind him, the kerosene lantern light picked out the features of Sergeant Major Fione Quinlan. Holten made a vague gesture that they took as an invitation to enter.

"I'll not be very good company," Holten cautioned them. "Although the idea of a good long pull on that rye suits."

"Then pull away it is," Donnovan declared with forced joviality.

Quinlan cleared his throat and spoke as though he had to force the words around some obstruction lodged in his vocal cords. "Yer not of our faith, I know, lad. Nor was that poor slip o' a girl. But, ye bein' gone when it all happened, like, I hope ye'll be understandin' the spirit in which 'twas done. When they was puttin' her to rest in that heathenish manner o' theirs, me an' some o' the byes got together an' said a few prayers fer the repose o' her soul."

Unaccountably Holten found large drops forming in his eyes and he had to blink to banish them. "Th-thank you, Quinlan. I *do* appreciate it and I know *Susweca* would, too. You . . . you're a good man. All of you are."

"Here, swig some o' this down, Mister Holten," Donnovan urged gruffly. "What's the use o' a good wake if ye can't get roarin' drunk?" One knuckle dug at a persistent bit of moisture in the corner of his left eye.

The jug went the rounds. "She had a nice turn o'

ankle, did she not?" Quinlan remarked wistfully.

"Fione!" Donnovan exclaimed, pronouncing the name *Fine* in the manner of the Gaelic language. "Mind yer manners."

"Fact is she *did* have nice ankles," Eli replied, cheered a bit by this sincere companionship. "And a sweet, smiling face. A good cook, too."

"Awh, God, 'tis a pity far one to be taken so young."

"Only the good die young, ye know that, Donnovan," Quinlan snapped back.

"What are we sitting around being so maudlin about?" Eli inquired. "Pass that jug and let me have a drop more."

"Now that miserable coward o' a shave-tail," Donnovan began in a lowered voice. " 'Twouldn't surprise me much if he were to choke to death on somethin' he et, before we're back to Fort Keogh."

"What? An' have that heavy on yer conscience, Donnovan?" Quinlan demanded.

"Sure an' 'twould rest there lightly as a feather, I'm thinkin'."

"Not for the likes o' me, it wouldn't," Quinlan chastised.

"Nor me," Holten added. "I've a feeling he'll get what's coming to him without any effort on our part. Let's forget the little bastard and enjoy this good whiskey."

Who stampeded the buffalo? Terrible pain thumped and thundered inside Eli Holten's brain. The early morning sun, muted a soft pink by fleecy white clouds low on the horizon, stabbed at his eyes like the talons of an eagle. Why had they, when the rye ran out, gone on to

Quinlan's Irish whiskey? And the sutler's Swamp Rot provided by Cpl. Leonard Stacey, B Company's trumpeter? Which, with a jolt of distilled terror, reminded the scout.

"Stacey," he murmured softly in order not to burst his eardrums, "Don't for Christ's sake, blow that thing if I'm within five hundred yards."

"Sign a man's gettin' old when he can't hold his likker, Mister Holten," Stacey replied grinningly, stiff-pecker proud at twenty-five.

"I'll personally see that you get one hundred hours extra duty in the goddamned stables when we return to Rawlins, Stacey, if you don't lay off."

"Uh, oh, sorry, Mister Holten. I, ah . . ."

"Never mind. God, I'd sell my soul for a cup of hot coffee and some of Frank Corrington's brandy."

"Column of fours . . . to the left . . . Yooo!" Captain Phalan called out.

Colonel Miles had put the cavalry in the van, and on both flanks, with his mounted infantry covering the rear and forming the center of the column. It provided maximum mobility and an instant response to any unexpected attack. Herded between the horseback units, the infantry, supply wagons and Sioux captives moved at a steady pace. Holten took the far point with two other scouts.

Who said hell was hot? the scout wondered a short while later. His saddle must have been carved from a block of ice. Cold sapped him and the furies with their little brass hammers did their utmost to destroy his skull from inside. What he didn't need was any form of delay, surprise or difficult decision to make. With some luck they'd reach the Big Snowies by mid-day tomorrow.

What Eli needed, he admitted, was not some, but a great deal of luck.

A benevolent God smiled on him. The day passed, as did his hangover, without untoward event. The camp bedded down and spent a peaceable night. Dawn came clear and cold. Higher drifts of snow began to appear as the army column came within ten miles of the rugged Big Snowy Mountains. Riding ahead, Eli first encountered their initial obstruction.

In a series of three drifts, each better than fifteen feet high, hard-packed snow blocked their trail. Holten and his two assistants searched to both sides of the passage between sheer rock walls, laid bare by erosion, and now bridged by the enormous piles of white.

"Shit," the scout grumbled. "Miles is going to love this. Parker, head back and inform Colonel Miles of what's up here. Stu and I'll trim some lodge pole shafts and try to probe for the easiest way through."

Chapter Twenty-one

Clouds of snowflakes mounted into the air while the shovels of the infantry troops bit into a high face of layered drift that blocked passage through the splintered rock formation. It sat astride the only usable trail toward the Big Snowy Mountains. For three hours, with pick and prybar the way had been tested for strength at several levels. Heavy compacting and a thick, hard freeze provided a passageway some twenty feet down from the top of the cut. Nearly half of the needed debris had been removed.

"Slide! Snow slide!" a wailing voice announced a fraction of a second after a sharp cracking sound from above.

Rumbling and gathering momentum, the mass on the left side of the man-made excavation gave way and plummeted downslope. The vibrations it set up caused the accumulation on the right embankment to jar loose and collapse inward. Men and animals scattered in confused disorder, while billows of snow encased them like a thick fog. Sharp-edged chunks of ice slammed into the soldiers' backs and heads, felling several. Their comrades turned to aid them, only to stumble away helplessly while tons of material fell atop the victims.

"They're trapped!" a young corporal yelled. "There's men caught under that."

"To be so damned close and have this happen," Miles grumbled.

Not one to give in to defeat or to complain unreasonably, Miles' attitude surprised his staff officers. When repeated, in essence if not verbatim, it moved the men to work even harder. No damned snow would give the general a setback, they vowed.

Long hours of tedious, dangerous work at last exposed the first of the buried men. He was dead. Little hope remained for the others. Three more came out, huddled in a group. None of them had survived. Five tense minutes went by. A hand appeared, then an arm and shoulder.

Working like men possessed, the rescue team uncovered another victim. Although unconscious and badly scraped by sharp bits in the slide, he still breathed. One alive so far. It seemed impossible. With renewed vigor the soldiers returned to their task.

"We've got another one," they sang out a minute later.

"And one here," a second team declared. "He's alive."

"So's this one," the first group reported.

Swiftly now the passage cleared and a total of five surviving troopers huddled around a fire, gulping coffee and shivering. The toll had been high, too high, Eli Holten considered. For all that, the way lay clear now.

"Find a place to make camp the other side of this ridge," Nelson Miles informed Yellowstone Kelly and

Eli Holten. "After that catastrophe the men are too tired to move on today."

"We're moving away from Fort Keogh," Grant Brockton observed in a whisper following the evening meal. "At this rate, God knows where they're going to take us. We'd better be ready soon to make a break for it."

"We have to have help," Ralph Lockwood complained. "What's being done about that?"

"That lieutenant you were so anxious to make fun of has made a lot of progress toward that goal. There's more than one man in his former command who thinks Clarke got a bad deal. Two of them are willing to take a risk to help him. So," Brockton said smugly, "when he goes, we go along."

"How soon?" Ralph wanted to know.

"Another day or two. Hard to tell. If it hadn't been for that snow slide, we might have been able to carry it off tonight. Now, we wait."

"And wait, and wait . . . for how long?"

"When I know, you'll know, Ralphy," Brockton informed him condescendingly. "Meanwhile we bide our time until Lieutenant Clarke thinks it is practical."

"Jist so he doesn't wait too long, I'll go along with that," Ralph put in, trying to retain some fiction of importance among the conspirators.

"Go along with it? Face it, Ralphy-boy, you haven't any choice."

"Stars onna ground," little Tommy Gower muttered through cracked, bloodied and frost-bitten lips. "Ova there."

"What? What did he say?" a woman asked weakly.

"Nothin', nothin'," Tommy's older sister responded in a thready voice. "He's seein' things."

Huddled together in the terrible biting cold of the cloudless night, the survivors from the ruined fort at Haven fought the elements in a pitiful attempt at survival. Two elderly women and three of the children had died during their long trek. Now they built walls of snow to shelter from the wind and bundled in close under an assortment of coats and blankets. Many, like twelve-year-old Lena Gower, had abandoned all hope. She hugged eight-year-old Tommy to her breast in a mothering gesture that conveyed defeat and resignation.

What could Tommy have seen? Lena worried over it, for want of something, anything to keep her mind from turning off entirely. There, maybe he had seen some sort of brightness. Yes, way beyond where she and the others clung together to conserve life. Little yellow dots. They did look like stars. What could it be? There were no towns out here, no farms. Slowly the image began to waver, then to swim before her drooping eyes and Lena slipped off into a sleep of exhaustion.

A pink glaze shimmered on the crusted surface of snow beyond the treacherous pass that had claimed the lives of nine troopers. Where the ground had been patchy with fading snow before, now it remained uniformly covered to a depth of a stout horse's knees. Shortly after sunup, Capt. Walter Brice of C Company sent out a cavalry patrol to sweep the immediate area so that the column would not have any unpleasant surprises. They returned abruptly, at the gallop, bearing a rather wondrous burden.

"They say they're from Haven, whatever that is," Lieutenant Carmoody told a group of eager listeners while his men lowered frail, nearly frozen women and children from the saddles in front of them.

"It is, or was, Ab Brandywine's place, a small stockade and trading post to the west of here, near the foothills of the Great Snowy Mountains," one gray-haired matron informed the soliders. "I'm Matilda Winston. The Sioux attacked. We are the survivors."

"Get these people into tents," Lieutenant Hildebrande, the OD, commanded. "Find them warm blankets, clothing if any will fit, and get some coffee and hot soup down them at once."

The arrival of the refugees from Haven made a sudden change in Nelson Miles' plans. Once they had recovered enough to make intelligent answers, the colonel sent for several to tell their story. When they had completed it, Miles looked to Yellowstone Kelly and Eli Holten for advice.

"These people have suffered, that's for certain, and at the hands of Sioux hostiles," Miles summed up. "How's this fit with you two?"

"Sounds like *Pisko* wanted awful badly to send us some sort of message," Kelly suggested.

"What would that be?" Miles inquired mildly.

"None of the women or children were hurt outright. You heard what that Mrs. Winston said. *Pisko* knows that you, personally, are on his trail. His talk about not making war on women and kids could indicate he wants to pow-wow."

"That would fit," Eli Holten added in support of Kelly's theory. "Then, again, it might refer to those renegade whites we captured the other day. If he wanted to say that the raids on white settlements and isolated homesteads would continue until they were stopped, he might choose something dramatic like this to emphasize his determination."

"Eli's got a handle on it, too, General. Could be either way."

"On the other hand, something isn't entirely on the up-and-up with this," Eli injected. "We know what he really wants. He wants his people turned loose. Why bother to make such a display, why kill the menfolk at Haven, if the result is to get the army to come after him with all the more determination? Night Hawk's not a lunatic, nor a fanatic. He should see clearly that this would only make matters worse for him. Before we go off hunting him, which I'm sure you're going to order, Colonel, I'd like to make a reconnaissance in force with a company of cavalry and Lieutenant Strickland's company of mounted infantry."

"To what purpose?"

"To see what's over the other side of Greathouse Peak. There's no question that all sign we've had of *Pisko* and the war party lead that direction. I don't like what I can see as the only reason for him wanting us to come that way."

"Such as," Miles urged mildly. His knack for drawing the best from his men functioned at its greatest today.

"Ummm. It's sort of hard to put in so many words, Colonel. Sort of . . . say *Pisko* wants us very badly to follow at all possible speed. Why? To do that, we'd have to sacrifice a lot of scouting activity. We'd go into those mountains, hot on his trail, without the least damned idea of what lay ahead."

"Ambush?"

"Exactly, Colonel. That's why I want to scout it out before we move. There's a good eighteen miles to cover to the foothills. If you move the main column that far, while we're out, well and good. Then we can get a better picture of what's likely to happen."

"Go to it, then, Mister Holten."

"Thank you, sir."

"Jim, have the appropriate orders cut for this," Miles informed his adjutant. "Verbal will have to do," he added in dusty humor.

"We're going too far to the west," Grant Brockton complained in a whispered conversation with his fellow conspirators. "We'll have to go through with the plan right away."

"Holten has left camp, taken two companies and most of the mounts with him," Ralph Lockwood informed the group. "While they are short-handed is the best time."

"I agree," Brockton replied, then directed a question to Charles Clarke. "Thing is, can you get those turncoat pals of yours to steal the keys by tonight?"

"I'm . . . not sure. Within two days is more likely."

"Hell, we'll be in those mountains by then."

"You can be fairly certain that the supply column, along with the captive Sioux and ourselves, will go no further than the foothills. Too easy for wagons to get destroyed in mountain passes. I'll give the army credit there. They have better sense than the immigrants who flock through here. Miles will establish a base camp and conduct operations from it."

Brockton jostled Clarke's shoulder in a friendly manner. "It's nice having our own military advisor, isn't it? So, then, what you'd advise is to wait until that camp is set up, then make our break?"

Charles Clarke gave it slow, careful thought. "That would be best. Fewer guards, fewer men free to pursue us once we're missed."

"I like that. Unless something interferes, we'll do it that way," Brockton declared flatly.

Chapter Twenty-two

Eli Holten rolled a long, thin cigar between the fingers and thumb of his left hand. His right held a cup of coffee, brewed over a small, enclosed fire that could not be seen more than twenty feet away. A hard day's ride had taken the detachment to a place well north of Greathouse Peak. From here they could ascend the mountains tomorrow, circle behind and come up on the route chosen by Nelson Miles.

If *Pisko* had planned any nasty surprises, they could be undone with ease. At least, that's the way the scout had it figured. He had little trust in the weather, though. Thick layers of cloud shrouded the peaks and Holten had little doubt that they unloaded tons of fresh snow. By the time his force had reached that altitude, they might find the way blocked. Eli placed the cigar between his full, sensuous lips and struck a match against the clever little sheetmetal stove Corporal Stacey had invented.

A thick ball of smoke slid down to his lungs as he inhaled the aromatic tobacco. Holten enjoyed an occasional smoke. These cigars were of the best quality, ordered especially by Gen. Frank Corrington. Whenever the scout went on a difficult mission, which was to say nearly always, the general saw to it that he had a generous supply. Eli had five left after this one.

"Better enjoy it, 'cause things are likely to go downhill from here."

"What?" Lieutenant Random asked, shaken from a reverie about his girl back home.

"Nothing important, Dwight. I was just making noise to hear my lips flap. From the looks of those clouds, we could run into a hell of a mess tomorrow."

"Not to mention the effort of making the climb. Greathouse Peak is over eight thousand feet. Air's sort of thin that high."

"That it is. I think I'll finish this and turn in."

"Good idea."

"Snow or not, we're going to need all the energy we can muster," Holten concluded before he drained his cup, doused the cigar and crawled into his chilly bedroll.

Adhering to a straight-line approach, Nelson Miles and his troops entered the foothills of the Great Snowy Mountains shortly past noon the next day. Dark, burning eyes watched their progress and a sensation of elation stole over *Pisko*. His plan was working.

Only one narrow pass lay ahead. The soldiers would have to take it. Once deep inside . . . ah, then they would be made to pay for capturing the village. His people would be free again.

"Look," Big Hands pointed out. "They have the long-shooting guns."

"They had them before. Like when we attacked the rolling-wood lodges, they'll not be able to use them. As Red Hair says, we will fall on them. The sides of the pass will fall on them. They won't have time to work the long-shooting guns."

"These blue-legs are many," Elk Tail observed soberly.

"The more scalps to be danced when the fighting is over," *Pisko* said lightly. "See. They're making camp. Tomorrow they will start to climb the pass. Tomorrow we'll have a big victory."

Increasing altitude began to take a toll on the men and animals. By mid-morning the next day, the column of mixed cavalry and mounted infantry had strung out far ahead of the marching troops. Two of the half dozen light six-pounders had been left with the base camp. The remaining four lagged far behind. Harry Belten, the gun sergeant, cursed the plodding mules, his breath labored, the usual blistering oaths delivered with far less than the regular vehemence.

"Wrong-headed, useless, oat-eating sods! Keep moving, damn you. Pull this thing, pull, damn your black hearts."

"Hell, Sarge, even the infantry's movin' faster than us."

"Keep yer yap shut, Brewster. I'm in no goddamned mood to be told how slow we're going," Belten snarled.

Unseen by the laboring soldiers, two bronze-skinned watchers kept close account of what progress the disjointed column made. "It is good that Night Hawk sent warriors to attack the camp," Raven remarked.

"Yes," Sun Boy agreed. "When they hear the fighting start, they can sweep through, take the people away and catch the soldiers in the rear."

"Many blue-legs will die before this day is over."

"It's for Night Hawk to decide which day the soldiers die. The harder it is for them to climb, the easier to defeat them. But, surely, the time will come for them to die."

Black shadows already filled the valley through which Eli Holten and the troops filed. Above, the sky remained a bright blue. They would be forced to stop before long. Weariness tugged at every man and horse. Their full day's climb had brought them above the six thousand foot level when they came to this long, narrow valley.

Fortunately, the rate of incline decreased. Pines, cedar and fir grew in profusion, along with the bare-limbed skeletons of aspen and sumac. A stand of birch had been gnawed by hungry deer. A profusion of tracks indicated a large number of the foraging animals to be about. No one complained when the signal came to halt.

"I want two parties of three expert marksmen to make a swing to each side of the valley. I'll take two men and go straight ahead," Eli Holten requested of Captain Phalan. He pointed to the denser thickets ahead. "We ought to jump those deer somewhere along there. At least enough to make a good feed for tonight."

Even the bare suggestion of fresh venison raised the spirits of the troops. They went about the usual camp chores with renewed vigor. Firewood accumulated in large stacks, big rocks formed fire rings, and the tents went up in record time. With sentries posted, and the mounts picketed, the men took turns rubbing down their animals. Oats and water came next. The last of the ninety-three horses crumped and chomped at their feed when faint, distance-muffled shots sounded.

A scant bit past fifteen minutes later, the hunting parties returned. Seven good-sized white tail deer lay over the backs of pack horses. Such a bounty of fresh meat greatly cheered the soldiers in camp. An ample number of volunteer butchers showed up under the limbs of the trees where the dead game had been strung up.

While the work progressed, Eli Holten warmed himself at the fire. "Hope someone brought onions along. I've a hanker for fresh deer liver and stewed onions."

"There should be some in the officers' mess box," Lieutenant Strickland suggested. "Have some coffee and take the chill off." While Holten poured, the young officer talked away. "How far do you figure we've made today, Eli?"

"Better than half way, Brad. This valley's angled the right direction. I think we can follow it right on through."

"Won't the hostiles have scouts out looking over this area?"

"You've been out here long enough, Brad, to know Indians don't do a whole lot of scouting, or put out many sentries. Chances are we can get into position where we want to be without being seen at all. Oh, they'll be watching the main trail through Greathouse Pass, I'd guess along about the foot of the peak itself. They could enfilade our boys that way, have advantage of the high ground and be able to ride down on them. That's where we'll come in. If there is a trap laid, we can spring it by hitting the Sioux from behind."

Anxiety over their escape kept Grant Brockton awake far into the night. He listened to the silence with the unease of a condemned man hearing the wind moan through the gallows tree. When a thump came against the tail gate of the wagon, not particularly loud, but shattering to him, he started violently enough to send sharp pain up his arms from his manacled wrists.

"Take it easy," a gruff whisper came.

Brockton recognized the voice as that of one of the men Clarke had induced to help them. A moment later a dark figure swung a leg over and entered the crowded interior. He located Lieutenant Clarke and crouched between him and Brockton on the opposite side.

"I brung this stuff now. We can't be coverin' your break and have it here at the last minute."

"Good planning, Peters," Clarke whispered. "What have you got?"

A metallic tinkling came to Brockton's ears. "Keys fer them irons. Also two revolvers. There'll be rifles waitin' with the horses. Don't get too eager to use these things. Once we tangle with the Injuns, there'll be plenty of confusion. That'll be the signal. Burle an' me have decided to go with you. Ain't no sense in stayin' here and take the chance of being caught out."

"All right. We can use all the firepower we can get in case the Sioux decide to chase us."

"Or the army," Peters replied. "They'll take a dim view of what we've got goin' here."

"You've done well. We'll make it up to you once we're away," Brockton inserted.

"Oh, we're countin' on that, you can be sure."

"Don't overestimate your worth," Brockton snapped.

"I'm not. But there's one thing sure's shit stinks, Mister. Without us, you ain't got a chance."

Chapter Twenty-three

Thick, gray clouds obscured the top of Greathouse Peak. They swirled like a dense fog down the slopes to conceal the advancing soldiers of Nelson Miles' Ninth Infantry and the lead company of the Twelfth. Even the clop of horses' hoofs and the rattle of loose gear became muffled into an unreal world of eerie silence. From time to time, a flurry of snowflakes blustered upon them, adding to the dampness of the tangible wisps of vapor that brushed the faces of the men. Through this blind universe, Yellowstone Kelly rode back to report to his commander.

"The lead element will be clear of the treeline in another five minutes. Still no sign of the Sioux."

"From the tone of your voice, Mister Kelly, I assume you suspect they aren't there to be found," Miles responded dryly.

"It's a possibility. Or they could be waiting for us to string out more in this damned cloud cover."

Miles studied the sky, which seemed to be brushing the top of his head. "Any chance of this clearing?"

"No way of telling. My guess is that it could hang around here for a week. Or be gone by noon, if the wind gets up right."

"Have you or your scouts crossed the divide as yet?"

"Nope."

"Then it's my suspicion that it's there they'll be waiting. Sergeant Major," Miles called out. "Pass the word back to slow the column until the rear elements catch up. Ready weapons and ammunition and keep a sharp lookout. There's Sioux around here somewhere. I can almost smell 'em."

"Why do we skulk on the back side of the mountain while the enemy comes closer all the while?" an impatient Teton warrior named Rain demanded as the day wore on.

"It's Night Hawk's plan," Snake Chaser told him quietly. "With each step the soldiers grow weaker. See, over there. Two more of them have fallen to the side of the trail for want of air to breathe. Our time will come. Think of the honor that's yours. You've been chosen to be part of the lure that draws them into that steep passage behind us. We'll be exposed to all their guns at one time. What stories will be told of our daring."

"You're young and foolish," Rain snorted.

"And I will count *coup* before we trick the soldiers into following us."

"I say we should attack now."

"You are not the leader."

"There's no honor in what we do."

"Go complain to the trees. I am *Pisko's* man and I do what I'm told."

Eli Holten cantered up to where Captain Phalan waited with the troops. "We're past the divide. Over there's the trail that has to be the one through Greathouse Pass. The peak's behind us now."

"You've done an excellent job, Eli. Any sign of the Sioux?"

"No, Art. That doesn't mean they aren't here. Once we reach the trail over there, there's a good ten miles or more between us and the column."

"We'll turn east, then, and join up when we can. I'll send a dispatch rider ahead."

"No, I don't think that would be a good idea," Holten countered tactfully. "Right now we're a surprise element the Sioux know nothing about. Let's keep it that way."

"Good enough."

Half an hour later, the troops who had been under forced march for the past two days crested a low rise on the trail. Eli Holten stopped them once more, this time with his hand raised in the signal to halt.

"Art, if you would ride forward with me, I have something to show you."

"What is it, Eli?"

"I think we've found the main body of hostiles and I'm fairly sure I can make a good estimate of what they have in mind."

"Let's go see it, then. Lieutenant Random, take charge of the company. Lieutenant Strickland, you're in command. First Sergeant, if you'll ride along?"

"Yes, sir," echoed his subordinates.

Three miles ahead, at the foot of a sharp incline that led to a sheer-walled cut in the pass, Eli Holten dismounted and led the way on foot. At the crest, he and the two soldiers removed their hats. Eli nodded toward the area beyond.

"In there. Quite a reception they're planning."

In stricken silence, Art Phalan studied the situation

in the narrow canyon. He gave a shiver of unease and slid backward a short distance. Phalan mopped at his running nose with a rumpled kerchief and shook his head in wonder.

"Not the usual thing you'd expect from the Sioux. According to some of the After Action Reports to come out of the Southwest, that's how the Apaches go about makin' war."

"Effective, too," Eli assured him. "Now you see what we're up against. At any time now, Miles and his troops can come around that far bend and into the defile. From my way of thinking, we'd better bring up the rest of the companies mighty fast and make ready to pull the blanket out from under *Pisko*."

It took no effort of consideration. "First Sergeant, my compliments to Lieutenant Strickland, and have the two companies brought up here with all dispatch. But, quietly, Sergeant, very quietly."

Sergeant Dononvan had barely reached his horse when the distance-distorted, oddly mixed sounds reached their ears. Battered back and forth over the convoluted walls so that the exact source could not be determined, horses whinnied, shots erupted and men yipped and yelled in a jumbled medley.

"What the hell?" Phalan blurted. "Don't tell me this is just a reserve force?"

"I . . . don't think so, Art. Though it does sound like the fighting's some distance ahead of here."

Below them, in the rocks, the Sioux tensed as a small band of warriors galloped into the narrow passage, firing behind them as they rode. Coming hot behind them, troopers of C Company rushed into the trap, weapons blazing despite the scant chance of hitting their intended targets. Beyond them, at a fair distance, a bugle sounded the call that sent infantry forward at the trot.

Yard by yard, the unsuspecting soldiers followed their cavalry escort into the vicious jaws of the ambush. A quick glance over his shoulder assured Eli Holten that B Company's troops, and those of Strickland's mounted infantry, came on with what speed they could. Would they make it in time though?

"We're going to have to hit the saddle and attack at once," Holten advised. "Let's get down to our horses. Have Corporal Stacey sound the *Charge* the moment they get up to us."

"Looks like I'd better split the company and sweep around the rim on both sides."

"That'll do it. Only leave a sizable force on the trail at the summit, to cut off any retreat. That way the Sioux ambush will turn into a trap for them."

"If only we could signal Colonel Miles."

"Unless we were in shoutin' range, that would be impossible. And if we were, we'd be in some deep shit."

"Don't I know it, Eli."

So far it had worked. *Pisko* could barely contain the howl of triumph that raised in his throat. If only his warriors would wait.

Up to this point, the blue-legs had not entered the deadly canyon. Would the bait turn in time to catch the fish? He wondered on that, consumed with a fiery impatience. Where were the blue-legs? Did they run forward with their knives in the ends of their rifles? Or did they wait in patient ranks, not in the least fooled by this trap? There! Ah, it began to happen as he had seen.

Near the western end of the defile, the fleeing Sioux turned their horses and fired a ragged volley at their pursuers. Only a few warriors, as he had ordered, joined in from the sides. Their charge blunted, the point outdistancing the body of the company by a hundred yards, the troopers reined in and dismounted. Some chose boulders, the others the living bodies of their horses for protection. Solid, dependable moves, *Pisko* observed. These men were experienced soldiers.

At once the Sioux began to return fire. The elongated string of the cavalry stretched toward them. Time seemed to freeze. Where were the blue-legs? More of the Sioux braves exposed themselves and engaged the enemy. He couldn't keep them in check much longer, *Pisko* thought regretfully. Faintly heard, a bugle sounded. The blue-legs would come now.

From much closer, another glittering string of notes filled the air. Above him, not below, *Pisko* realized with a start. Behind, not ahead of him. What could it be? Had he made a mistake about the number and position of the soldiers? Hoofs rattled in the rocks and pony-soldiers began firing down onto the Sioux positions.

"Sound the *Charge*!" Art Phalan commanded.

With the first staccato notes, the cavalry burst over the edge of the canyon and began to fire down on the startled Sioux. Bronze bodies fell among blood-splattered rocks. Some of the more self-possessed warriors managed to steady themselves and send leaden defiance at this unexpected trouble. All around the boulders exploded into slashing shards where the 405 grain slugs of the .45-70 Springfields struck. Ricochets moaned through the canyon. A bugle sounded again, louder and clearer, this time from where *Pisko* had expected it.

Bear Coat Miles' infantry had arrived. But now, instead of being the game, they had become the hunters, turning the trap effectively back on its inventors. All sense of order or design disintegrated for the Sioux.

Here and there prepared mounds of stones and boulders rumbled down-slope toward the blue-uniformed forces. Had all the cradles been dumped at once, as *Pisko* had intended, the soldiers' resistance would have ended quickly. Now their superior firepower and aimed, disciplined marksmanship took command of the field.

War whoops echoed off the stone walls, while insults in English answered them. Oblivious to the steady hail of deadly slugs, braves rose up, lance and shield in hand, and charged into the close ranks of the infantry. Mounted men raced from place to place. Smoke clouds drifted lazily over the scene of carnage as each side sought to inflict enough injuries to tip the balance their way. How badly *Pisko* wished he had not sent a fair-sized force off to attack the wagons. He needed them here and now.

For all the wild melee in the canyon, the sounds of battle came faintly to the huddled Sioux captives and everyone in the supply train at the base camp. It signaled the beginning, however, for Grant Brockton. Smiling with anticipation, he unlocked his manacles and leg irons and passed the keys along to the next man.

"Won't be long now," Brockton assured the others. "Rub your wrists and ankles, get the circulation back quickly. I'll have one of those sixguns, if you please, Lieutenant."

Charles Clarke handed over one of the Colt Army revolvers without hesitation. His eyes held a far-away cast and he cocked his head as though listening to something of demanding interest. Would he be visualizing the battle? Brockton wondered. If so, it would no doubt be with considerable trepidation, not to mention gratitude at not being there. Clarke grew suddenly pale as the sound he audited increased in volume and clarity.

Yips and howls and the thud of unshod hoofs swelled around the wagons. Men shouted the alarm that verified the horror Charles Clarke envisioned.

"Indians! Hostiles attacking from the south!" came the cry from outside the wagon.

"More Sioux to the east!"

"This is it!" Grant Brockton shouted. "This is our chance. Let's get out of here right now!"

"N-no! They'll k-kill us!" Clarke wailed.

Brockton's lips twisted in disgust. "Come along or stay, it don't matter to me, you yellow bastard."

Shots barked from close by their covered vehicle. Rifle fire answered from a distance. Charles Clarke began to shake like a palsied man. All the same he stood in turn and jumped from the rear of the wagon.

"Over there," Ralph Lockwood shouted, pointing to six saddled mounts beyond the cook tent. "Our horses are ready."

"Halt!" an infantryman called out.

Brockton turned part way around and shot the soldier between the eyes. His emotions soared toward giddiness. Freedom! It beckoned from only a few yards away.

Individual fighting, hand-to-hand combats of intense and savage nature, had taken over the canyon. Here a soldier locked his hands in a death-grip around the throat of a hostile Sioux. There a warrior swayed as though in a drunken dance with a blue-uniformed infantryman, each grasping the other's right wrist, to prevent a vicious blade from piercing skin.

Draped across a boulder, a cavalryman with a broken leg howled in terror as a snarling Miniconjou drove a war lance into this abdomen. Rolling in the muddy debris of the canyon's floor, like two ravaging dogs, another pair of opponents struggled to gain that precious split-second which would spell death for the other. As the men of B Company streamed down the sides of the canyon, Eli Holten saw a gaudily decked out warrior rise up to strike Yellowstone Kelly in the back of the head with a stone war club.

Holten's Winchester fired almost without his willing it. The .44-40 slug smashed into the left side of *Tasa*'s chest and burst his heart. He fell backward, legs kicking a final spasm of death. From the east end of the canyon, a rider came splashing through the small stream, flailing the air with his hat and shouting, though none could hear him. Eli worked his way closer.

"The supply column's been attacked. Send some relief!" the soldier bellowed.

"Relief hell," Holten heard a young lieutenant remark. "We're up to our armpits in Sioux and they want a relief mounted."

A voice sounded resoundingly to Holten's left, deep and resonant, speaking well-modulated Lakota. "You! I command you to single fight, Tall Bear of the Oglala. Face me or be named coward. I am *Pisko* of the Miniconjou. I have killed twelve men, taken nine scalps and counted *coup* thirty times. My deeds are great! Flee in despair or face me and die!"

"*Maka kin le, mitawa ca!*" Eli shouted defiantly. Right then, charged with a drenaline by the ferocity of battle, he felt like he *did* own the earth.

Each man drove heels into his mount's flanks at the same instant. Like animate locomotives they hurtled over the rough terrain that separated them. Night Hawk held a war club in his left hand, a brass tack-decorated Winchester in the right. The braided horse hair rein he clamped in his teeth. Eli Holten had dropped his reins and guided Sonny by the pressure of his knees. He kept a two-handed hold on the rifle he sighted, watching the figure of his challenger bob wildly in and out of the sight picture. Less than twenty yards separated them when Holten fired.

Hot and speedy, Eli's slug ripped a deep gouge out of the deltoid muscle of *Pisko*'s left shoulder. The force spun the Sioux war leader around and he slipped from his mount's back, landing with a bound. Holten kneed Sonny around and slowed him. Flamed to a killing lust, the scout acknowledged he had to make one more try.

He slipped from the saddle and came forward, weapons ready, until only five feet separated him from the Miniconjou war leader. "Stop the fighting now, *Pisko* and go to the reservation in peace."

"You know me?" Surprised that the white brother of the Oglala recognized him, he nonetheless held his warlike stance, challenging, though blood ran in a thick rope down his left arm.

"Twelve seasons ago we danced across the sacred pole from each other in the *Wambli Gleska* society at the Sundance," Holten calmly told him. "You had only thirteen summers that year."

Stunned, *Pisko* tottered slightly and the word "brother" formed soundlessly on his lips. "A Dakota is forbidden to kill a brother. Why do you war on us?"

"Order your men to stop and we can talk, brother."

"No! No, we must fight to be free," *Pisko* stubbornly insisted.

"To fight now is to die. Choose to live, Night Hawk."

"I . . . I don't know how to . . . to say stop."

"Don't let it be with your scalp in my hand."

Memory of the tall, handsome, sun-browned youth who stayed long after so many others had fallen, swarmed in *Pisko*'s mind. It was he, Tall Bear, who had given the skinny boy of thirteen courage enough to continue one more round, to wind his twisted rawhide tether into the giant braid that decorated the Sundance pole. He had done so and collapsed. His last sight had been the compassionate, yet joyful expression of Tall Bear, as though the young adopted Oglala wished him well. Tears flooded *Pisko's* eyes and he threw down his weapons.

"Stop! Enough! Lay down your arms, brothers of the Miniconjou. From this time forward, *Pisko* will not fight. Stop, I say! I command you to hear me. Stop fighting!"

Radiating outward from where Eli Holten and Night Hawk stood, arms around each other's shoulders, the sounds of the conflict diminished. Gaining momentum, the cease fire swept the length of the canyon. At last a tense silence hovered over the panting contestants. Nelson Miles wiped blood from his cheek and blinked owlishly.

"Well . . . I'll be . . . goddamned," he declared in a hushed, awed voice.

Chapter Twenty-four

Captain Brand broke the spell of incredible silence. "The supply column. We've got to get back there. Hildebrand'll have a hell of a time holding off an attack."

"Send the cavalry," Nelson Miles commanded. "Mister Holten, will you accompany them, please, sir?"

"Uh, of course, Colonel."

"We'll see to disarming and rounding up these new candidates for the reservation."

The true meaning of *Pisko*'s surrender reached a deeper level of Eli's consciousness then. Off to a reservation. All of the fighting, the killing, and in the end, a life of restricted movement and handouts from the government, if and when they arrived.

For a long, sad moment he wondered if maybe, just maybe, it wouldn't have been better to leave these few hundred people free to roam the plains for the short years left before the white men turned it all into neat farmsteads, with fences and pretty little houses. A shiver of premonition ran along the scout's spine. He clasped *Pisko* affectionately by the shoulders.

"There are no Sundances on the reservation, my brother. But the free Cheyenne sometimes hold them. One day I'll come and we can slip away together and go and watch and remember."

Still dazed by the enormity of his actions, Night

Hawk returned the embrace and spoke dreamily. "I'd like that. Yes, we will do it . . . some day."

Captain Brice had C Company ready to go. Holten reloaded his Winchester and replaced two expended rounds in his Remington revolver. He bent and lifted *Pisko*'s feather-decorated war lance from the ground. He'd carry that along as a convincer, in the event they reached the supply wagons in time. Then Eli swung into Sonny's saddle and took his place at the head of the column. Although sorely tempted, he did not look back as they trotted along the canyon floor toward the trail down to the foothills.

"They just keep coming!" Sergeant Bascomb of K Company shouted as the Sioux wheeled their ponies and started back toward the defensive ring of wagons.

"They're not as many as when they first attacked a week ago," Lieutenant Hildebrand returned with false joviality.

"Yeah," Bascomb agreed. "That only makes it harder to find a target."

"If we don't get help from the main force soon, they're gonna ride right over us, Sergeant."

"I know it, sir." He reached out and pressed downward on Hildebrand's shoulder. "Duck. That sonofabitch is gonna jump the barricade."

Riding low and close to his pony's neck, a Sioux warrior broke directly for the place between two wagons where the defenses were most vulnerable. Hildebrand and Bascomb crouched low and turned to follow the brownish blur. This one had to be stopped and quickly.

Fully half of their command had to be put to guarding the captive Miniconjou. Were an armed warrior to get into that group, it could result in all sorts of mischief. Bascomb fired first.

Four hundred and five grains of lead erupted from the muzzle of Bascomb's Springfield and smashed into the left shoulder blade of the intruder. He appeared to vault forward and disappear in the midst of the captive Sioux contained under the rifles of the infantry.

A great cry of lamentation went up, which the beleaguered troops spared little attention, compelled as they were to holding off still more hostiles. At the defeat of this strategem, the warriors pulled off a way and sat studying the situation.

"The rolling-wood lodges are harder to defeat than we thought," Big Hands observed, panting from the exertion of their repeated assaults on the soldiers.

"They don't have to be careful about our people," another Miniconjou remarked. "We're made weak by attacking from only one side."

"What you say is true," Big Hands admitted. "Any idea of how to break through and free our people?"

"We must become twice our number," a wise old warrior suggested.

"How is that?"

"Some must stay and fight fiercely, make much noise and don't let the blue-legs know the rest have gone from here."

"Gone where?" Big Hands asked impatiently.

"We'll go up the creek a way, swim across and come back down. Once we are behind the soldiers, we'll swim back and go in among our people. In the same way we can free them while we're fighting the soldiers."

Big Hands smiled broadly. "It's a good plan. We'll do

it that way."

Trumpeter Culhane of C Company put the nickel-plated mouthpiece of his instrument to his mouth and pursed his lips to form the first notes of the *Charge*. Sharp, clear bell-tones sparkled across the distance to the beleaguered supply column. Sweeping down the hill, the company spread out into a double line "as skirmishers." Their Springfield carbines drawn and ready, a volley of .45-70 fire crackled on command.

Consternation raced through the ranks of the Sioux. There shouldn't have been any cavalry to ride to the rescue. The ambush in the canyon was to have finished off all the blue-legs and pony-soldiers. How could it be that they were here, in considerable strength, firing with withering accuracy into the crowded cluster that waited while their brothers crossed the stream and freed their people? Confusion turned to panic when Eli Holten rode out ahead of the troops, waving a war lance.

"*Pisko* has surrendered," he shouted in Lakota. "See this! See Night Hawk's lance. Lay down your weapons or run while you can," the scout yelled to them.

Those caught in the water naturally gave up without any show of resistance. The remainder, still mounted and well-armed, fired a few token rounds, then fled or surrendered, as the mood struck them. Their medicine had failed them. But, most rationalized, there would be another day. The relief column entered the defenses to the cheers of the soldiers at the barricades. It took Eli Holten only two minutes to discover that Lt. Charles Clarke, along with some seven others had escaped.

"I'm going after them," he announced.

"You can't go alone," Capt. Walter Brice protested. "Besides, this has to be reported to Colonel Miles."

"Someone else can do that. I want to get after them while there's some chance of catching the lot."

"I'll send a platoon."

"Thanks, Walt. I'll go for that."

"Good luck, Eli."

Snow began falling before Eli Holten had made five miles along the trail left by the fleeing fugitives. They had not taken any precautions to hide their passage. Overturned rocks, broken stalks of grass and twigs on sage and lupine, clear, sharp hoof prints in wet ground, all pointed the way for the scout's keen eyes. The latest flurry of white flakes he considered only to be a momentary hindrance. He quickly outdistanced the patrol, gaining ground on the most laggardly of the eight horses. Confident of the ease with which the escaped criminals would be overtaken, Holten nearly let his incaution cost him his life.

Rounding a bend, Eli jerked in the saddle as a bullet snapped past his ear, uncomfortably close. He dove into the cushioning protection of a small snowdrift and came up with his Winchester in his hand. Snow crystals blinded him momentarily. Slowly indistinct images began to form, dark objects against a white background. Holten sighted in on the nearest one.

"He went down somewhere around here," Paul May called out. "I must'a popped him right in the head."

"Find him an' let's get the hell outta here, Paul," came a nervous reply. "They gonna send soldiers after us, too."

"Yeah, but they can't find their butts with bull fiddles compared to that scout. With him finished for sure, we're plumb free."

Eli Holten squeezed on the trigger of his Winchester. A loud, grating sound followed. Swift as a rattlesnake, Paul May brought up his own weapon. Flame blossomed at the muzzle. Snow kicked up beside Eli's shoulder as he abandoned the damaged rifle and clawed out his sixgun.

"He's still alive!" Paul May shouted.

"Get him!"

Holten's Remington barked twice, closely spaced shots that sped true to their target. Two black holes formed a figure eight on Paul May's heavy coat. A dumbfounded expression washed over his face and he leaned backward so that he sat awkwardly and suddenly on his rump in the snow.

"He . . . killed . . . me," Paul May declared in wonder.

Not one to wait for retribution to catch up to him, Paul's partner in crime scrambled under the low, snow-laden branches of an ancient pine and hurried to where the horses had been tied off. He came into the open and made three long strides before Eli Holten had reached Paul May's corpse and relieved him of the stolen Springfield rifle.

Wayne Hollis made two more paces toward his mount by the time Eli had the thick butt plate rammed against his shoulder. He eased back the hammer, opened the trap and inserted another .45-70 round. The bolt mechanism back in place, he put the weapon on full cock and took aim.

Only four steps to go, Hollis rejoiced. So far Holten hadn't shot at him. Must be he didn't have a long gun. Then a great white nothingness expanded inside his head and he flew forward, his face blown away, blood, fluid and gray matter showering the ground as he fell into his own gore. The sound of the shot echoed off the hills.

Holten waited until the rolling crack subsided into silence. Then he retrieved all the ammunition Paul May had for his Springfield, gathered up Sonny's reins and swung into the saddle. Six more to go, he considered, looking uncomfortably at the increase in snowfall.

"We could get lost in this stuff," Ralph Lockwood protested.

"You can stay here if you want," Grant Brockton informed him in an indifferent tone. "That way you can say hello to the army for us when they catch up to you."

"Won't they lose the trail in the snow?" Ralph asked anxiously.

"For a while, maybe. We've not been exactly over careful to hide where we've been. A good scout, like Kelly or Holten, will be able to track us for at least two, three days after we've been through an area. And make no mistake, the army will send someone after us."

Lt. Charles Clarke sat a short distance away with the two deserters who had aided in the escape. He'd heard enough of this petty bickering. Clarke's self-confidence had returned after the harried flight from the besieged supply column. He felt nothing but contempt for these crude border trash. The time had come, he felt certain, to part company. To that end, he leaned close to Private

Peters and whispered conspiratorially.

"Next good blind turn in the trail, blaze a tree or something easy to spot and head off away from that bunch. Muller and I will follow your mark. Then we'll head down onto flat country, get away from these idiots and the snow."

"I've gotcha, Lieutenant."

To the civilians, Clarke raised his voice to say, "Peters is going to ride point for us, check the trail ahead. This snow could make things difficult."

"Good idea, Lieutenant," Brockton replied.

Moaning through the trees, a heavy wind came up, picking the new-fallen flakes up into whirling miasmas of white oblivion. Within ten minutes the small party of fugitives could not see each other over a distance of five feet. Another twenty minutes went by before Grant Brockton, Ralph Lockwood, and Ephram Sprague discovered that they had become separated from the three soldiers.

"What do we do now?" Ralph inquired, justifiably frightened by the prospect of being lost in a blizzard.

"What else? Keep going," Brockton responded.

"How can we? If we've lost the three of them, we could get separated, too."

Brockton considered Ralph's words. "Perhaps you're right. There's trees enough around here. We can surely find some firewood and use branches to form a shelter with our ground cloths."

"Right here on the trail?"

"Of course not. If we're twenty, thirty feet away no one could see us in this storm. I figure we should walk our horses fifty paces into the trees. That should be safe enough."

"Let's hurry, then, I'm freezing."

Eli Holten detected the odor of woodsmoke first. In the whipping, whirling snow he saw nothing. He'd have to let his nose lead him, he decided.

That worked well enough. He came within thirty feet of the small camp before he discovered it. A less experienced trail guide might have passed it up entirely. Quietly he dismounted and walked Sonny back along his previous route for a safe distance, then tied the reins to a pine branch. He left his useless Winchester in the saddle scabbard and started forward with the Springfield cradled in his arms. During the short stalk to the campsite, he came to the conclusion that shock and surprise could be his best allies.

No telling how many of the fugitives might be there. Were he to call out to them, one or more might be able to slip away, circle around and shoot him in the back. Walk in on them and bluff his way through seemed the best alternative. Rich aromas filled his nostrils and his stomach growled in protest. Whoever might be up there had found a way to cook their rations.

Hunger caused the scout to salivate profusely. Damnit all. Well, he'd finish off with them, then help himself to a meal. Ten yards to go and it would be all over.

"Don't anyone move," Eli commanded as he walked into the sheltered pocket that contained three men.

"How?" Ralph Lockwood blurted, one hand reaching for the rifle at his side.

Holten put a round from the Springfield into young Lockwood's arm, shattering his elbow. Ralph howled in agony and writhed on the ground, clasping the wound.

His noises changed to a pitiful whimper as the scout spoke again.

"I mean what I said. Be smart and you'll live through this."

He lowered the rifle and drew his Remington. The sear ratchet sounded abnormally loud in the confined area as Eli thumbed back the hammer. Grant Brockton considered the odds and decided that to act would be better than submitting humbly to capture. He all but made his move when a muffled voice called out from the direction of the trail.

"That shot came from over here, Lieutenant."

Holten fought to keep the trio from seeing the relief he felt. "You didn't really think I came alone, did you?" he asked in an offhand manner. "Now, one at a time, stand up and turn your back to me. I'm going to tie you up." The scout raised his voice and shouted toward the unseen pathway. "Over here. It's Holten. I've got three prisoners."

Chapter Twenty-five

With the prisoners securely in the custody of Lieutenant Anderson's platoon, Eli Holten filled his belly on jerky stew and ranged out ahead again. He'd seen indications that the remaining escapees had split off deliberately and wanted to return to the point to study it more. The patrol would follow behind, with blazes of colored cloth to guide the way. Eli located the spot with a bit more difficulty than he had anticipated.

He left a bright red bandanna tied to a limb to indicate the direction he would take and set out along the new trail. He discovered the error of his planning within half an hour. Instead of passing over, as many such storms did, the snow intensified and turned into a localized blizzard. As the altitude dropped, the snow changed to sleet. Ice glazed the tree limbs and sparkled from his hat, shoulders and Sonny's mane.

Numbing cold affected Eli's memory. Had he left another marker where he'd turned to the south? How many miles separated him from the patrol? What time of day was it? Ice rimmed his eyebrows and the curled ends of his long, yellow locks. His toes had no feeling at all. When he blinked his eyes it took several seconds for the scene to steady again and come into focus. Lethargically, the scout came to realize that he was suffering from frostbite, and was numbed almost to the point of freezing to death. He had to find shelter or else.

That, with a sinking feeling, he realized might not come at all. Two or three times, he lost count easily, he thought he saw a tiny spot of bright yellow wavering in the distance. It could be anything, including his brain playing tricks, Eli acknowledged. Still instinct guided him toward it.

There. Once again, and larger this time, a fuzzy-edged circle of yellow. Eli swayed in the saddle, no feeling from his shoulders down or in his legs at all. With each stiff-legged stride of his Morgan stallion, a soft grunt came from his blue, chapped and swollen lips. For a moment everything went gray.

How easy it would be to . . . just . . . close his . . . eyes and . . . sleep . . .

Solid impact awakened Eli. Sonny stood astride of him, his soft muzzle sliding over Eli's face. How had he gotten on the ground? Tingling splinters of pain radiated from his legs and arms as he struggled to come upright. He hung onto Sonny's long, sorrowful head and forced his feet under him. Around him the world had turned solid white. He had to keep moving.

Floundering through the snow, head down to break the savagery of the scything sleet, Eli ran face-first into a graying slab of wood. For a long while he stood staring stupidly at it, then recognized it for what it was. Gloved fingers brushing the surface, he traced his way along the adze-shaped beams until he came to a corner.

Rounding it, he soon located a door and began to pound. Before he heard an answer, blackness came stealing over him.

Rich, savory cooking odors roused him. It took the scout several long minutes to recall his name and what he had been doing before the long blackness. It had to have been for a long while. The snow had stopped, the wind had gone and he felt warm and dry. Entwined among the confused, blurred images of his immediate past he faintly made out the face of a lovely young Sioux woman. Try as he might he could not bring forth a name for her. He felt a yawn coming on and stretched luxuriously, opening wide and letting his eyelids flutter upward.

"Yipe!" he squawked when he looked directly into a forest of eyes.

"You youngun's get away from there, you hear?" a well-modulated voice commanded.

Then a vision of sheer, red-haired loveliness came into focus, as the collection of curious orbs fled to all points of the compass. "Oh, you are awake. I thought that was Peter being funny."

"Uh . . . Peter? Er, who are you?"

"I'm Malissa Thorne." The thicket of big, blue, staring eyes, each set likewise topped with scarlet mops, slowly returned. "What's your name?"

"It's . . . Eli Holten. At least that's the name that seems to fit."

"You've been out for two days, Eli Holten. Poppa an'

I bathed you in snow water to take away the frostbite. Then bundled you up. Oh, these are my brothers and sisters. Matthew and Mark, they're seventeen. Luke's fifteen, John's thirteen, Peter, twelve, an' the littlest, Paul is ten. The girls are me, Doreen, who's sixteen, Samantha, fourteen, and Susanna, fourteen, and Helen eleven."

"My, that many of you? Your folks must have kept right busy . . ."

"Poppa's all that's left. Momma died birthin' little Paul."

"Small wonder. I suppose that the chore of mothering all this brood fell on you?"

Malissa looked weary and sad for a moment. "Sorta. I was eight at the time." An expression of chagrin crossed her lovely face. "Shame on me. You'll want some soup. Johnny an' Peter shot some rabbits. It ain't much, but it's real good. Let me bring you some. The rest of you get on outta here."

Most of the flock fled. Samantha remained a moment, staring boldly down toward the location of Eli's crotch. "My, but you're a *big* one," she said in a soft, sweet voice. Then she giggled and ran off toward the big stone hearth where a cheery blaze crackled away.

"Big . . . one?" the scout muttered aloud.

"Sure," Paul said, returning with a huge grin plastered on his freckled face. "We'd never seen anyone so bad hurt with freezing before, so we all watched while Poppa an' 'Lissa cared for you. At one point there, while they was pouring snow melt over you in the washtub you sprung up mighty big, I'd say. Wish I was that well hun . . ."

"Dangit, Paul. You might be the baby an' all an' spoiled rotten, but that don't mean you can't keep a civil tongue in your head. Think of your sisters."

"I am thinkin' of 'em. Of what they said, at least."

"You li'l brat! I'm gonna yank down your britches and spank your bottom raw."

"No you ain't," Paul teased. " 'Cause if you do, I'll tell 'im what you said to Doreen about it. So there."

"You'll have to excuse us, Mister Holten," Matthew apologized, in a voice that rambled between small boy and adult. "We're a wild bunch and mighty direct about a lot of things, bein' raised without a Maw an' all."

"I understand," Eli answered politely, though he didn't really.

Malissa brought him the soup. It had a heavenly aroma of onions, peppers and rabbit. Chunks of potato floated in the broth and yellow tidbits of corn. His hand shook so badly Malissa covered it with one of her own to guide the spoon to his mouth.

"Ummmmm. This is the best rabbit soup I've ever had," Eli enthused when he'd managed four rapid swallows to cut the edge of his ravenous appetite.

"You finish it all up, then we can talk some. I'm bakin' fresh bread. Poppa should be in any time now. He's mendin' harness in the barn."

Feeling stronger with each bite, Holten industriously worked his way to the bottom of the bowl. He sat quietly then, eagerly awaiting a thick slab of crusty, home-baked bread, slathered with butter. The door slammed open and a stout man stomped inside in a bluster of snowflakes.

His flaming red mustache, beard and long hair of the

same scarlet color were shot with gray so that he looked a good sixty, rather than the forty-six years of his actual age. The smile he produced was warm and lively, revealing blunt, still-white teeth.

"Our visitor is among the living again, I see," he bellowed in a good-natured tone.

"He is, Poppa. His name's Eli Holten."

Crossing the room, his arm and hand extended in welcome, the powerfully built man brought with him the aroma of pipe tobacco. "M'name's Gabrial Thorne, Mister Holten. Call me Gabe. You ain't from around these parts, is you?"

"No, Gabe," Holten responded, taking the offered hand. "Make it Eli and we'll be on even terms. I'm from Fort Rawlins."

"T'devil you say. That's a far piece from here. What brings you out our way?"

"Indians. The renegade Sioux. Two companies of cavalry from Rawlins were detached to assist Nelson Miles in his round-up of off-reservation Sioux."

"Had any luck?" Gabe inquired, head cocked to one side, eye agleam with humorous mischief.

"Yep. Mostly bad. But we rounded up near onto three hundred, counting Night Hawk and his warriors."

"M'God! Night Hawk you say? Eli, I'm not prone to call any man a liar, but if you mean what you say, then ol' Bear Coat Miles was blessed by all the angels and the saints to boot."

"There was some fighting, but we've got them all rounded up now. Which reminds me. There's a patrol of cavalry out there somewhere. They're looking for me. Or I'm looking for them. One way or the other.

And some fugitive white men, three army deserters. Seen anything of them?"

"No. Can't say I have. Storm only blowed over yesterday. Think we oughtta search for them?"

"I do, Gabe. They're not at home in this country. I'll get dressed and we can start out . . ."

"No, no, no you're not. Land sakes, Eli, you darn near froze solid out there just three nights ago come sundown. Not a chance I'm gonna let you out of here for a while yet."

"He's right, Eli," Malissa supported her father. "You've got another long soak coming this afternoon. A warm one this time. After that, it'll be at least another day or two before you can get out of bed."

"I can't stay here that long. Lieutenant Andrews is a stranger to this country, like I am. I've got to round up that patrol, then I have to track down those three men I told you about and get started back to the Pine Ridge reservation with the Miniconjou."

"Not 'till you're able to sit a horse you won't," Gabe injected into Eli's protest. "You just listen to my li'l 'Lissa here. She knows what's best for you. Now," he went on, rising as he changed the subject, "let's thank the Lord for what we got and fill our bellies."

After the meal, Eli had another bowl of soup and the bread he'd been promised, Gabe organized a search for the missing patrol and the fugitives. His instructions came crisp, sure and firm.

"Make sure you boys bring at least fifty cartridges each. If we run into those deserters, there's liable to be some shootin'. An' we want to be able to fire signal shots whilst we round up them soldier-boys. Don't worry, Eli, we'll be back with your missing troops in no time."

All of the older Thorne boys went with Gabe; Matthew, Mark, Luke and John. That left only Peter and Paul, Doreen, Samantha, Susanna, and Helen, besides Malissa, who fussed busily around the kitchen corner of the huge cabin. At last as though an afterthought, Malissa clapped her hands and pointed sternly to the door.

"You boys run to the barn and get the big tub. Put on your coats, mind."

Eyes alight with eagerness, they raced outside. Malissa turned to Eli. "Your soak, like I promised. That's what all that water's for. You girls, get into your warm things. You're going out to the barn to do chores."

"Awh, we wanna watch," Samantha and Susanna chorused together.

"You already did."

"But he wasn't awake then," came the immediate protest.

"What about the boys?" Helen inquired in a tiny chirp.

"They're going with you."

"*You* can't stay if we can't," Samantha challenged.

"Well, of course I am. I've gotta. To see to the right temperature of the water, to help with his rub-down." That brought immediate giggles from the three younger girls. "None of that now. Get dressed warm right now."

By the time the boys returned with the tub, the younger Thorne girls were decked out in coats, mittens and scarves. They didn't look the least pleased by the prospect of an afternoon in the barn. Malissa shooed them out and had the boys help her with the water.

Then she sternly chased them off too. She bent, then, and touched a tentative finger to the steaming liquid in the tub.

Quite a tub it was, Eli had noticed when it first came in. An oval-shaped, copper device, with high sides, and wooden handles on each end, large enough to hold two healthy sized adults or several children at one time. Smiling, as though at some secret, Malissa crossed to the bed. An eager glow danced in her eyes.

"Off with that nightshirt, now. It's time for your soak."

"I, ah, er, that is, uh . . ."

"I have a nice warm towel here for you," Malissa offered.

Eli climbed from the profusion of down quilts and turned his back. Hesitantly he pulled the hem of the long night shirt up over his long, lean body and removed it. With a nervous glance he reached out for the towel. This he wound around his waist and padded barefoot over to the steaming tub. He spread the fluffy cloth, stepped into the eye-tearing hot water, and let it drop as he sat down. Quick as lightning, Malissa came up beside him.

"Now for the best part of your soak," she said brightly as her fingers flew along the buttons of her dress.

It took Malissa no time at all to get naked. Holten's eyes widened, blinked, bulged. Beneath the plain, simple dress of a frontier woman hid the stunning body of a voluptuous wanton. Ripe, full breasts, not overlarge, but globular and firm, with dark red aureolas and thumbtip nipples jutted from her dramatically flared chest.

A thin tracery of ribs could be seen beneath the

alabaster skin when she raised her arms above her head in a languid gesture of feline grace. Her flat, teasingly rounded belly quivered slightly with each breath and the soft fur-like golden hairs around the small knot of her navel caught rays of the yellow lamp light, striking stars that shone in Eli's avid gaze. Flaring hips, below a narrow waist, arrowed downward to the slightly furred pubic mound.

Dewy droplets shimmered there in an auburn thatch, framed between classically rounded thighs that Rodin would have envied. Malissa's legs were long and trim, ending in feet that might be a bit too wide across the front, but bore a resemblance to those of the Indian girls who were raised in moccasins. Despite the shock of her rapid disrobing, Eli found he had a fantastic erection.

Malissa discovered it, too, and gave him a swift, secret smile that promised far more than a therapeutic bath. She pulled up a three-legged stool and plumped down on it.

"First your back. Bend forward."

Eil complied, stifling a groan at the raging fire in his groin. With hands soft and gentle, Malissa spread water over his shoulders and kneaded the muscles that had become rigid under her initial touch. The pleasant interlude passed on to his arms, chest and legs. Like the mast of a sunken ship, his rebellious member thrust up out of the water.

"Stretch out, I want to do your belly," Malissa cooed.

"Oooh," Eli moaned. "I . . . I, ah, don't think that's too good an idea."

"Oh, yes, it is. You never know what damage can be

done by near freezing. Your belly now and . . . I'm saving . . . the best . . . for last."

In order to expose his stomach, more than half of his pulsing phallus would be above the level of warm water. It had to be some delirium brought on by being lost in the howling storm. Yes, a dream—like the ones he had as a boy, when lovely, willing girls came to him and did all sorts of fanciful things, and he woke up all wet and sticky. His mind was kidding him.

No it wasn't! he discovered quickly when Malissa took firm hold of that solid shaft and held it away with one hand, while she used strong fingers to articulate the vibrating muscles of his abdomen. Eli knew every delightful moment that he was wide awake and this was actually happening, as she progressed downward.

"Now, for the best part," Malissa murmured dreamily as she rose and straddled the tub. Then she stepped into it and lowered herself over his steely phallus. Bit by bit she came closer, deft fingers guiding the tip of his maleness to its ultimate reward.

Warm, moist and inviting, her blossoming cleft opened and received him. Paroxysms of sheer delight shook the scout and he thought for a moment he was shivering with cold. No, not cold.

Heat so intense it threatened to scorch his skin radiated from his loins as Malissa impaled herself on his magnificent lance. Eli groaned and undulated his hips.

"Yessss," Malissa hissed. "Yes-yes-yes. Deeper. Fill me, you big, wonderful man. Fill me up! Doreen, an' Susie an' Samantha all want you, but they can't have you."

"My God. All—all of you?' the scout gulped. "Th-

they're just little girls."

"Big enough. And more than ready. Too bad for them, you belong to me."

"What if I don't want . . ."

Malissa did some magical things with the muscles surrounding her fiery passage that robbed Eli of speech and even his thoughts. In the next instant they were fully joined. Hips undulating in concert, they gleefully entered the lists on the field of Eros and contested for which could draw more delight from the other.

New universes unfolded before them and the world whirled at such a speed that they became giddy with its motion. Water sloshed over the lips of the copper tub, floorboards creaked and groaned. Malissa's squeals of delight grew more strident and more often. She thrashed her head from side to side and plunged downward with unbridled passion.

Before his own reason fled in the oblivion of completion, Eli had one farcical thought. Odd, but love in a bath tub could be all sorts of fun. Shrieking in delight, Malissa preceded him over the peak. Her swaying body came down on his chest, her soft breasts providing a thrilling sensation of their own.

They lay like that for a long while. Then Malissa pushed herself upright. "Let's get dry and we can use the bed. It's fun like this, but being loved on a goose-down comforter is a lot better."

"Do you . . . do you think I've got strength enough for more?" Eli asked weakly.

"Oh, sure you do. Hurry now, I can't wait."

Eli hurried and found he did and much more. Some time during the long, ecstatic afternoon, Eli heard

Malissa murmur words that excited him beyond all prospects.

"If you're really good, and promise not to tell, I might let you sample Doreen. If you make me happy lots of times before you get well enough to leave, maybe even Susie and Sam. It'll be sort of a present for them. Poor Helen, she'll have to wait. She's a bit small yet."

"My God, girl, what do you think I am?"

"More man than any of us have ever had before," came her prompt reply. "Now get those other girls out of your mind. We have lots more to accomplish before I'm done with you."

Chapter Twenty-six

Tingling, jangling sensations of pure delight spider-legged along the well-strained nerves of Eli Holten's body. A day and a half had passed and he was getting yet another "treatment" from Malissa Thorne. She knelt now, nude and pink and pretty, between his upraised knees. Her supple lips did marvelous things to his rigid organ as she worked her head up and down. Her tongue did remarkable service as well. Eli had enjoyed quite a lot of "treatments" during the intervening time.

His most bizarre amorous therapy had been a two-on-one arranged by Malissa and employing the talents of her sister, Doreen, while the remainder of the red-headed flock had a snowball fight in the yard. First Malissa, then Doreen, had straddled his hips, impaling themselves on his mighty member, while the opposite one lay atop his heaving chest, his face buried deeply in their auburn-thatched clefts, while lapping away with clever tongues at the junction point between the scout and the other sister. It had taken Eli some while to accustom himself to such care, and he never lost a residual bit of trepidation. Yet he couldn't deny the sheer splendor of it all. Reflecting on that signal occasion, he let himself slowly ascend the incline to euphoria as Malissa labored over his fiery rod.

"Ah, 'Lissa, 'Lissa, that's fantastic," Eli panted.

She stopped long enough to ask coyly, "Like to get Dorrie in again?"

"Uh . . . it was grand and all, but, uh, I don't think so. Wouldn't the other kids get suspicious?"

"Awh, they all know what's goin' on," Malissa retorted. "Ain't a one of 'em hasn't played around a little. 'Cept Matt an' Mark an' Poppa."

Her admission made Eli decidedly uncomfortable. "Is, ah, this what you do for family fun?"

"Naw, it ain't like that, much anyway. Usually we find folks passin' through, or such. Neighbors from back a way, come a barn raisin' or the like. Helps pass the time, don't you see?"

"Uh . . . yes, yes I do."

Malissa resumed her tender attentions. Eli soared upward to the crest, only to lose that fine, sensuous edge when the door banged open. Peter stood in the opening, grinning like a ninny.

"Poppa's comin'. He's got him a bunch of sol'jer-boys with him. Best get fixed around so's all is normal."

"Thank you, Petey," Malissa said calmly.

She rose and began hurriedly to dress, not the least put out at the presence of her little brother. Peter, for his part, didn't make any effort to avert his eyes from the scene he had encountered. Holten, not at all to his surprise, found himself blushing and turning away to shrug on his borrowed nightshirt.

Gabe Thorne arrived with a loud halloo. "Hey, Holten, you up an' about as yet? I got some of your friends out here. A Lieutenant Andrews and some of his troops."

"I'll be there in a minute," Eli called back.

He climbed from the bed and began to pull on his buckskin trousers. In a warm flannel shirt, his feet stuffed into moccasins, Eli walked a bit unsteadily to the door. Had he not gotten so many "treatments," he thought ruefully he might have had better control.

"Eli!" Tom Andrews exclaimed when the scout stepped out onto the porch. "We'd given you up for dead."

"Damned near was, Tom. Good to see you. Are the others still missing?"

"No. Once we got together again, I sent them back to the colonel's base camp with the prisoners. We still have three to hunt down, you know."

"Yeah. And a cold trail to work, too."

"Matt an' Luke cut fresh sign leadin' toward a steep bluff to the southeast yesterday. Might be your deserters. They're checkin' on it an' oughtta be back here by nightfall. I told Lieutenant Andrews here that he could put his men up in the barn for the night an' you could all get a fresh start tomorrow."

"That sounds reasonable enough," Eli responded warily. *If half of what Malissa had revealed to him was true*, he thought, *those soldiers were about to get their brains screwed out*.

"You hadn't ought to be out in this nippy air so long, Eli," Gabe complained. "Go back in there an' sit by the fire. You look a bit peaked."

"I think I'll do just that," Eli agreed gratefully.

No mistaking the cause of the smug smiles on the faces of the seven troopers the next morning. Nor of the happy glow in the eyes of Doreen, Samantha and

Susanna.

"Awh, damn, why don't they have drummer *girls* in the army," Eli heard Peter complain miserably to Paul.

Some family, the scout summed up. Maybe it was the red hair, he speculated as he and Lieutenant Andrews walked their horses away from the farmyard. People said that was a sure sign of a warm nature.

His departure from Malissa had certainly been warm. She clung to him with a strong arm around his neck, her soft, moist lips against his in a long, delicious kiss. Her lips parted and their tongues fenced heatedly, while she rammed her free hand down the front of his trousers and squeezed hungrily at his manhood. As usual it had roused to the occasion and Malissa urged him to steal a few minutes away with her in the barn to attend to this obvious affliction. He had to speak roughly to her, if it did include a promise to return if possible, to prevent her suggestion from becoming action.

Now he tried unsuccessfully to purge his memory of the incredible hours he had spent in Malissa's arms, her tight, firm passage encasing his steely maleness, and the wondrous nectar of her and Doreen in their hour of madness. And it had been madness. How could a whole family, at least the greater portion of a family, be so dedicated to the pleasures of the flesh? For the time being, Eli preferred not to think about it. Matt and Luke Thorne led the way.

They had returned shortly before nightfall and reported that definitely three horses had made the tracks they had followed. One had a cracked shoe, which jibed with what Eli had developed before the storm. So the youngsters had volunteered to direct Eli and the patrol to where they had first picked up the trail. Once there, Holten forged on while Lieutenant Andrews brought the cavalry along behind. He'd covered some eight miles when he saw a thin spiral of smoke lifting from about two miles ahead.

"Why didn't they raise a flag and wave banners?" Eli groused aloud at the carelessness of the fugitives.

He rode on another two miles, then dismounted and led Sonny in a wide, circuitous path that would put him close by the hunted men at an unexpected angle. Moving through sparse stands of lodgepole pine, blackjack and elm, he managed to evade discovery. He smelled brewing coffee and wondered again at their ineptness. Eli slid his repaired Winchester from the saddle scabbard and crouched low.

To his surprise, he made it to within twenty yards of the camp without raising an alarm. Were they blind? Voices drifted to him.

"We really shouldn't be stayin' around here like this, Lieutenant," Peters remarked in a complainer's whine.

"We've got to, Peters. We have to have landmarks to go by and that means waiting until the snow melts some."

"Chust zo," Muller agreed. "Only dey haff people out looking for us. Ve cou't get caught."

"You're a fence-sitter, Muller. First you agree with me, then you agree with Peters, all in the same breath."

"I tell you, it's important, Lieutenant. That scout, Eli Holten, could find us if he's out looking."

"Holten? That cowardly incompetent?" Clarke sneered.

"You're way off on that, Lieutenant. Why, it wouldn't surprise me if he was lookin' down the sights of a rifle at us right now."

"I am," Holten's voice came to them from not ten feet away in a clump of elm. "Keep your hands in sight and stand up slowly."

"*Liebe Gott*," Muller shouted as he dove for his Springfield.

Eli's Winchester cracked and Karl Muller howled in pain, a .44-40 slug through his right thigh. The rifle blast galvanized the other two to action. Peters flipped over backward and rolled to where he'd left his weapon. Charles Clarke spun around, clumsily drawing his revolver.

Clarke's Colt spurted flame and a hot slug nipped a small limb from an elm beside Holten's face. Fragments of bark stung his cheeks and a bit caused one eye to water. The sabre wounds Clarke had given him ached when the scout cycled the lever action of the Winchester. His second round snapped between Clarke's legs and thudded into the snowbank behind.

With a yelp of fright, Clarke dove for cover. That left Holten and the wounded Muller exposed. Little winks of yellow-orange revealed the muzzles of Peters' Springfield and the lieutenant's revolver. Forced to move, Eli cut off at an angle, placing his assailants between him and the sheer lip of the bluff. He fired twice on the move, then sprawled out behind a little hillock of snow.

Immediately he slithered over the crusty surface to another location before rising up. Muller had dragged himself to his rifle and held it awkwardly. He sensed movement and swung the muzzle in Eli's direction. Calmly, the scout shot him in the chest. Blood and bits of Muller's uniform greatcoat flew in a spray as he flopped backward, legs reflexively spasming in his death throes. Holten sidled away before more incoming fire could pin him down.

"I'll kill you, Holten!" Clarke shouted, his ragged nerves on the edge of dissolution.

"You had your chance and blew it, Clarke. Now I'm going to bring you in slung over your saddle."

"You can't kill me for desertion."

"You're right, I can't. I'm going to kill you for what you did to *Susweca*."

"That damned squaw!" Clarke spat. "They'll swing you for that. I have a witness."

Eli had steadily been shifting his point of vision as he bantered with Clarke. A quick flick of his eye picked up a blur of motion off to the left. Peters had been creeping away from the area of the confrontation and now apparently decided he had a commanding position. He rose, Springfield to his shoulder, hammer back and ready.

Holten pumped two slugs into the deserter. Peters flung his weapon away in a reflex gesture and flopped like a beached fish. Eli calmly inserted three rounds through the loading gate and returned his attention to Clarke.

"No you don't. No witnesses, just corpses . . . like you're going to be real soon."

"You can't do this to me!"

Driven to the panic point, Charles Clarke rose from behind a snow-covered log, firing wildly until his Colt's Army Model clicked on an empty chamber. None of the bullets came close to Eli Holten, who now rose and advanced on his enemy.

Horror glazed Charles Clarke's eyes. He dropped the

revolver and raised his hands as though to fend off a blow. "Please . . . you can't . . . I-I'm not armed. Y-you wouldn't kill a helpless man, would you?"

"Move to your left. Over there," Eli Holten commanded. "Pick up Muller's rifle."

"I-I-I can't, I won't."

"Pick it up or I'll shoot you in the balls," the scout demanded in a dreadful voice.

Droplets of perspiration sprang up on Clarke's forehead. His hands trembled and he unknowingly voided his bladder. His knees quivered and threatened to give way. The look on Eli Holten's face reminded him of drawings of the devil in his long-ago Sunday school books. An uncontrollable whimper escaped from his throat.

"*Pick . . . it . . . up!*"

Terrified beyond the ability to resist further, Lt. Charles Clarke bent downward in a convulsive move and snatched the cocked Springfield from the ground. He'd barely touched it when Holten's Winchester barked.

Pain jarred up Clarke's arms from the impact of the slug. The side plate of the Springfield lock cracked and the guts spilled out. That could have been *his* insides, Clarke thought disjointedly. Unguided, he began to back away from the menace that faced him. With a wail of dejection he hurled the useless rifle at Eli Holten.

Eli easily batted it out of the way with the butt stock of his Winchester. Lips in a feral snarl, he continued to advance. Clarke backed further. Holten uttered a growl deep in his chest. Clarke sobbed and mewed weakly. Eli took another step. Clarke countered with another backward move.

Charles Clarke's eyes went wide in astonishment as his heel came down on nothingness. He swayed for a while, then tottered over the edge. Immediately he began to scream as he plummeted toward the ground far below.

He screamed a long time, for it was a long way to go.

Exhausted, sapped by his many recent wounds and the ordeal of his night in the blizzard, Eli Holten stumbled to the bluff and looked over. Goodbye, Lieutenant, he thought, not without considerable satisfaction. Clarke had lived a coward and died like one. It fit the scout's sense of justice. And, he acknowledged with relief, he had not had to fire the fatal shot at an unarmed man.

Goodbye . . . and good riddance.

It took all but the last of Eli's strength to gather the corpses and tie them over their saddles. By the time he had completed the task, Lieutenant Andrews arrived with the patrol. Eli made a short, terse explanation, giving only scant details. Andrews didn't press him. Eli, he knew, would write a complete report when the time came. In subdued quiet, the small column started off.

Eli thought of the spartan comforts available at Fort Rawlins, so far, far away. Even those appeared most appealing, compared to his present condition. What he needed was a long, hot soak in a big copper tub, plenty of good, red meat to eat and a woman to love away the hurts. He knew, too, where he could find all of them.

When the patrol reached the turn-off to the Thorne cabin, Eli halted while Matt and Luke said goodbye to Lieutenant Andrews. Then Holten cut Sonny away from his place beside the officer and lifted his hat.

"I'm still a little, ah, shaky, if you know what I mean," Eli told the young cavalry officer. "I think I'll ride on in with them and catch up a little more recuperation before joining Colonel Miles and his column. Let him know for me, will you?"

"Glad to. Are you sure you'll be all right?"

A hint of a wistful smile lifted the corners of Eli's mouth. "Oh, I'll manage."

He turned his mount and rode off with the Thorne boys, reflecting that there was a time and a place for fighting and serving the army. But that time would come later, much later. Gladly, his mind filled with the image of the amorous welcome Malissa would give him.

WHITE SQUAW
Zebra's Adult Western Series
by E.J. Hunter

#1: SIOUX WILDFIRE	(1205, $2.50)
#2: BOOMTOWN BUST	(1286, $2.50)
#3: VIRGIN TERRITORY	(1314, $2.50)
#4: HOT TEXAS TAIL	(1359, $2.50)
#5: BUCKSKIN BOMBSHELL	(1410, $2.50)
#6: DAKOTA SQUEEZE	(1479, $2.50)
#8: HORN OF PLENTY	(1649, $2.50)
#9: TWIN PEAKS – OR BUST	(1746, $2.50)
#10: SOLID AS A ROCK	(1831, $2.50)

Available wherever paperbacks are sold, or order direct from the Publisher. Send cover price plus 50¢ per copy for mailing and handling to Zebra Books, Dept. 2103, 475 Park Avenue South, New York, N.Y. 10016. Residents of New York, New Jersey and Pennsylvania must include sales tax. DO NOT SEND CASH.